A SAPPHIC TABLETOP RPG ROMANCE

DI🎲CURIOUS

Di-Curious

1

JUNE

I f only I had my orc fidget toy for this phone call. A fan made it for me, and when I squeeze the little guy, he makes a squeaky grunt, and his axe chops forward. It's quite cathartic. "Come on, man. It wouldn't be weird for me to be on Zoom for this game. You've done it before for other players."

I would squeeze the hell out of that orc right now.

Todd—game master of a semi-popular Dungeons and Dragons streaming group—lets out a sigh from my phone's speakers, echoing around my car where I sit in my friend's driveway. "Junie...it's just not going to work. The whole draw you have rides on your look. Your cosplays. It's why we invited you. If you're playing over Zoom and can't afford to travel, people on our YouTube won't be able to see your face or costume. We don't have the set up."

It's one of those rare, warm Georgia days in early March, seventy-five degrees, and the interior of my black car is getting hotter by the second in the sunlight. But I need to save on gas. It's not like I have a great revenue source right now. Sad as it is, the free dinner tonight at Aiden and Lyssa's will help.

"I think I offer more than just a pretty face. You said you watched the stream of my last campaign. Awe kicked ass."

Awe is my best friend—and also imaginary.

Awe Danamark the Sparkling. The best bard in all the realms and my all-time favorite character to play. A master of lore, she can play a mean lute solo, heal up her friends from certain death, and throw a fireball straight into the middle of an enemy camp.

"Yeah, uh-huh. But—"

"But *what*? I know you want me to be there in person. But you're holding the game in California, and I just moved." Back into my parents' basement in suburban Georgia. Ugh. "I can't make flying out work right now. You've Zoomed in other players before. It can't be that much of a dealbreaker."

He sighs again. "The long-distance issue is only part of it. Awe is very cute and funny. But the other producers and I have been talking, and we're going in a different direction. A grittier direction."

Wait a minute. He just said how much he liked Awe's look and why that was the reason I couldn't Zoom into the game. This is double-talking bullshit. I don't want to directly call him on it, though. It's always easier when I can solve my issues through charisma checks.

"Come on, I can be gritty." I look up from the steering wheel and glance out the car window, trying to get a peek at the people in the yard. I'm late joining the party, but Aiden and Lyssa won't mind. They know what I've been dealing with. I just have to convince this asshole to let me do the thing he already agreed to.

"Junie, you have pink hair. Your character is known as 'The Sparkling.'"

Him calling me 'Junie,' like I'm a close friend, gets under my skin.

"Yeah, she sparkles, but she also kicks ass. Come on. I need this. My sponsor at NerdyPodCasts is counting on me to have a show ready for them to start editing in two weeks." And I'm counting on their financial support. I hate living with my parents.

Not to mention the fact that playing a game with Todd's celebrity group would look great on my resume for *Dungeons and Dreams*. A real, lucrative career doing the things I love would be my dream—and that reality show could catapult my channel to Todd's level—or beyond.

He chuckles. "Yeah, yeah. Look. I don't know how to tell you this. But the decision's been made."

The decision to cut me from the group. Maybe it doesn't matter what I offer to change. "By who?" My voice rises in volume—totally unprofessional. I need to get my emotions under control.

"We never made an official agreement. You didn't sign anything. I didn't sign anything. I'm not paying to fly you out to California, and if you can't make it to the in-person sessions yourself, we need to go in another direction. Zoom isn't going to work. If things change and we need a cute little long-distance bard, I'll let you know, okay? Mmm kay. Buh-bye."

"Fucking asswipe sexist bastard," I mutter. What a jerk.

"I can still hear you."

I yank my phone from the cubby on my car dash and jam that disconnect button so fast, I'm surprised I don't split the screen. Yeah, I really need my squeeze orc. And I'm supposed to get out of my car, join a party, and socialize? Fuck.

I press my forehead against the steering wheel. What am I supposed to do now? I need a podcast. Of an entire D&D group. That continues once a week for at least twelve episodes. Yeah, maybe that was possible when my friends and I were kids, but getting a regular adult tabletop role-playing group together is as impossible as finding an actual portal to a fantasy world.

I shove my cell in the pocket of my rainbow print over-alls and get out of my car, slamming the door behind me. Aiden and Lyssa graduated high school with me eight years ago. And they have this adorable white house and an adorable new baby and adorable perfect relationship and...

I have absolutely nothing figured out. It doesn't matter how many people online think I do.

There are six other cars here at the small ranch-style home. They're even hosting people. Man. When did they grow up and I didn't?

I trudge down the green grassy hill of Lyssa's front yard. One of the perks to living in the South. Some of the grasses turn green extra early, and we get spring days like today which are lovely. Of course, it'll turn back to cold in a day or two. Lyssa texted me earlier that since the weather is so good, they decided to have a cookout in the backyard, around the back of her house and through the gated chain length fence. The aroma of burgers on the charcoal grill and peals of laughter float in the air.

They also have supportive families. My parents let me move back in but waste no opportunity to comment on my life choices—and gave me a hard move-out date of July first, the day they're moving into their new home in the country. Not that I blame them. I lecture myself more than anyone else.

I reach the bottom of the hill, heading to the side of the house with the large backyard gate.

"Rose! Dang it!" Lyssa's voice echoes off the home and hill. "Seriously?"

A reddish blur of fur, floppy tongue, and doggy slobber streaks past me. I adore Rose. She's some kind of mystery mutt—the build of a golden retriever, the color of an Irish setter, and the personality of a sarcastic elderly woman with nothing to lose.

"I'll get her!" I call as I turn, jogging after the beast. She's doing circles around the front yard, tucking her tail in as she hauls her entire forty pounds in what Lyssa calls hurricane-ing. She'll tire in a moment. I hope.

I jog up to block the suburban neighborhood street, cutting off Rose's chance of getting into actual danger.

A person with short brown hair and wearing a button-up navy shirt with printed oranges, long tan shorts, and sandals comes running out of the smaller, less-used gate on the opposite side of Lyssa's yard, clicking their tongue. "Rose!" More clicking. "I got a piece of burger with your name on it."

Rose regards me as she slows in her circling. I hold my arms out like I'm guarding the road the way I would a basketball hoop in middle school. *Don't even think about it, ma'am.* Never mind I was terrible at basketball.

Rose looks back at the person with the burger. Then to the patch of woods on the right of Lyssa's house, where I know she's been in trouble before for digging up disgusting fungus. The gears are turning in her doggy mind.

"Come around this way!" I call. "She's gonna go for the woods!"

Citrus-shirt runs up the hill between the dog and the woods.

Ha. We got ya now.

"Come here, sweet girl. Look what I got."

Rose sees the piece of burger now in their hands—it seems she's considering whether capture is worth the taste. Still holding my hands out, I make my way closer.

Oh! I know this person! Nova Dawson—oh my God, I've missed her so much. We haven't talked in person since the time I ran into Nova at the local gaming store while visiting my parents' home the year after high school graduation and...damn. That's been seven years. I can't even think of the last time I talked with her on social media either. In high school, Nova and I were close enough to spend the night at each other's houses. And then I lost so many friends as collateral damage to me trying to please my awful ex. Never again.

Nova looks so different—no more heavy emo makeup rimming her eyes. Instead, her face is clear, and her light brown hair is short rather than dyed bright blue, hanging in her face and down her back. A swooping bang in the front brushes her forehead. She gives a slight lopsided-smile at the dog, whose attention is now rapt on the treat in Nova's hand.

I snag Rose's collar as she sits for Nova. For a second, I think the dog is going to sprint again, but I guess her desire for cookout wins. I don't blame her. My stomach is growling, too.

"Good girl." Nova feeds the dog the taste of burger while grabbing her collar. "I got her."

Our hands brush on the blue collar. Nova smells like oranges and cream. Must be a shampoo, or body spray, or something to match her shirt. That's adorable.

I try to catch her eye. "Hey! Nova, it's been a while."

She doesn't look at me and moves her hand away from mine to the other side of the collar. "I'll take her to the backyard."

I let go of Rose. "Sure. Then let's catch up. I want to hear how you've been."

She just grunts, leading the dog to the backyard's side gate.

That's weird. But Nova could be a bit closed off. It used to take some time for her to come out of her shell when we'd hang out. I'll find her in a few minutes.

Not wanting to interfere with getting the dog back in the yard, I go around the other side of the house and enter the main gate.

"June. Glad you could make it!" Lyssa hugs me. Her long, dark brown hair is in a messy braid over her left shoulder, and she's in a pretty yellow sundress only a little stained with what I'm guessing is baby spit up down one side. She's amazing—how does she have the energy to do this with a three-month-old?

"Sorry I'm late. I was on the phone with an asshole." I look around the yard. Some people, Lyssa's brothers I think, are playing a ring toss game while holding beers. Aiden's father is "manning the grill," something which Lyssa, Aiden, and I have joked is his excuse to do as little as possible during gatherings.

Lyssa smiles. "You're good. It's a drop-in thing anyway. Want some food?"

I've been so thankful to get to rekindle my friendship with Lyssa—and Aiden and now Eleanor, their little baby. When I lived out in Charleston, it was like I was on an island. Just me and Parker. Ick. I should've never listened to him about putting space between myself and my friends to work on our relationship. I'll never let a guy do that to me again. Even if it means living with my parents for a few months while I figure things out. I've been saving, but it takes so much money to get an apartment these days without a traditional job, from the deposits to the proof of several months' rents.

"Yeah, I'm starving." I see a hint of concern in her eyes, and I put my hands up as I explain, "Like, not *literally*, don't worry about me or anything."

She laughs. "I know."

I pretend to wipe sweat from my forehead. "Phew."

"You're a social media star. You gotta be rich." She winks at me—a joke between us.

"Well. *About that.*" I proceed to share all the bullshit that was my call with Todd.

Lyssa rubs her temples. "What a sexist bastard."

"I know, that's what I said!" I shake my head, watching the smoke from the grill puff up to the sky. "Another item in the long list of things fucking over my life. I really could've used this revenue from NerdyPodCasts, plus the exposure. And it was a pain in the ass to get Todd's whole crew to each give permission to stream the game."

"I'm not fully caught up on all the videos on your channel or on how the online gaming community works, but could you still do your streaming show but with different players? You said NerdyPodCasts wanted a show about Awe. Can't you use her character and play with a new group?"

"Yeah, I mean, it's a good idea. But how am I supposed to find a regular D&D group that can commit to basically every Saturday night for several months? Especially on this short notice. My stream was to begin in two weeks, and NPC was to start adapting it as soon as the stream ran."

Lyssa shrugs. "I know we're not internet celebrities or anything, but you could rejoin our group. We used to come up with great stories."

I haven't played with Lyssa and Aiden's group since high school. But she's right—wow, did we. It was what sparked my love for role-playing games. After I moved to attend college and got serious with Parker, that all ended, and they kept playing without me.

That was also why I started my channel to begin with—so I could still do all the things I loved about my favorite game. I started with timelapse videos of myself painting game figures, then moved to cosplay, then people began collaborating with me online, and I started playing in internet games. Awe is level fourteen now after several campaigns and a few years.

"Who's in your group now?" I ask.

"Well, myself and Aiden, of course. Drew, who you probably remember."

Drew was Aiden's best friend growing up. When I met him, I thought he was non-verbal. Until the first time I played D&D with him.

"And Nova. She's the DM. She's phenomenal."

Nova. With the swooshy hair, shirt with oranges on it, and matching orange-scented soap or whatever. Mmm. "Oh, I saw her earlier! I need to find her again and catch up. It's been years. She's kinda hot now."

Heh, I must really be low in blood sugar for my filter to be that gone.

Lyssa raises her eyebrows. "Oh, is she? Well, I know for a fact she's single after breaking up with her girlfriend several months ago..."

Girlfriend. But I'm in no place to ask anyone out. I roll my eyes. "Shut up—I'm straight."

"Are you?"

"Are you?" I echo back. I'm actually not sure if I am. My options have been pretty limited. I only had one serious high school boyfriend, then after we broke up, I started dating Parker the summer after high school. I dated him almost eight freaking years. "I mean, despite what people say, no one's *really* like, all straight, are they? Is that even possible?"

Lyssa chuckles. "You know only bi people say that."

Is that actually true? I'm too hungry to ponder it properly.

Lyssa smiles, putting a hand on my shoulder. "Go get some food. I'm going to find Aiden and the rest of the group and ask them if they mind appearing on your channel for our next game. But I don't see it being a problem for anyone. You know we're all big fans of yours."

Real friends. This was another big part of why I moved back to Georgia.

Lyssa's plan isn't a bad one. NerdyPodCasts didn't sign Todd or his friends—getting a semi-famous group was a bonus for them. They didn't want his "gritty" character bullshit. They want fun. They want Awe. And I can give her to them.

No one needs to know the mess behind the scenes.

2
NOVA

Damn, there are way too many people here. I pick at the sparse grass under the shade from the deck of Aiden's backyard. Maybe there's just one person too many. I'd known June was going to come, and I thought I'd be fine. That I'd ignore her.

Now I'm in even worse of a situation. I should've said something when she gathered the D&D group to ask about playing on her streaming channel. How am I supposed to deal with seeing her so frequently? I close my eyes and pat Rose's fluffy head. She sits next to me, panting. Ever since I fed her a piece of burger, she's my best friend.

"Hey, there you are." Aiden walks up to me, baby Eleanor strapped to his chest facing outwards. She's kicking her little feet as fast as they'll go, like she's running through the air. He and his baby look like someone control-c-control-v'd with their matching deep tanned skin and tight curled short hair.

"You talking to me or the dog?" I ask, taking a sip of my hoppy craft beer as I study shapes of the tree line.

"I know these big social things can be a lot for you.

Lyssa and I appreciate you coming. If you need to go, it's fine."

I shake my head, still looking at the trees and how the light makes the colors of the branches darker the more they're silhouetted. Aiden's right. A huge gathering is a lot for me. But I'm happy to be here to support Lyssa and Aiden and celebrate—albeit three months late—the birth of their new baby. Even with June in attendance. But now...

"Nova. Come on. Say something. Are you uncomfortable about June streaming our game and felt like you couldn't speak up? Because I promise, we're not going to be mad at you if you don't want to be filmed while playing."

"I... That's not why. But..." Fuck, why is it so embarrassing to say? If I'd told Aiden and the rest of my friends months ago when it happened, I wouldn't be in this situation. I doubt Aiden and Lyssa would've asked June to come today much less agreed to play D&D. "Hold on. I'll tell you. Let me think of how to explain."

I close my eyes and take a breath, petting Rose again. I'll pretend I'm talking about someone else.

"Okay. I know you remember my book?"

It was a dream to get *Curse of Dragon's Gate* published eight months ago. After I went to school for creative writing, I poured all my craft knowledge into making the fantasy book I'd always wanted to read. One with diverse characters, a plot that yanked readers on a wild ride, and a trippy-yet-classic fantasy aesthetic. I even got a Dungeons and Dragons approved setting.

"Yeah—it rocked. Lys and I have, like, ten copies."

I swallow, glancing at Aiden and Eleanor, who's cooing now, still strapped to her dad's chest. "I'm glad you feel that way. I loved the book too. Obviously. But unfortunately, my sales numbers didn't reflect those feelings. The publisher didn't sign me for more books and my agent dropped me. Not just because of the sales numbers, but it's why I'm ghostwriting and editing for other people right now."

"Aw, that sucks. I'm sorry to hear it."

I shake off the sympathy. "It's fine. It's the industry. Well, it's not fine. Ugh." I'm so bad at explaining these things. Best to just spill it. "You know how I hate social media?"

"Hashtag same."

"Funny. Like, two years ago, when I first sold *Curse* to the publishers and they did the publishing announcement blurb about its release, a dude from my college alumni paper asked me to do an interview. After we started the interview, I kind of guessed he was making fun of me, but I'm pretty used to that, so I didn't care."

I did care, a lot. But it's how I deal with these things—pretend I don't.

"He was grilling me on tabletop RPGs in general, you know, trying to make it sound like I was a fake geek and just trying to write in the fantasy genre for the money." *Ha.* "And he started talking about all the editions of D&D. He asked if I'd ever played the original game, you know, first edition. And I said no. Because I haven't. I've played version three, three point five, four, which was terrible, and now five." I tick them off on my fingers on the hand holding the beer. "And Pathfinder. And several other tabletops. But during this exchange, he got a direct quote of me saying I've never played D&D. Whatever, fine. It's a school paper. However, two months before the book released, someone on Twitter found an archived version of this interview."

It was awful. I walked around breathing embarrassment and didn't leave my apartment for more than two weeks, barely eating and sleeping.

Aiden says nothing, holding Eleanor's tiny fist. I don't want his pity—I wish I didn't have to bring this up to anyone.

I take a breath and continue, "Well, that was bad enough. Then the review bombs came in from the sexist 'men's rights' trolls when the article spread the fact that I present...female. Ish. Even though I'd written under a pen name to disguise that. But I rolled with that too."

Rolled into a ball and ate ice cream for dinner.

"Then, four months later, just as all that bullshit was dying down, guess which pink-haired bard decides to talk about my book on her channel, stirring up that fucking article all over again? It was at that point my publisher was done."

Hearing June, a person I once trusted more than anyone else on the planet, talk about the article was even worse than the first time it spread. I realize I'm clenching my teeth and relax my jaw.

Aiden's eyes are wide. "Fuck. Did she know it was you?"

It doesn't matter. "I'm pretty sure she didn't. Even the article doesn't give my real name. The douche interviewer calls me 'she'—that was enough for the incels to pile on. When I saw June today, she was all excited to see me. I doubt she'd be that way if she tanked my career on purpose. Unless she's as fake as her cotton candy hair color."

Maybe she always was. Even when we were young. She was my best friend in the world and she left me behind, after all.

Aiden shakes his head. "No, no, she's not fake. Clueless, it sounds like. Just...damn. I'll go ask her to leave right now and tell her playing with our group is out of the question."

"No. Please. You can't ruin this for Lyssa. Not only is she thrilled June moved back to town, she really seems excited about being on a podcast. I know having D&D night is important to her, especially since y'all just had your baby. I just... I'm not sure if I can play with June. Maybe I should bow out."

"Nova, you're not replaceable. When I tell Lyssa, she's going to understand and support you too."

My heart lifts a little at his words. *You're not replaceable.* I went through my childhood feeling like I spoke a different language than everyone else. Only in college did I seek help for what I thought was depression and realized I wasn't depressed—just neurodivergent and trying to function in a world not designed for me. Like a computer running a different operating system. Autism and ADHD. The diagnosis has been both a grieving process and a key to freedom.

"You tell me what you want to do, and we'll support you. All the way up to murder. Of fictional characters only." Aiden smiles and rubs Eleanor's head. "You know, in one of June's previous videos, she put in an open call to any player who wants to attempt to kill her character, saying they're welcome to try it."

He winks at me, and his baby gives an approving "ahh-oo."

"Heh. Yeah. But so far, she's always won those challenges." Murdering Awe Danamark the Sparkling *would* be quite cathartic, though. I take a sip of beer. "You know, maybe you're onto something. I would like to off Awe."

"Well, you're the DM. Now's your chance."

"Ha. No. I'd just make myself look bad. A good DM is

impartial, and June is a kickass player who uses a powerful build. She's unlikely to die."

Eleanor starts fussing, so Aiden sways back and forth, doing a little dance in place as he stares off in the distance. "Hm. Then I'll DM a new campaign, if that's okay with you. I've been working on a campaign for a few months—a modified version of that official mega-dungeon D&D published. I'd love a chance to run it. You be a player. Pick one of the enemies Awe killed in one of her other campaigns and make that dead character your character's relative. Be a vengeance paladin and swear an oath of revenge."

That's...not a bad idea. Even the thought of confronting June makes my stomach turn. But in-game, killing her character could give me some closure. Especially if it's in front of her audience.

However, I've watched streams of her playing other campaigns. She's good. She can see a betrayal from a mile away. And other players have tried it—that's why she issued the challenge. I'll have to play my very best if I want a shot at her. "She always sees it coming. I'll need to make a charismatic character that can win her over first."

"Then a paladin is perfect. As long as you play in-character the whole time and disclose your past to me, the DM, you're not breaking any rules. If you pull it off, it'll be one hell of a show for June's viewers, so she couldn't even be that mad. Or she might. She's been playing that character for years."

"Yeah, I don't care." I ruffle Rose's soft ears. I do love a good challenge.

"We were talking about doing a session zero tomorrow. I know it's fast, but do you think you'll be able to come up with a character idea?"

"Of course. I'm ready now. My main character from my book—Hunt Wygarthe. Naturally, they need revenge. And I doubt if June has even read the book."

"Oooh," Aiden says in the tone of an onlooker to a playground fight.

It's better this way. Someone like June could never understand what she took from me by spreading her hurtful video, just like she didn't realize dropping me as a friend would hurt.

Maybe it's not the most mature way of handling the situation, but killing her character could be the only closure I'll get.

3
JUNE

Awe Danamark shoves the mansion's heavy double doors open as she walks into the fanciest home in the River District. "You summoned and I'm here."

Earlier, she blazed by the mansion's guards and butler—none tried to stop her. They must know better.

Garaxle Hafgobin, richest fellow in the city, gives a low bow. "My dearest lady of the lute, so glad you could join us."

Awe chuckles. Rich men think they can pay their way into and out of everything. But certain things are priceless—Awe's life being one of them. "If I'm understanding the carefully disguised wording of your letter correctly, you want me and probably some other poor saps to journey into the depths of the wizard's catacombs. I came to humor you, Garaxle, mostly because I'm bored. It'd take much to make me risk losing my head and horns."

Garaxle holds out a hand covered with lavish jeweled rings. "My dear lady, come into my fancy room and all will be revealed."

What a strange way for the owner of the house to describe one of its rooms. His parlor? Oh, well. Candles on the wall flicker as Awe follows the man—a half-elf with long black hair wearing an opulent purple robe.

Fancy room, indeed.

Two long couches of matching purple velvet are positioned around a roaring fire powered by magic. There are runes everywhere—fueling the fire, the candles, and more. Silver trays float around the room, holding figs, cheese, bread, and other delights most citizens of city could only dream of partaking.

Goddess knows Awe hates dealing with the ultra-wealthy, stuffy assholes of society's upper crust—unless she can swindle them.

On the couches, however, sit three decidedly not-stuffy beings.

A gnome, bald on top with wiry white hair on the sides of his head, wears the sign of... Is that Procan's crest? What an obscure deity for a holy man to wear. Of course, Awe isn't one to talk as she follows Leira, Lady of Deception.

An elf—oh, this is a woman Awe recognizes! "Solla Firestarter! How'd you get dragged into this?" Solla and Awe are good friends and have blown up many a brigand together.

Solla shoves her dark brown braid behind her back as she rises and bows to Awe. Her speckled cat familiar, the color of the night sky filled with stars, leaps up to ride on her shoulders. "I'd imagine the same way you did, my friend. I'm here to listen to what the elusive Garaxle has to say."

And the third person... Awe hasn't seen them before. Horns just like hers—a tiefling—but in a blue shade that matches their skin. A beautifully deep cobalt. They have teal hair cut short with a lock swooping over their forehead.

They stand and bow, their armor making a clinking sound. This knight wouldn't be stealthy while walking dungeon catacombs. They offer a warm smile to Awe, which makes her heart flutter.

Why is that? She's not interested—a performer through and through and not interested on settling down, even with an enticing tiefling stranger.

"Awe Danamark. I've been waiting for you to walk into my life."

It's strange. Somehow, Awe didn't expect such a warm greeting from this person. She imagined a cold reception, like this particular stranger would be the sort to whom you'd give a warm and hearty hello at a party and then they'd avoid you the rest of the evening.

Suddenly, all the snappy comebacks fly from Awe's brain. "Um, hello there." How embarrassing. She's the premier bard of the realms with a whole list of greetings better than that.

Garaxle clears his throat. "Excuse me. Awe, thank you for coming." The half-elf holds a hand out, making his cloak ripple as he gestures to the other three in the room. "You'll allow me to introduce you to a few of the companions I've gathered during the past several years." He steps next to the gnome. "We have Namfoodle Ningle, sky cleric of Procan and master of lighting." Garaxle nods at Solla. "I believe you know Solla Firestarter, wizard of both elf and dragon lineage. And this is Hunt Wygarthe, a paladin."

Hunt lifts Awe's hand and kisses it. The warmth from their lips is surprising, even in this well-heated room. It's been so long since Awe felt a stir like this.

Awe can recover and impress this admittedly cute holy

person in shiny armor. "You're like me, then?" Awe's eyes meet Hunt's—a rich hazel.

Hunt lifts a teal eyebrow.

"I mean"—she gestures to her own horns with a flourish—"one of demonic lineage. A tiefling."

"Oh, you're good at spotting us, then?" A flash of white teeth and playful twinkle in their eye.

Such a nice smile. Usually, Awe is the one catching others off-guard. "The large horns kind of gave it away." She leans in closer to Hunt's face. "One might even say you're horny."

Hunt doesn't back away. "And one might say that bards are notorious for that same attribute. And therefore, one might assume a tiefling bard is perhaps the horniest combination a being could be."

"One would have to buy that tiefling bard a drink first before finding out." Where did that come from?

They laugh, and Awe loves the sound. This person in a shiny mithril breastplate is an enigma—and damn, does Awe want to unravel it.

Garaxle clears his throat, and Awe realizes just how close she's leaning to Hunt. Oops.

"Well, then. Unless there's more of this, I'll share why I gathered the four of you here." Garaxle waves his hands and the lights dim ominously. "Magic...is fucked."

Awe leans back on her heels, staring at the rich man. "Did I mishear you?" What a strange way to phrase something. And what could he even mean with such a statement?

"The famous wizard Yhallister Darkmantle retreated into the catacombs under the city."

"Yes, we know this already." Awe waves her hand, signaling him to explain faster. "Not only has everyone in the city heard the news, you said as much in your letter. What does that have to do with magic?"

Garaxle paces across the room, lights magically flickering with his every step. "I gathered the three of you because magic is near and dear to every person here. You couldn't do what you do without it. Without magic, Namfoodle is a regular gnome, serving a god of the sea."

Namfoodle puts a finger up to interrupt the rich man's speech. "Oh, Procan is more than that. Have I told you about Procan? The Storm Lord. God of the wind and sea."

Awe has to cover her mouth not to laugh. Whatever she thought Namfoodle's voice would be...it's not that. Even though he's a gnome, it seemed he might speak in a serious tone not the nasally, amusing voice coming from his mouth now.

She smiles. "Please, do tell me more about Procan."

Hunt and Solla groan, sitting back down and sinking into the velvet couches.

Awe realizes her error when Nam continues on about his Storm Lord for the next five minutes.

"Nam!" Solla interrupts, slapping her palm to her forehead. "We just had a very rich man tell us magic is fucked. We need to parse if what he's saying has any basis in our reality, or if he's another rich asshole that we definitely wouldn't steal from and ditch."

Nam rolls his eyes, looking mildly offended. "Well, if you already know about Procan..."

Awe turns to Garaxle. "Please, friend. Tell us why you summoned us. We'll do our best not to interrupt again."

Garaxle gives a smug smile. "Oh, it's just a regular venture into the catacombs to stop a wizard hell-bent on merging the arcane and shadow magic weaves. It might leave magic stronger than ever. That's what Yhallister hopes. Or, the more likely scenario according to my calculations, is when he completes his ritual, all magic will cease to work. We may or may not end up in a completely different timeline. You see, Yhallister has been messing with time magic..."

I love a good role-play session. Under the table, I hit the button on my phone to cut off the three cameras and mics. Two hours ago, I arrived early to the session and set them up on stands around the table—one facing myself and Nova, one Lyssa and Drew, and one facing Aiden. Those suckers were expensive, and it took me forever to pay off the credit cards, but having good quality footage is invaluable to my channel.

Cameras off, I shake myself out and stretch my hands over my head. "And that's a wrap on session zero. Thanks, all. I can't tell you how much I appreciate it. Aiden— phenomenal DMing. I'd only read a bit about this module, but I can already tell you've put in a lot of work to customize it."

"Thank you, good Lady Danamark." Aiden twirls his hand and gives a bow from his chair.

I chuckle, looking around the table. It's great to play in person with friends again. "And I love the rest of your characters—it was so fun! I've missed you guys. Drew, I love Nam's voice. I had no idea you could act like that." I'm the only one in cosplay tonight, but I bet I can convince them all to embrace a few pieces for my channel's stream. Our chemistry was outstanding. They're all excellent role-players.

Drew smiles and shrugs, tucking a piece of his long hair

behind an ear. He gathers his dice and slides his Player's Guide into his backpack, then tucks the dice bag into the front pocket. Drew has always been so quiet. Lyssa mentioned he lives in an apartment in Atlanta and designs custom computers, but she also said he's brilliant and hilarious. "If we make it to the next level, fifteen, then the Storm Lord will give Namfoodle an eighth level spell, and he'll be able to control the weather. Imagine how annoying he'll be then."

I laugh as I try to catch the eye of the person beside me. Nova files her character sheet away in a binder and puts her dice in a small velvet bag. She's wearing a black punk band t-shirt tonight with cartoon characters of the band members—I guess a throw-back to her emo days. Still hot. Especially during that session when she lifted my hand to her lips to act out our characters' interactions, and when I leaned in to tease her about being a tiefling. And hearing her laugh...

Losing my friendship with Nova was the absolute worst casualty of my relationship with Parker. I have to fix it.

"Nova, I can't wait to hear all about Hunt and their history and motivations. I'm so intrigued already."

"Mm," Nova says as she continues gathering her things, not meeting my gaze.

I lean an elbow on the table. "I know it's late, but do you want to go to the Awful Waffle for old times' sake?" It's our nickname from high school about the all-night breakfast place, ubiquitous all over the south.

"No, thanks." She slides her binder into a leather bag and sticks the dice pouch in one of its pockets.

Well, then. Why'd she flirt with me in-game if she was going to act like this?

I guess she could be tired. Or ran her social batteries

low or something else I don't even know about. She used to like going places but sometimes would shut down afterwards. Perhaps playing in front of cameras was extra draining tonight.

She says goodbye to the rest of the table and hurries out the door.

Everyone cleans up, and it hits me. I'm an asshole. Nova doesn't want to talk to me outside the game because I dropped her as a friend. She acts tough and quiet, but she feels things in a big way. Of course, she doesn't want to be around me now.

I pull the costume horns off my forehead. If only I could go back in time and fix it. I was trying so hard to please Parker, I let my other friendships go. Lyssa was nice enough to reach out to me after she saw my video about Parker and I breaking up. Listening to him about dropping other close friends was the worst decision of my life. At one point, Nova and I used to spend every free moment together. Now I don't even know her.

I gave so much trying to be Parker's everything that I lost my entire self.

I look at the sculpted tiefling horns in my hand. Nova is unique and worth the effort. I want to know her again if she'll give me a second chance.

4
NOVA

I blink at my laptop screen, trying to make my brain get into gear and focus. *Come on.* I sit taller in my computer desk chair. The Adderall I took this morning is wearing off. I guess I could take another, but I was hoping to be done with work by now. I hate this story. It's not mine—an older man's with a famous name who hasn't written his own books in decades. I'm not even the only ghostwriter on this project. After the two of us writers turn in our chapters, a different editor will edit it into the man's distinct style, then run it through a software program that will help in mimicking the "author's" voice. After, another person will manually fix any odd-sounding phrases.

Someone knocks on the door to my apartment. I sigh and shut my laptop. Fine. I hear you, universe. I didn't finish the word count I wanted for today, but my brain is dry, burnt toast. I glance at the clock on my phone as I stand and stretch, walking to the door. Damn. It's after three, and I didn't eat lunch yet. No wonder my mind is gone.

Well...lack of food and also because of how I keep ruminating on June and her video. Why does my brain like to dredge up my greatest embarrassment, churning through it like a boat stuck on a tether making a circle? I stirred the thoughts up by telling Aiden at the cookout. Then playing D&D with June on Saturday... Ugh.

I slide in my socks along the faux wood flooring, making my way to the door. It's probably the handyman who's supposed to fix my dishwasher this week.

Without looking through the peephole, I yank the front door open.

June, in all her rosy-hued glory, stands holding two bags. Fuck.

"Hey, sorry to drop by unannounced." She smiles behind rainbow-mirrored wayfarer sunglasses. Her hair is in a high bun with little curly tendrils escaping down the side of her face. She's wearing an oversized sweatshirt adorned with a cartoon frog, cuffed linen pants, and oxford shoes. How is she so cute on a random Wednesday afternoon? Does she walk around like this all the time? I look like a bum in a gray 5k race tee, soft black pants, and no bra.

"Um..." Expert reply. What exactly should I do here? I opened the door already. If I close it on her, then that's blatantly rude, and it could mess up my plan to win her over in-game. I've already been impolite. I think. It was all I could do not to rush out of Aiden's house after the session.

"I tried to call and text you first, but you didn't answer," she says, shifting her weight to one side. "And I tried to find you on socials, but I found nothing."

"I don't have social media." Other than Discord. And that's solely to chat with the D&D group in Aiden's server. "Where'd you get my address?"

"The player roster and those copyright permission

forms you filled out. You'll need to update your phone number. The number I have saved doesn't work, and that's the same number on your forms."

I didn't expect June to be the one to go through the forms. I thought she'd have an assistant to help with that, or the podcast company would. "It doesn't work because I blocked your number."

She yanks off her sunglasses, glaring at me. "Okay. I get you're mad at me, but is it so bad you needed to block me? What the hell is your problem? We need to work this out."

She's raising her voice. Shit. Confrontation. My heart speeds, and I recoil. "Um. I...er, come in? My neighbors could hear."

"Fine." She steps inside and shuts the door, then sets the two bags on the divider counter to the kitchen without asking where to put them.

"What's in the bags?" A large brown paper bag has a savory smell. Take-out?

She points at the other, a canvas tote. "Professional bleach, hair dye, and all the stuff to apply it. And *this* one is vegetarian pho and tofu wraps. I asked Lyssa about what foods you ate and what your favorite was."

I swallow. My stomach growls. "I didn't ask you to buy me food."

"No shit! Apparently, you *blocked* me. I was doing my best to figure out what you might like. I'm just trying to be your friend." She puts her hands on her hips. She's a head shorter than me, and yet I'm intimidated.

No, I have to stand up for myself. This person contributed to ruining my life and didn't think a second thing about dropping me. Hungry or not, I need to have a spine.

"You shouldn't presume you're aware of what's going on in everyone else's lives. I had good reason to block you."

"I know you did." June's tone shifts abruptly from intense to miserable. She walks over to my brown faux-suede couch and plops down, putting her face in her hands.

She knows, then? She...spread that article about me on purpose? I'm frozen in place. I assumed she forgot about me and didn't know my pen name.

She sighs into her hands. "You're mad at me because I dropped off the face of the planet when I moved away. I get it. I was a shitty friend."

What? No. I was sad when I stopped hearing from her, but back then, I couldn't think anything bad about her.

I follow her and sit in the bucket chair across from the couch.

She drags her hands down her face. "You remember Parker?"

Of course, I do. I couldn't forget that asswipe. Definition of sexism and privilege rolled into one shitty frat-boy. I saw all her posts gushing about him, and even as a casual observer, I could tell he didn't appreciate her. I have no idea why June dated him. I guess they're broken up now, though. Aiden and Lyssa said as much. I realize I haven't answered, and June's looking at me. I nod.

"When we'd been dating around a year, I missed his fraternity graduation dinner where he was up for an award because I was playing D&D with our group. I thought the award ceremony was the following weekend, and I was so absorbed in what I was doing, I didn't see his missed calls and texts. Other than the time we broke up, that day was the only time I saw him cry. The only way I could think of how to fix the situation was to promise him I'd put space between me and my friends and focus on making our relationship work. I was young, ignorant, and in love."

If they were dating around a year, she was probably around nineteen when this happened—right at the time I was graduating high school at eighteen. What an asshole Parker was to think that was an acceptable solution for a single, understandable mistake. The timing makes sense, too—that's when I stopped getting emails and texts back from June and stopped seeing her at events. Yeah, it hurt, but sometimes I forget to text people back too, or life gets in the way.

She reaches out and takes my hand, looking up at me with red-rimmed eyes.

It startles me, but I don't yank back.

"Nova, I'm so sorry. I didn't mean to leave you behind like that. And I never meant to give you the impression I thought I was better than you or any of our friends. I'm not. I'm a fucking mess. For so long, I tried to be the perfect girlfriend and future-wife to Parker like my parents' church taught me, and all it made me was miserable. Like, I might *appear* successful if you watch my channel, but I can't even afford my own place. When Parker and I broke up a few months ago, I couldn't make the rent alone. I lived with him for another two months, then had to move back in with my parents. I've got a few months to come up with a down payment on an apartment and several months' rents before my folks move out of their house."

Must be rough. It's hard for me to scrape together enough money for this tiny place, and I have regular writing jobs. "Um, it's okay. It takes a lot to make it. You have nothing to be ashamed over."

"I'm really sorry. Please. Forgive me?" She squeezes my

hand. Hers is soft and warm, just like it was when I kissed it at the D&D session.

Dammit, this is so unfair. The universe had to drop a fucking adorable former friend at my doorstep. I'm hungry, and my brain feels like mush. The last thing I want to do right now is explain to her what she did to my career by spreading that article.

There's no way I can be her friend again. But what am I supposed to do now? She's pleading with me. And she brought me *food*.

I nod quickly. "Yeah, yeah, of course I can forgive you for falling out of contact."

June smiles and wipes her eyes on the back of her hand. "Good. Um. Also, after we eat, will you dye my roots for me? It's hard to get them even by myself, and I know you used to do wild colors when you were in high school. Honestly, you were part of my inspiration to go for it with the hot pink like Awe."

She didn't dye her hair the color of her character's until two years ago. I know. I used to watch every video on her channel. That meant...even years after we spoke, she still thought of me?

"Annnnd... I brought you some teal if you'd like. No pressure if you don't want to do it. I can help bleach yours first so it shows up really bright. I've gotten good at mixing it."

"Mine?" Wait...

"Well, as you know, tieflings go all the way." She smiles and points at where horns would be on her forehead if she were wearing her costume. "Gotta show your commitment to the character." She winks. "Solidarity, Hunt Wygarthe. But first, food!"

Oh, God. Now I have to dye my hair. I mean, teal is

awesome, and I might've done it anyway for the campaign. But to have June's fingers touching it...June's face near mine... I *should* hate that idea. I do hate that idea. This is just hunger. I'll be able to think straight again after I eat.

We sit at my little round table in the apartment's dining area, which looks out at my balcony of plants—in various stages of under or overwatering.

"I like your place," June says while passing me the plastic bowls and separate soup and noodle containers.

"Thanks." I put a pack of chopsticks and plastic soup spoon next to her place and mine. I can barely afford the one-bedroom third floor apartment, but damn, I love living on my own.

This broth smells divine. It's so hard to find vegetarian food around here—at least any with substance. I open the broth container and pour it over the tofu, rice noodles, sprouts, and herbs.

June smiles at me as I stir my soup and opens her broth container. "My pronouns are she/her. Can I ask yours? I want to make sure I'm using the right ones for you, not just Hunt."

This subject... I take a breath. "My gender is 'don't perceive me.'" One of my favorite jokes, at least that I make to myself. I hate knowing people assume things about me by my appearance.

June blinks and chuckles. "Um."

She's cute when she's nervous. I shrug. "I'm just kidding. If only. It doesn't bother me to be called she, and that's more accurate than he, but it feels like putting on a shirt. Inoffensive but not intrinsically a part of me the way I hear other people identify with womanhood or manhood. I use she or they. Hunt is they/them, so I get to try that on at the table, I guess. I'm nonbinary, too. And even though I'm not a woman, I still resonate with lesbian because of the history of gender-nonconformity in that culture."

Most people around here look at me like I'm some sort of alien when I try to explain, so I usually don't. But my identity isn't for them—it's for me.

June smiles. "Okay. I'll do my best not to perceive you." She winks.

I nod. "Thanks." I appreciate that she doesn't dig further.

The fragrant smell of the pho's spices and herbs touches my nose again. I wish she'd never done that fucking video. We could be catching up, chatting about D&D, and enjoying this meal.

"June, I appreciate the food. And I forgive you for falling out of touch. But I don't think I'm really...comfortable doing your hair. I'll participate by coloring mine, but I'd rather do my own, if that's okay."

Her smile falters, but she shakes it off. "Yeah, of course. Totally understand. You can still borrow my supplies if you'd like. I'm not going to be doing teal anytime soon, so you might as well."

"Thank you."

Once upon a time, I missed her. Forever ago, she was my closest friend. Now she's back, finally broken up with her loser boyfriend, and she seems to want to be my friend again. She even brought me food...

But how can I ever look at her and not see the way my career went to shit? How I'm stuck ghostwriting for an asshole instead of writing what I love? And she doesn't even realize it. To her, it was just another video.

Opening myself up, whether in friendship or anything else, just leads to heartbreak. Every time.

5
JUNE

It's four hours into session two, approaching one in the morning, and we're all about to die. Fuck. Aiden is a sick bastard in the body of a friendly young dad. He's sitting over there, perfectly calm behind his DM screen, holding Eleanor on his knee. Rose is snoozing on his feet, giving the occasional doggy snore, and Eleanor chews a baby toy that looks like a bee. She was asleep for the first two hours of our session, but according to her parents, she's in something called a "sleep regression." Another reason why kids are not on my life's to-do list.

I don't know what I expected from tonight's D&D session, but it wasn't a total party kill on our first day in the dungeon.

Nova looks determined, and she's scribbling notes quickly on her character sheet. Calculating something.

I peer over her shoulder, trying to see.

She covers it with her hand. "No metagaming, Danamark," she mutters, too soft for the mics to pick up. Our sessions are streaming live right now, but the podcast company will cut out all the pauses and edit the sessions into a more concise story later.

A smirk curls the right side of Nova's mouth as they chide me. God, if I thought they were hot before, that teal hair really seals the deal.

"Solla, you're up." Aiden points to his wife.

"Well, I have a spell slot left, so obviously, I cast Fireball. Rank four."

"Hm. You see your companions are in melee with the demons. As well as the other party of captives you've released earlier in the session."

"I spell sculpt it around the civilians and our party."

Aiden points at Lyssa with the back of his pencil. "You're short two humanoids—you can't sculpt around them all."

Lyssa looks at me and Nova. "The tieflings are going to be most likely to survive. Resistant to fire. And Hunt has a decent number of hit points left."

But Awe doesn't. I glare at her from across the table. "Solla, I swear, if you drop another Fireball on my head..." I'm still missing health from the first time. And I've used up all my spell slots from combat after combat, so I can't heal myself or anyone else right now.

"I've looked at the scenario." Lyssa points at the grid board at the center of the table displaying our characters' figures, the enemies' figures, and the non-playable characters' tokens. "It's our best shot at surviving and saving the hostages. You're out of spell slots, Awe. So is Nam."

Drew holds his hands together, pretending to pray. "Yep, Procan says he needs a breather. Even the Storm Lord needs a rest."

"Hunt used all their slots *and* their Lay Hands," Solla

continues. "You two tieflings are gonna have to survive this. Or else we all die."

Aiden looks at his notes behind his screen and grins wider. Fuck. I recognize that look coming from a DM. We're dead. I have so few hit points left already from fighting the swarm of ice demons we accidentally summoned. Aiden gestures to Nova and me. "Dex saves, tieflings."

Our twenty-sided dice clatter to the table at the same time.

Nova's teal die reads seventeen. With that high a number, it's an obvious save. And with Hunt's damage reduction, plus the tiefling fire resistance, that means they take no damage. My pink sparkling die doesn't paint as pretty of a picture for Awe…

Five. Why, dice, why? I've written entire songs begging them to work better, which I've featured on my channel. I've tried punishment, bribes, putting the offending die in time out, and still, I get this. I flip the bird at the die as it shows its pitiful number to the whole table.

Aiden glances at our rolls, then scribbles a number down behind his screen. "Awe, roll that d20 again."

I bet it's a death save. He didn't even bother to have Solla roll her damage yet—Awe's hit points are so low it wouldn't matter if each of Solla's Fireball's d6 damage dice roll ones. Awe is unconscious.

"Wait," Nova cuts in. "I have the Shield Master feat, and I'm already protecting Awe—I think logic dictates I should get a reaction to this."

Aiden shrugs. "That reaction Hunt gets from protection fighting style is if someone is attacking Awe, and you'd be imposing disadvantage on their attack roll."

"A Fireball going off on our heads seems like the same thing," Nova says.

Aiden nods. "I'll allow it. What do you want to try?"

"I want to put my shield over the bard, tucking my body around her to protect her from the flames."

I see the characters in my mind, Nova's Hunt pulling Awe close and tucking her to their chest. Back in high school, Nova and I used to physically act out what our characters were doing sometimes. This encounter would've been fun.

My heart is racing at the idea for some reason. Probably because I'm imagining dodging a Fireball.

"Hunt carries an Orrog shield—it's enormous," I remind Aiden.

His face is neutral. "Fine. Since Shield Master allows you to take no damage if you succeed a dex check against a Fireball, Hunt can dex save to Solla's Fireball at disadvantage while holding Awe. Nova, roll again, and Hunt takes the lowest number of the two rolls to determine if this move succeeds. Difficulty class fifteen."

I pluck my die from the table. "I didn't mean it, Pinky." Blowing on it, I shake it between my hands, then give it a kiss. "Here, use this! She usually comes through for me in a pinch."

Nova has a slight smile on one side of their face as they take my die and roll it on the table. Their paladin doesn't add any bonus to dex. Fourteen... Dammit, Pinky.

Aiden glances at it. "The fire comes down on your heads. Hunt tucks Awe into their shield but, unfortunately, takes the brunt of the heavy blast from the wizard—"

"Bardic Inspiration," Nova says. "Hunt remembers the song Awe sang before the battle, and it inspires them to survive."

Aiden smiles. "You hadn't used yours yet—I was wondering. That adds two to your score, which puts you over the threshold. Barely. Solla—what's the damage to the surrounding ice demons?"

Lyssa rolls a cup of d6, tallies them up, scribbles a number down on a piece of paper, then hands it to her husband, a wicked grin on her face.

Aiden nods solemnly, then flips over the remaining monster pieces on the board. "Good game, everyone. The demons are dead. The paladin and the bard live to fight another day. *Barely*. We'll pick up right here in a week. For now...sleep calls." He looks at his baby, still sitting on his knee. "If the cutest dragon spawn in the world will cooperate."

Phew. I hit the button on my phone to turn off the cameras and mics. "Thanks for that save, Nova."

"Mmm." She nods, picking up her figure depicting Hunt and putting it into a small protective case.

"Yeah, that save Hunt pulled off is *pretty* interesting to me, too," Aiden says, closing his books.

Nova pauses, narrowing her eyes at Aiden. Sheesh, she's still so cold, if not the completely icy demeanor she had before. Even after I brought her food and apologized, and after she said she forgave me, she barely talks to me outside the game. And I think she still has my number blocked. Not that she owes me anything.

In the campaign, as Hunt, they're warm, even flirty, with my character. Hunt saved Awe's life tonight. But as soon as we take a break or the session ends, Nova freezes me out. What gives?

Everyone—with the exception of Nova—chats while gathering their stuff.

Lyssa scrolls on her phone. "Anyone know a player that might want to join up? We could use another martial class. The god of this land is a sadist."

Aiden holds one of his hands in a small circle over his head like a halo and smiles at his wife.

"I'll hold Eleanor if you want while you get a snack and get ready for bed," I offer Aiden and Lyssa.

"Sure." He passes her to me, and she gives me that suspicious baby look.

I cradle her in my elbow. "Hey there, mini sorceress." I snatch up the baby toy Aiden left on the table and wiggle it in front of her face. "Look! A bee!" Heh, she gives me the exact same glare Lyssa does sometimes.

I walk Eleanor in circles around the kitchen, keeping her entertained as I wave goodbye to Drew and Nova. Only one of them waves back at me, and it's not the player of my paladin protector. I sigh. I guess they're not interested in interacting with me. It shouldn't bother me so much that they don't seem interested in friendship.

Eleanor fusses, so I face her outward like I've seen Aiden do, holding her while I walk around the house. Oh, their bookcase is full of good stuff. Fantasy books of all kinds. Some statues on display. Funny—ten copies of the same book, all in a row.

I read the spine. *Curse of the Dragon's Gate* by N.H. David. It's familiar, but I can't place it. The bottom of the thick spine has a Wizards of the Coast seal—D&D related—so maybe it was something I read a while ago for my channel.

"You read that one?" Aiden asks as he walks up to me, holding his hands out for Eleanor.

I pass her to her dad. "Maybe. Looks familiar." I pull a copy from the shelf.

"It's my favorite book." There's something off about Aiden's tone. It's harder than normal.

Oh, shit. "Wait. Is this the book I did a review of a few months ago where the author had never played D&D?" I probably offended Aiden with my review. I stare at the front cover's art and blink. It's a tiefling in mithril armor with teal hair. Reminds me of Nova's character.

I flip the pages open. *Oh my God.* Hunt is the main character. Nova totally ripped this off. Unless... *Shit.* Where's the author bio?

It's printed on the back flap—sparse, with no real identifying details. *...N.H. David is a recluse wordsmith living under the mountains in the realm of King George...* Ah, thank God. They're an English author. It's not like Nova's pen name or something. That'd be terrible, and she'd probably hate me forever.

"Oh, you showing June our favorite book?" Lyssa walks up, going on her tiptoes as she kisses Aiden's cheek. "I bet she's been too busy doing her channel to read anything."

"I read!" Well, I try to, at least. Something's weird about Lyssa's tone as well. What am I missing? I stare at Hunt on the cover again.

Oh, God. I'm such an asshole. Lyssa's right, and I see what she's implying. I didn't even read this book, and they all must love it. I bet Nova's character is an inside wink between all of them. That day I posted the video about this book, I told Parker I wouldn't marry him, and we argued for hours. He tried to guilt me and make me think I was the one in the wrong. I just needed to make one video, *any* video, so my standing in the algorithm wouldn't plummet because I didn't post. I searched for D&D scandals and chose a random one.

I shake my head. "You know what, you're right. I didn't read this one, and I understand why you both must be frustrated if it's a book you love this much. I'm sorry."

Lyssa crosses her arms, shifting her weight to one leg. "Aiden and I only saw your video recently. Between the pregnancy, Eleanor's birth, and both of our jobs, we didn't get to watch every single one of your videos from that time."

"Is that why you dropped the Fireball on Awe?" I tilt my head, studying them both.

Lyssa is mad. *Aiden* is mad—I've made Mr. Sunshine angry. Must be some book.

Lyssa gives me a tense smile, lifting her eyebrows. "Maybe. And don't think that Aiden doesn't know how to properly tune encounter difficulties."

That hellish fight was totally to give Awe a chance to go unconscious—or give Hunt a chance to... What? Take some kind of revenge.

Oh. It's making more sense now. The three of them did plan this—including Nova naming their character Hunt. But Hunt didn't let Awe die, shielding her instead with their body. Why?

Aiden taps the front cover of the book with his arm not holding Eleanor. "This book is fantastic. Best fantasy I've ever read. Too bad we'll never get a sequel."

"What? Why not?" I stare at the beautiful cover art. I can see why Nova wanted to play this character; Hunt is striking.

"After all the backlash online, the author's publisher dropped them. Then their agent did."

Shit, really? "Why didn't you tell me before?" It's clear I'm the last one to know. Like I'm always the last to know everything.

I look at the thick novel in my hands. This had to be years of effort and world building. And all it took was a few assholes online to tear it down.

I hate that I'm one of them.

6
NOVA

I should've got out here on this trail earlier in the morning. It's eleven A.M., and by the time I get back, my day will be halfway over. My feet beat a steady rhythm on the soft trail dirt as trees go by. Just a mile or so, and then I'll be done. Not sure what I'm in a hurry about, as the only things on my to-do list are editing a first-time author's query letter and ghost writing an article for a home goods influencer.

I wipe my forehead with the back of my hand. It's slightly teal. Even days later, that hair dye June brought me is still bleeding onto my skin. I forgot about this part. Guess June deals with this all the time but in pink. Pink would be easier.

My watch buzzes with a notification, and I glance at it.

Cristy. Why is my ex texting me on a Thursday morning? I touch her name, and the full message pops up. *"Call me."*

Ugh, why? I hate calling people. Just text me.

"why?" I text back using the watch.

"Can't text it all," she replies.

I sigh and slow to a walk, hitting pause on my run recording app. Once, I thought Cristy might be the one. She's so genuine and kind. But a few things were going against us. For one, her inability to tell her conservative Catholic family we were dating. I didn't think I could be someone's "roommate" for the rest of my life. And she wanted me to open up and tell her all my feelings after my book release disaster...which, I guess, was legit. That one was on me.

I pull out my phone from my hip pouch and press her number from my favorites list.

She answers on the first ring. "Nova!"

It makes me feel a little guilty how excited she is to talk to me. "Hey, just running."

"Ooh, you getting all sweaty?"

"How is that an 'ooh?'"

She laughs. "So...have you checked *Curse*'s book chart ranking lately?"

"No. I told you. I had to disconnect from all of that—it wasn't healthy."

"You might want to."

"Or you could just tell me."

"Where's the fun in that? I want to hear your reaction. Maybe I should video call you to see your face."

I look skyward. I can't stand being observed, especially when there's some sort of expectation. "Well, I'm out in the woods, so you should tell me if you don't want to wait a few hours." I put it on speaker so I can still hear her while I look this up. Of course, I'm going to check it immediately. I might act like these things don't bother me, but they do.

They really, really do.

The site fills in the search bar with my book title—like my phone remembers how obsessively I used to check the ranking and is judging me.

"You're looking it up now, aren't you?" Cristy asks through the phone's speaker.

Hm. Weird. Number five in the Sword-and-Sorcery category? "The publisher is probably running a sale or something. Clearing off old books. Or they got their BookBub promotion to go through months too late."

"Oh my God, you're such a Boomer. 'I Don't Do Social Media.' I'll save you the time guessing. Your frenemy, Awe Danamark, made a new video about it."

"What?"

"Okay, now I really want to see your face," Cristy giggles.

"I gotta go. Thanks for telling me. Bye." Why couldn't she have texted all of this?

I hit end on the call and open up YouTube. Ugh. It also remembers my login. And I'm still subscribed to June's channel, even though I haven't used the app in months. Her newest video is the first one listed.

"Friends!" June's excited voice starts, the world around me fading away as I focus on her face. She leans in close to the camera with dark circles under her usually perfect eyes. "There's a reason why you haven't heard from me in three days. So, I had a long list of things I was supposed to get done." She lifts a dragon figure still in its box and shows it to the camera. "I was supposed to put this together." She tosses it behind her onto a bed with a dragon-printed quilt. "Instead, I've been reading for three days straight. I know. Usually, you all make fun of me for how short my attention span is. Not that I'm disagreeing. Ooh, a bunny ran by my window!" She waves. "Just kidding. But...this book is going to blow your mind." She shoves a copy of *Curse of the Dragon's Gate* up to the camera so it shows the whole book cover. My stomach drops. Oh no. "Wait until I tell you about this story."

Shit! I reach up to touch my teal hair—just like Hunt's on the cover. If people see this video, see my character's name, and realize I'm affiliated with June...they perhaps could put together my actual *name.* Especially since June's been calling me Nova on the stream, and our real names are in a few places.

When I chose to use Hunt's name for my character, I assumed anyone who saw the stream or listened to the podcast would most likely not recognize them, or if they did, they'd think I was a fan of the book. But now, with June bringing attention to it...

How could she be so careless? She might've figured out I'm the author. And why I'm mad at her. But this is how she decides to fix things rather than talking to me?

Well. I did block her. And I can't think of a time I've used my last name or any other personal identifying info, so the chance of someone actually finding me is low. Still.

"Normally, I hate political intrigue, but this book actually managed to make it personal. And paladins? The worst, right? Overpowered, chauvinistic assholes. But Hunt stole my heart. They were so real and sincere, and every painful decision they made actually tore me apart. I cried, y'all. Real tears. Three times. Also laughed, and I"—she coughs —"*self-cared* more than once." She moves the book cover and gets in the camera's face. "It. Was. Awesome."

Self-cared? Oh. *Oh.*

June's smile falls. "Now for the hard truth. I've said lots of shit in my life out of ignorance. While I'm a diehard feminist—that's right, trolls, I said the f word—and I try to be an ally to all and do my best to be an anti-racist, I still cringe at some memories of things I've done or said. One of the worst things I ever did was publicly jump on a bandwagon of hatred set against this book"—she waves it again—"by some asswipe interviewer who misquoted the author on purpose to make it sound like they'd never played D&D. Back then, I hadn't even read the work. And I trusted the integrity of a wannabe journalist who was trying to get clicks." She looks down and frowns. "I guess I was trying to get clicks too. So, I'm sorry, and I'm gonna try to do better. Y'all go buy this book, and I'm going to go to sleep." She stares into the camera again. "And to the author, if you're seeing this, I'm sorry. I'm really sorry."

The video cuts off. I glance at the views listed under it. Holy crap. If only a fraction of these people go buy the book...

I go into my phone's messages and start composing one to Aiden and Lyssa. *"Hey, did either of you tell June I wrote Curse? She did a video on it and it's blowing up."*

"No," Aiden texts back. *"I actually don't think she realizes you're the author, but you know June. She can be clueless sometimes even when something is right in front of her face. She saw I had ten copies on the shelf and took one home."*

"We'll let it be your call on when to tell her. You holding up okay?" Lyssa asks.

"Yeah, I'm fine. Just was curious," I reply.

Lyssa sends me a heart emoji.

I'm not sure how I feel about any of this. I still have stress dreams sometimes over an angry incel finding me in real life. Even though I've moved apartments since publishing my book.

On one hand, it feels good to hear June say how much she loves my story, especially since she doesn't know it's me and therefore has nothing to gain by posting that video. But on the other, it doesn't really undo the damage she already did. It's not like her apology will bring back my contract. I have to move on. Having a friendship with her will only do the exact opposite for my life.

I put my phone back in my pocket and resume my run.

7
JUNE

I send off an email reply to a sponsor from my laptop as Mom slides a bowl of...something green across the table. A smoothie bowl, maybe? It looks textured. There are pumpkin seeds, chia seeds, raw coconut flakes, and blueberries on top.

"Give that a taste." Mom is in her yoga gear, her reddish-blonde hair in a high ponytail. She crosses her arms, showing more impressive muscles than mine. "It's kale, spinach, avocado, flax seed, and frozen bananas. The blended bananas make it like you're eating a bowl of ice cream!"

"Thanks, Mom!" Ice cream made in hell, maybe. She doesn't have to do this. She *really* doesn't have to.

But this is her way of trying. I'm the middle of three kids—and the only one who needed to move back home. My older brother works as an engineer and is married with a kid of his own, and my younger brother is a music leader at a mega-church at twenty-five.

I try a bite. Texture aside, it tastes surprisingly decent.

"You need to eat more. I checked your fridge and freezer downstairs, and all you have is frozen stuff and cold coffee."

I eat another spoonful. "Diet of champions." Grocery shopping has been low on my priority list. I'm still behind on creating content after my three-day book binge last week. We had another session on Saturday, and Nova didn't speak to me at all when we were out of character. Guess my apology went over like a lead balloon. I've had to remind myself it's not about me, and no one who likes the book is obligated to forgive me over it. Still...it'd be nice.

Mom chuckles. "I know we don't always understand each other, but I worry about you sometimes."

The doorbell rings, and we both look up. A salesman, maybe? I glance out the window and see a sports car in the driveway. A familiar blue Subaru BRZ.

It's Parker. Why is he at my parents' house? Should I bolt for the basement? Mom would understand.

"I'll get it," she says, patting the back of my hand.

I haven't spoken with Parker in...shit, almost three months. I've finally stopped crying, even occasionally.

I hear Mom open the front door. "Hey, Parker."

"Hey, Mrs. Bishop. Junie around? I don't need anything, I just...wanted to say hi if that's okay with you and her. And I brought her this 'cause I thought she'd like it."

"June?" Mom calls. She always liked Parker. I guess to my parents, he looked like a decent guy. He never yelled at me or anything. By all outside perspectives, he treated me well. I never told my parents about my agreement with him to see less of my friends. Or my endless cycle of trying to please him.

Sighing, I get up from the table.

I step in next to my mom. "It's okay, Mom. Hi, Parker. Yeah, we can go talk on the porch."

He's looking...better than last time. A recent haircut, his ashy light brown hair styled with some kind of pomade. "I saw this at the game store and thought you might like putting it together." He holds a purple dragon figure, still in the box. It's a figure I've wanted to buy for myself but didn't have the funds to justify.

Despite our problems, he was always good at small, thoughtful things—moments in our relationship where I felt like he got me and appreciated me. They were why it took me so long to leave.

It feels wrong to accept anything from him, but when I moved out, we both promised we'd be civil and friendly. He gave me space, so I guess I can talk with him for a few minutes. I force myself to smile at him as he hands it to me. "Thanks."

We walk out to my parents' covered front porch and sit on two swivel chairs. I don't ask if he wants to come in—I have a to-do list a mile long.

"I, uh, wanted to stop by and share a few things. I took a job at my company less than an hour from here. Hope that's okay." He smiles. I used to find him so handsome. And he is by any typical standard. But there are no butterflies anymore. "I realize now that I was a bad partner."

What? I bite back the response of "no shit," staying quiet to let him continue.

"And I see why you had to end things. I'm not, like, here to ask you out again or anything. I want to do better and for us to be friends again. Junie, you weren't just my girlfriend; you were my best friend. My only real friend. And, um, I wanna tell you that I intend to try to do better. If you'll allow me to."

He's actually nervous, looking at his hands. He meets my eyes. "I'm sorry. I didn't pull my weight in the relationship and took advantage of you. It didn't hit me how much you were doing until you were gone."

If he'd been able to realize *this* a year ago, perhaps we never would've had to break up.

Well, it'd also depend on if he could follow through on these words. But he's trying here. And I know how much it sucks to apologize and receive nothing but cold silence.

I smile. "Forgiven. Absolutely. I agree, moving forward, no relationship, but we can be friends."

He laughs nervously. "Um, know anyone around here that might want to hang out?"

I shrug. "Nothing that you'd like doing. I'm afraid I don't get out a lot besides gaming."

Parker never had any interest in D&D—or any role-playing game, tabletop, or video game, often telling me how first-person shooters were the only video games worth playing. We made a whole series of videos for my channel about the subject years ago. I thought the fan reactions would be telling me how cute and relatable we were as a couple, but the most common comments were about how I needed to do better and date someone who respects me.

"Oh!" He sits up straight. "I should've told you first!" He points at the box he brought me. "The reason I had that dragon figure is I've been going to the game shop in Charleston regularly. Basically ever since we broke up. They've been teaching me D&D and a few other games. I was wrong about that, too—tabletop RPGs are a lot of fun. And I beat that Dragon Age video game you loved and always wanted me to try. I played a fighter with a big sword. You're right—it's way better than Medal of Honor and Halo."

I blink several times, thinking I must've misheard him. *Parker* playing RPGs?

He rubs the back of his neck. "Yeah, so, like, if your group needs another player, I'd love to join. I can even bring food or whatever. I'm learning to cook, too. I can make a mean frozen lasagna. It's a work in progress."

We both laugh. This...isn't that bad. I'll never want a relationship again with Parker. But friendship? Yeah, it might be nice.

"So," I begin, "I don't know if you're following along with my stream or not..."

He nods. "I am, actually."

"We're getting lit up by Yhallister's traps. Our party is a little light on the martial side. I'd have to ask the rest of my friends, but if they're cool with that, would you be willing to appear on my stream?"

His eyes light up. "Oh man, I never expected this!" He leans forward and hugs me around my shoulders. "Thank you!"

I pat him on the back lightly, and he releases me. "Yeah. Of course! You said you liked playing Dragon Age as a fighter with a big sword? We could really use that."

One of the reasons I moved here was to get away from Parker. Am I making a big mistake by giving him this chance?

Nova

June's cheery voice comes through my computer's speakers as I sit on my couch Monday night, playing my favorite PC game where I'm tromping through the fjords as a tough Viking woman. "So, what do you guys think? Is it okay for Parker to come on Saturday?"

The group is quiet over Discord. June asked us to hop on to discuss adding a player. But fuck, Parker? I mean, it shouldn't surprise me. Don't plenty of people end up going back to their familiar-yet-shitty partner? My chest feels like it's burning inside.

"June...are you sure about this?" Lyssa's voice is incredulous. With all those red flags June shared with me, and I'm sure with Lyssa too, how could she think this is a good idea?

"Yeah. Like I said, he was super sincere with his apology."

With no one to watch me, I indulge myself with an epic eye roll. Yeah, right. He just wants to weasel his way back into her life. I should speak up. Tell her right now what a bad idea this is.

"As far as the campaign goes," Aiden starts, "your party *is* hurting now. I'll reiterate, I created this campaign to be a challenge. One you have all the resources for, to be sure, but a challenge."

"I'm fine with it," Drew says. "We can let him try."

I pause my PC game and minimize it, pressing the buttons a little harder than needed.

Please, no—playing with June's ex sounds awful. But I don't want to be a dick or sound like I'm gatekeeping the game. I hit the computer's push-to-talk button to speak on Discord. *Just say something.* I have to keep my voice even and sound nonchalant.

"I don't think it's a good idea. He's a new player. He might be more of a detriment than a help. It's not like we have a lot of room for failure after the last two sessions."

"Yeah, but we were all new players once," June replies. "He's been practicing for months. He sent me his character sheet. His character looks well-made—albeit with a cliché name. He didn't choose any bad feats or anything."

"Yeah, send that to me," Aiden says. "I bet I can make it work with the plot. Anyone else with a reason to not let him join?"

Everyone is silent over the channel. Dammit.

"Cool. And y'all good with me being the final decision maker after I look at that sheet?"

"Yes, of course," June says.

"Yep," Drew replies at the same time.

"Nova?" Aiden asks.

I make a noise of frustration no one can hear before taking a breath and pushing the push-to-talk button, calm again. "You're the DM. It's your call." This is exasperating. I flip back over to my computer game.

"Hey, Nova?" June's voice.

My character leaps from a high ledge, stabbing some hapless flunky to the story's villain. "Yeah." I can't properly ignore her when we're on a chat like this.

"I sent you something. In the mail."

"Okay."

"Let me know when you get it. I'd just text you about it, but…"

I still have her blocked.

"Okay," I say again, making my character run away from a gathering crowd of enemies. Ugh. Fine. I hit pause. "I'll go check for it now if you want to hold on."

"Sure! Hop down in the other channel and we can chat about it."

Her name jumps down to the private chat room in Aiden's Discord. I click it to join the channel.

"I'll be right back," I tell June. "I gotta run to the apartment mail room at the clubhouse."

"It's a package."

Odd, but okay. I slide into my sandals, leave the apartment, and jog toward the clubhouse building.

Less than ten minutes later, I'm carrying the medium-sized package as I shut and lock my apartment door again. I sit on my couch and pull apart the box top, peeling the packing tape back. It's addressed from June's house. Inside, there's a smaller box—plain cardboard with the words "gargantuan gold" printed in block letters.

"Nova, you back yet?"

I hit the push-to-talk button. "Yeah. I'm opening it now. Gargantuan gold?"

"Yep! It's a dragon figure by a smaller sculpting company—should be a statue with gold scales. I noticed you had a few different fantasy figures on the shelves of your apartment when I was there a few weeks back. It's a freebie a sponsor sent me."

I lift off the lid...and am *not* greeted with any kind of dragon I was expecting. It appears to be a very detailed, enormous, textured dildo in a silk lining. It has ridges and scale-like edges. Maybe someone's idea of what a dragon's dick would look like? Sometimes...there are no words. I blink for a few seconds.

"You still there?"

"June..." I swallow. "Where's the rest of the dragon?"

"What?" She has no idea. Oh my God.

The humor of the situation overwhelms me all at once, and I burst out laughing. Oops—I'm still holding the button.

"What's funny?"

"You..." I'm laughing so hard my eyes are watering. I think from the sheer shock of it.

"*I'm* funny? You know, I was trying to do something nice. If the figure is broken, I'm sure I can find another—"

"Oh, it's not broken. It's very, very whole." And it appears uncircumcised. "Uncut." I still can't stop laughing.

"I'm gonna need more context, Dawson!"

I wipe away some tears, still unable to stop giggling. I'm a real mature adult. "Hold on, I'm unblocking your number and sending you a picture." I snag my phone from the coffee table and do that, lifting *the item* out of its box so she can get a good idea of the sheer heft of it and snap a picture. It looks like under the thing, there's a carrying case and some sort of strap. To go on the wall? To go on a person? Who knows.

"Did you get the picture?" I ask a moment later.

Silence.

"Juuuunne," I prod over Discord.

"Oh my God, I'm so embarrassed I could die!" she yells so loud her voice distorts from my computer speakers. "Fuck me!"

"With this thing? Looks too big for actual use. I dunno. I think you might be playing an entirely different dungeon-based game."

"Ah! No! I mean, not that there's anything wrong with—"

"I'm messing with you." I cut her protests off. "Obviously, you sent me the wrong package. Heh, package. Though now I'm curious just how many dragon dicks you have in your home." I can't help it. God, she's so fun to tease. I know I shouldn't enjoy it, but during our game nights, teasing her is my favorite part. Always was.

She groans. "Ughhhh, as if I wasn't embarrassed enough. Look. I have an OnlyFans account that I post on occasionally under the name Juno D. Mark. Not like super risqué stuff, but I review adult toys with fantasy themes and do more...adult cosplay. I had to have gotten the boxes confused."

I open the browser on my computer and run a search.

"Say something," she says.

"Hm? Oh, I'm subscribing to your OnlyFans."

"*What?*"

"Why, does that bother you? Not trying to make you uncomfortable. I thought since you were putting it on the internet and telling me about it, you wouldn't mind."

"I-I don't mind. Go ahead. In fact, I *dare* you to subscribe."

"Fine. Let me know if you need me to send you more pictures of me with the dragon dick."

Fuck, that was too much. I realize it as soon as it leaves my mouth. What's wrong with me? One, she's straight. Two, she's probably getting back with her ex-fiancé. I feel like I either overshare or undershare in absolutely every human interaction.

"Yes, please," she squeaks out.

"Really?"

"Ah, er, I can come get it! I mean—ugh, I'm so embarrassed. But I probably should post photos reviewing it. It was in my sponsor agreement. If you think you can send me videos of yourself, like, without your face while holding it, that's fine, too. But then you'd be appearing in my Only-Fans. And I'm not asking you to do that. And...I'm going to go die of embarrassment now and hope we both wake up in the morning with amnesia."

Discord makes the disconnect noise as June signs off.

I grab my phone and send her a text, still chuckling to myself about the 'gargantuan gold.'

"Gotta hand it to you. A man might send an unsolicited

picture of his junk. You just mailed me the whole dick. I admit, I'm impressed by the size."

The dots appear, indicating she's writing something, and I'm nervous.

"Haha! If you want to be technical, you're the one who sent the dick pic, and guess what? Since I gave it to you, it's your dick. AND it was your first text to me in four years, ten months, and eleven days. A dick pic."

The familiar sting to my heart hits again—like it does every time I think of June. I should be immune by now. *"You counting?"*

"Maybe." She sends a winking face with its tongue out.

I'm such a fool. I should block and delete her number before I let her break my heart again. *"Inventory check, Awe. How many different types of dicks do you own?"* I send the eggplant emoji.

"You'll have to come over and find out."

A noise escapes my throat as I imagine it. I don't want to be attracted to her. Are we flirting? Is she even able to consider me that way?

I stick the ridiculous toy back in its box and close the lid.

8

JUNE

The cacophony of the orc market buzzes around Awe and her traveling companions. Orcs of all types bustle around, anything from small orcs to massive ones and everything in between. The smells of roasting meat, sweet baked breads, spices, and other foods that Awe has never tried float on the air, and she's hearing at least five distinct languages going at the same time. When the group stepped through a portal hidden in a painting in the dungeon, this was *not* where Awe expected to go.

Namfoodle haggles with a vendor over the price of an enchanted cape. It'd be nice to amass some magic items—and offload some of the finds from the dungeon. "Have I told you about Procan?"

"The Storm Lord," Awe, Hunt, and Solla all say in unison, looking at each other and grinning. They've heard the gnome mention his god no less than fifty times over the journey so far.

"God of the wind and sea? Well, he can be quite generous to those who help his followers." Nam flashes his holy symbol, printed on his ritual book. "And quite smitey with those who don't."

The orc decides to agree to Namfoodle's price.

"Great." Awe claps her hands together. "That should help Nam's ability to blend in and make him harder to hit. And we still have enough money left to hire someone to help us with the rest of the wizard's sprawling, whacked-out dungeon."

Hunt sighs.

"Copper for your thoughts, my paladin friend?" Awe asks. She's been waiting for a chance to confront them.

They straighten. "Apologies. I was just remembering something."

"Something about your great-uncle perhaps?"

"What?"

Awe takes a few steps closer to Hunt, tracing her hand along their mithril breastplate. "Oh, don't think that I don't know who you are. I knew something was up with you the first day we met. When we were in the enchanted library a night ago, we were able to ask an all-knowing book a question—and I asked it about you."

"I'm afraid I don't know what you mean," they say with a smile. "I'm your guardian."

"Right—and that's what doesn't make sense to me." Best to get it all out in the open. "It was because of a situation of my making that your beloved great-uncle died. Sometimes, when I listen in on what you mutter before battle, you speak of vengeance. By all rights, you should want me dead. And yet. When we were down on our luck, you could've let me get singed to a crisp by Solla's Fireball, and you didn't. Why?"

Hunt grins wider. "My lady, I'm a paladin."

"And?" Awe leans in to where her face is inches from Hunt's.

Hunt doesn't back away, their hazel eyes staring into Awe's. "I'm a person of honor."

"Mm. Yes, but I'm not."

Hunt bites their bottom lip, looking Awe up and down. "That much is obvious. Wearing stolen armor and a magical lute plundered from a red dragon's horde."

"Then why not let the blast kill me?"

"It wouldn't be honorable to let a stray fireball—"

"Hey, isn't someone going to hire me?" A rude voice cuts in.

Awe and Hunt turn. Solla and Nam are already staring at the source of the voice.

A tall man is standing near them—covered in tattoos with shoulder-length white hair and a huge sword strapped to his back.

"Do we know you?" Hunt's voice is hard.

"Oh, she's about to." The man winks, then moves forward to put an arm around Awe's shoulders.

Awe wants to tell the newcomer man to back off. But perhaps this particular man might get his feelings hurt if she's too rough with him. Perhaps he's new to the...market.

"The name's Jerald of Rivera. I'm a mercenary for hire."

Hunt rolls their eyes. "Ah. That's the first time I've ever heard a name like that."

Awe moves the man's arm from her shoulders and takes a step back. "We are looking for a hired sword, as luck would have it."

"Great. Then I'm your man."

Jerald has the gall to demand a large chunk of the party's money, but Awe is able to argue that the majority of the party's treasure will come *after* they leave the dungeon, as their deal is with Garaxle, richest person in the city, and they agree to hire Jerald.

The next few hours of time in their world are...difficult. Jerald kills two people in the orc market who look at him wrong.

The group is barely able to flee from the guards through the portal they came in and doesn't have a chance to fully restock their rations—something they could've used.

And when they're trying to listen for enemy footsteps in the corridors of Yhallister's dungeon, Jerald won't stop bragging. "My armor class is so high nothing could hit me."

"I don't know what an armor class is, but I can assure you, this is *not* the time," Hunt's tense voice hisses.

Jerald barks out a laugh. "Heh, you don't know? Man, I thought you guys all knew more about this than me."

"Friends—I'm detecting magic." Solla sounds strained. "There's a chamber here, hidden away, where we can rest. And we certainly all need it."

Turning in early sounds good to Awe, too.

My friends glance at each other around the table. They're annoyed—and honestly, so am I. We ended the campaign early. It's not even midnight yet. I didn't expect Parker to play perfectly, but I thought he'd do better than this. He said he played with a group in a game shop before.

He grins. "Yo, that was fun! Thanks for letting me come. I kicked some ass."

Nova grinds their teeth, twirling their pencil back and forth. "Parker. When you played in Charleston, did anyone ever tell you about the term 'murderhobo?'"

"No, why?"

Nova sighs, touching their fingers to their temple. "Fine. I'll tell you. A 'murderhobo' is someone who wanders the land with no connections or ties to the greater world, indiscriminately killing and looting whatever the fuck he wants."

"Haha, that's awesome!" Parker laughs. "Yeah, sounds like my character."

Nova cuts their glare my way.

I shrug. "Er, I think what Nova is saying is, you'd have more fun if you'd interact with the world with...words. And also try to connect with some of our characters."

"Oh, yeah. I'm gonna connect with Awe so hard."

"Parker." Aiden closes a DM guide and points the book at Parker. "How about you give me a call or set up a time we can chat on Discord? I have a few...ideas for your character."

"Yeah, sure, man!"

"Well." Nova stands, putting a hand on the table. "I need to head out."

"Hey." I touch the back of their hand. "You want to do something tomorrow?" Ahh, what the hell am I doing? They're about to turn me down in front of everyone. I have to save face. "I mean, any of you are welcome to come. There's this game-themed bar in downtown Gainesville. I keep meaning to check it out. They have an open call for people playing Rock Band—you know, the game where you control instruments—as well as card game tournaments every Sunday evening."

"I wish we could, but I'm afraid we can't leave Eleanor for that long." Aiden shrugs with a sad smile. "Sounds fun, though."

"Yeah, little sorceress won't take a bottle these days, and bringing a baby into a loud bar sounds like a bad time for everyone involved. Raincheck for about two months from now when Grandma and Grandpa can watch her for longer than an hour?" Lyssa asks.

"Thanks for the invite, but I have a standing online raid group on Sunday nights for World of Warcraft." It's funny how serious Drew sounds—then, when we're playing D&D, he uses such a hilarious voice as Namfoodle's.

Parker lifts his glass, about half full of the lager he poured earlier. "I'll go with you, Junie. Music and beer sounds fun. I can even pick you up."

That's just fan-fucking-tastic. Now I've set myself up on a date with the man it took me months to leave. No one else is going to come. Why'd I have to open my freaking mouth?

Nova's and my eyes meet. *Help me*, I inwardly plead.

She leans on the table. "Um, I was about to ask June if she could drive me, actually. Parking my car is a pain in the ass downtown."

Nova wants to come with me. My stomach flutters at the thought. She drives a small sedan, and I doubt she has trouble parking it anywhere. Does this mean she made that excuse to ride with me?

Parker downs the rest of his beer and laughs. "I don't have a problem parking. Decks, parallel, you name it. Maybe having trouble parking is a woman driver thing."

"Oh, good grief!" The words burst out before I can stop them. "Shut up and stop misgendering my friend." I told him Nova was nonbinary and to be respectful of that. Why is he such an ass? "And if you're so proud of your driving, just drive yourself."

Stunned silence hangs across the rest of the group.

Parker puts his hands up. "Okay, okay. I'm sorry. That was a real dick thing to say. Forgive me, Nova? And June, what time do you want to meet at the bar?"

Nova nods thanks at me and starts gathering their stuff.

I guess it's good he apologized. He's trying, even if his best isn't great. But I wish he would've backed out of tomorrow's plans entirely. I don't know how to reply. "Um, let's say six-thirty at the bar. Nova, I'll pick you up at six?"

They turn to me, a ghost of a smile on their lips. "Yeah, sure."

Am I winning her over a little? I texted her a few D&D memes throughout the week, and she replied every time. She even sent a few teasing comments about the gargantuan gold. Still can't believe I was so foolish to send her that without checking the contents of the box.

With every interaction we've had, missing her gnaws at me more. I want more time with grown-up Nova. Maybe this could be our new start.

9
NOVA

I'm waiting in the apartment complex parking lot when June comes to get me, pulling into a spot in a ridiculously sized white pickup truck. Somehow, it's the last thing I expected to see her in. She lowers the window and waves. "Hey!"

Heh, tiny June driving something huge like this. I guess she notices the look on my face because she adds, "It's my dad's, and if he were here, he'd add that it's a hybrid, not a gas guzzler, and Mom insists everyone knows it." She rolls her eyes, grinning. "My car is leaking something, and I need to fix it. I mean, it works when I need it to, but since Dad wasn't using the truck..."

"No judgment here." I nod at her and walk around the truck. God, why do I find it so cute she's so small? She's straight and practically on her way to going out with that douche again. I open the passenger door and pull myself inside.

This evening is the perfect temperature to wear anything. June's light-purple dress could fit in at a Renaissance Fair, with puffy sleeves and a ribbon lace-up bodice.

It does good things to her figure. But I shouldn't look. I glance instead out the passenger side window as she backs out of the parking space.

"Thanks for the save, by the way," she says.

"The time I saved Awe's ass or yours?"

June says she doesn't want to date Parker. Yet. But she defended him over Discord. And she didn't disinvite him from our game after he was an ass.

She laughs. "I guess both. Like, I know Parker is trying, but I do *not* want to go out with him ever again. Not in any way."

I wish I could believe her. But it's not the first time I've been burned by liking a straight girl. By liking June.

Wait. No. I don't like her. She ruined my life, and my character has an oath of vengeance against hers. Hunt's just biding their time. Shit.

"Was he always like that?" I find myself asking before I can get my brain to stop the words. I glance at her.

She frowns as she pulls out on the main road. "Parker? I dunno. Maybe?"

We ride in silence for a moment. I shouldn't have asked. It doesn't matter—and I don't want to talk bad about a dude she's probably going to get back together with.

"Well," June starts, "looking back now, it seems silly I stayed with him as long as I did. I mean, a dude who encourages his girlfriend to stop hanging out with her hometown friends is like *big red flags for sale!*"

I chuckle. "Yeah. But, you know, sometimes love puts blinders on us, right?"

Her eyes cut to me as she pulls up to a redlight. "Totally. And now I have a hard time trusting my own judgment, especially when Parker is involved. I'm working on breaking my bad habit of people-pleasing, but it's tough to shed old dynamics."

Yeah, I knew it. She still likes him. Of course. It shouldn't bother me, but dammit, it does. "Rolling at disadvantage on your checks with him, then? It's okay; I'm pretty sure I roll all social interactions at disadvantage." Especially with her.

"Okay, we have to talk about the elephant in the room. Er, the truck. I mean, it's large enough for one, but we'll feel a lot better if we talk about it. I'm talking about *Curse of the Dragon's Gate*."

Oh, shit, she does realize I'm the author. She has to— I've been playing the main character.

"I dunno if you watch my channel, but I read it recently. For the first time."

"Yeah?" My voice sounds too strained to be natural. I should've driven separately. I don't want to be trapped while rehashing some of the worst moments of my life.

"I know it's a special story to you, Aiden, and Lyssa. Even after apologizing in my most recent video, I still feel guilty about what I said when I trashed it."

What? She thinks we're all superfans or something?

The light turns green, and we start moving again. "I swear," June continues, "I'm not that type of person. Someone who piles on with hate. I...was having the worst day of my life. Not that it excuses it or anything. Parker and I'd been fighting more and more. Including some really bad ones. I got behind on posting. I knew if I didn't post *something* that got decent traction, I'd lose my place in the YouTube algorithm, as well as TikTok, so I literally searched 'recent D&D scandals' because I knew that'd be my quickest way to views. I put zero effort into fact-checking or researching because I just wanted it to be done. And I was an absolute ass for doing so."

I try to process her words, looking out the window as we get onto the ramp to merge onto the interstate toward the city. It doesn't necessarily make the situation better for me...but I trust that June had no malicious intent in posting that video.

Of course, she didn't. She couldn't be malicious if she tried. Here she is, trying to give this awful dude another chance even though he's hurt her before.

"What were you fighting about?" I ask.

June blows air, making her cheeks puff. She turns on her blinker to go around a slow car in the right lane. "You name it. I'd graduated the previous year with a degree in marketing, but instead of getting a traditional job, I was putting all my effort into growing my channels. I think Parker was a bit jealous all my attention was going there instead of to him. And at the time, he hated all RPGs, so he didn't understand it all or why I cared so much. He wanted me to be a more traditional wife. And I responded by telling him I couldn't marry him."

I scoff, then get control of myself. She doesn't need to hear my detest for Parker.

She glances at me as she twists her hands on the steering wheel. "Yeah, it sounds really bad, and I guess it was. I don't think he was or is *trying* to be an asshole. That's how his parents raised him, you know? Under all of that, he's this super sweet guy. He made me laugh. When we were together, he told me good things about myself and tried to help me build self-confidence."

"June, a super sweet guy doesn't ask his girlfriend to give up her friends or make her feel guilty for doing something she loves." Not to mention all the absolute sexist bull-shit behind the definition of a 'traditional wife.'

"Yeah. Maybe so." She shakes herself, getting back in the right lane. "Regardless, we weren't a good match. I held on for too long. The day I posted the video was the day I realized that our relationship was broken beyond repair. There was no amount of therapy or changing that either of us could do that would make us compatible. I was engaged to him—and in order for me to find any personal happi-ness, I was going to have to give up him, give up his family, and give up the future family that we planned. For good. Even if that meant not being able to afford my own place. Hence living with my folks.

"I mean, I have plans to get out. When NerdyPodCasts produces the podcast version of my show, the royalties should be a steadier income along with my usual revenue, and I'm hoping to get my own apartment. Or maybe one of the many jobs that I applied for will come through. I applied to the all-star D&D reality show they're casting. Did you hear about it? It'll be like a gameshow within D&D with a chaotic eye monster as the host. Though I'm not really famous enough that they'd want me."

"It sounds cool. You should keep trying. Freedom is always worth it." Even though it's stretching my budget, I love living alone in my own apartment. "I'm waiting on a few applications, too. An MFA program and scholarship." Unlikely to ever happen, but it didn't stop me from applying.

"You were such a brilliant writer in high school. I bet you're fantastic now."

"Er, thanks." Taking compliments is always tough, even about my writing. I should tell her now that *Curse* was my book. But then what if it makes the evening weird and ruins this tenuous understanding we seem to have?

"What about you? You, er, have better luck in love than I did?" She sounds nervous about asking.

"Uh, yeah, probably so, since you dated *Parker*."

We both chuckle. Damn, I don't want her to go back to him...

"June. Don't date Parker again. You know that's why he's at our D&D table." She has to know.

"Oh, I'm not interested in that. I already told you. I'm just trying to be nice. He needs friends."

An annoyed sound comes from my throat before I can rein it in. "You just give me the signal when Hunt needs to murder his plagiarized character." Though she probably thinks I'm plagiarizing too. *Tell her.* But the words stick in my throat.

"Why, thank you, my gallant paladin." She reaches over the huge truck cabin and squeezes my knee.

Butterflies again? *Stop it!* I tell my body. I don't like her.

"Well." She puts her hand back on the steering wheel. "Spill it, then. You better tell me."

My face burns. Tell her what? Does she suspect I'm the author? Or perhaps I'm easier to read than I thought, and she can see that I find her attractive. Did...she always know? "Um. Tell you what?"

"You're embarrassed!" She cackles. "I'm asking about your love life, you dork. Who are you blushing for?"

"I'm not." I shake my head. Good. Then she doesn't realize. Not that I feel anything but *completely normal* attraction to a pretty woman. Who's straight. I clear my throat. "It's not like that. I, er, needed to tell you there's a good chance my ex will be at the bar tonight."

"Mmmhm?" June turns down a street that has the sun shining in our eyes and pulls down her shade.

"I dated Cristy for about a year and a half. We lived together for a year."

"Oh?"

I don't really want to get into talking about all the details. I tug on my t-shirt collar. It's too damn hot in this car. "Yeah. She ended things, but we're friends. We still talk a few times a week."

"A few times a *week*? Then why are you giving me crap about being friends with Parker?"

"Wha—?" I sputter. "I-I'm not! And it's different! The queer social scene around here is much smaller than the straight dating pool. It's not like Cristy and I had a bad break-up or anything. We just…"

The memory hits me hard and has me clenching my fist against the truck seat. Cristy had tears running down her beautiful face, smearing her dark mascara. I hadn't left the apartment for going on two weeks at that point. "This isn't sustainable! If you can't talk to me about what bothers you, Nova, then it's not a relationship! Please." She tried to take my hands, but I pulled away.

I flipped over on our bed to where she couldn't see my face. "Don't blame this on me! It's not like it was ever a real relationship if you're telling your family we're just room-mates!" I was lashing out, trying to turn it around on her, when I was the one who couldn't find my way out of my own head.

Bringing myself back into the present, I shudder. "It was a hard year for me in several ways. Cristy and I didn't make it as a couple. But she's still a close friend. She has another friend group that meets up at that bar for the card tournaments every Sunday. We might see her there. You'll probably like her."

I don't want to make June feel bad by mentioning it, but Cristy has almost as much of a vendetta against June as I did. Do. I definitely still do. Damn, I have to remember I have a grudge against her.

But June apologized—twice now. I look at her profile as she turns on her blinker to exit. Maybe that could be enough for us to start again as friends. Of course, that'd make me a fool. I broke my own heart by having such a huge crush on her when we were younger and she dated scumbag dudes.

"Well, at least I won't be the only one feeling awkward around my ex. Tieflings stick together, right?"

"Together into trouble, maybe."

Trouble of more than one kind.

10
JUNE

Some dude's off-key voice blasts through the speakers on the bar stage. The three guys playing Rock Band chose Freebird. Why is it always Freebird? I scoot my wooden chair a few more inches away from Parker. It's sticky-hot in here. I'm sweating under my boobs in this dress, and the puffy ruffles at the bottom make me stick out like a sore purple thumb.

It's like the universe is conspiring to annoy me. The game bar is otherwise nice enough, and the food and game-themed drinks are good, but Parker keeps trying to sit too close. Earlier, he insisted on buying dinner for our table. I mean, I need all the financial help I can get, but still, it feels icky. Maybe Nova's right, and he's doing all of this to weasel his way back into a relationship.

Don't date Parker again. Nova's voice was so serious. Why do they care, though?

They're laughing and playing games with their ex. What's the difference?

Cristy has gorgeous, shiny black hair, great style, the common sense not to wear a poofy Renaissance dress to a game bar, and an infectious laugh. After dinner, she imme-diately drafted Nova into playing Last Imagination, an RPG card game.

Cristy and Nova sit at a table across from two other players, competing on a two-person team. This is a compli-cated game with rules I don't know.

Parker and I have chairs pulled up behind them, watch-ing. He scoots closer to me again, acting like he's trying to get a better view. Why am I such a fool? Nova was right. I really should've known his whole reason for trying to join our game and probably even moving here was about getting back in with me.

"Pssst," Cristy beckons Nova closer, then whispers something in her ear.

Nova laughs, covering her mouth with her hand, her short fingernails decorated with black nail polish. "No way." I love the way her new teal hair contrasts with her black shirt and nails. I was the one who convinced her to dye her hair. She'll have to explain that to her ex. Right?

Cristy raises her eyebrows and nods like she and Nova are in on a secret.

And why wouldn't they be? They're still close. Nova said they were.

What is this ridiculous tight feeling in my chest?

"Hey, you want to get another drink and take a walk outside?" Parker puts a hand on my lower back.

No, that's the last thing I want. How do I get out of this? I didn't want to go on a fucking date with Parker—I don't want to be with Parker! This is the worst. I just wanted an excuse to come to this bar with Nova.

I watch her as she slams a card down on the table, pointing to a number on it.

The two men on the other side of the table competing

against Nova and Cristy both groan, leaning their foreheads next to their beers and cards. Nova high-fives Cristy, who cackles and grips Nova's hand tight in hers. I want to be the one she conspires with. The one to make her smile and laugh.

Do…I have a crush on Nova?

The thought has me sitting bolt upright.

"June. Did you hear me, honey?" Parker rubs a little circle on my lower back.

"What?" I stand, taking a step away from Parker and his uninvited hand.

"Let's get a drink and take a walk."

Shit. I look around, needing an excuse. Any excuse. "No, I really wanted to play Rock Band. It's why I wanted to come to this bar." Ridiculous, but I hope it's a good enough excuse for now. I step forward and tap Nova's shoulder.

They turn, mid grin. I know it's about the card game, whatever inside jokes Nova and their ex have, and not about me at all, but the sight of their smile makes my heart skip.

"Come on, let's tell them we want to go next!" I point at the stage, where two huge TVs, one in front and one behind, are set up with the Rock Band game.

She puts her hands up. "Oh, no. I don't do stuff in front of people."

"Please? I was going to pick Fall Out Boy. I saw it on the list when someone else was choosing. And I know no one else that knows all the words by heart like you do."

Nova drapes an arm over the back of her chair as she angles her body toward me, narrowing her eyes. "*You* know all the words, too. Don't pretend you don't. We used to belt their songs while driving around."

"But I'm not coordinated enough to do the guitar parts

and sing at the same time!" I complain. "Come on. Please?" I give her a fake pouty lip and pull on the hand she put over the back of her chair.

Nova rolls her eyes but stands. I don't drop her hand. Maybe she'll let me hold onto it longer. "Um, guess that's it for me on Last Imagination," she tells Cristy. "Maybe you could teach Parker."

Cristy looks back and forth between Nova and me. Damn. She knows what I'm trying to do, and she's going to say no. But instead, she laughs and shrugs. "Eh. Sure. Why not?"

Parker is in Nova's chair in an instant. "You would? This game looks fun." Parker sounds excited? Maybe he's not completely faking it about liking RPGs now.

Which means...I can escape this situation! Yes! Must've rolled high on my charisma checks.

"Come on!" I pull Nova toward the stage. The guy running the Rock Band games sits nearby. Nova and I dodge around other people in chairs or walking through the bar. I squeeze their hand tighter. They don't drop it until we get in front of the announcer's small table.

The man is a little older than us, with no hair on top, sitting behind a laptop. He glances up at me. "There's about an hour wait right now if you want to play Rock Band." He leans closer, pointing at Nova. "Unless you're getting her to sing. In that case, you can go next."

Nova rolls her eyes. "Dan, just put us on the list, and maybe June will get bored and give up before it gets to our turn."

"Nova's gonna sing? They can take my spot!" A guy with glasses and spiky hair calls from a nearby table and then laughs with his friends. They're also playing Last Imagination. Must be a group Nova knows.

Nova's face is red. "Cristy and I used to come here a few times a week when the place first opened," they mutter to me. "I've never been on the stage before. A lot of people have tried to get me up there."

I'm the one who convinced them? I grin, raising myself on my tiptoes to look into their eyes. "It's because you can't deny the call...of the emo."

She looks skyward. "Christ."

I grab her arm. Another excuse to touch her. I can't help myself. "Don't worry. I'll be up there with you."

"That's actually more of why I'm worried. I played Rock Band at your house when it first came out. Did you...get any better?" She doesn't push me away.

I stick my tongue out at her.

She brushes hair from her forehead with her other hand. "Ah. We're screwed, then."

I might be.

Freebird is finally, *finally* ending. What kind of masochist put that song in the game, anyway?

"Well, get up there." Dan shoos us onstage. "I'll be your third. Want to play guitar or drums?"

Drums are way harder. "Guitar!" I take the plastic instrument controller from the Freebird guy who had it before. I haven't played this game in years.

Crap. I'm about to make a big embarrassment of myself. In front of a lot of people. Somehow, I didn't calculate for this when I was trying to get away from Parker...and get Nova to stop laughing with her ex. I glance out over the crowded bar and restaurant. Cristy is watching us while talking to Parker and pointing to the numbers on the cards.

I acted that way because I was jealous.

Why? It shouldn't matter if Nova has other friends. It's not like there's a limit on how many friendships a person can have. And Lord knows I don't want to act like how Parker used to with me. But I wanted a night for Nova and I to...what? Rekindle a friendship? Get...closer? My throat is dry, and these colored stage lights are already making me sweat.

"June." Nova nudges me. They're holding the silver mic, and they look so hot up here on the stage with their teal hair, black eyeliner, and that black tee with the perfect fit. With the blue and purple lights on them, it's like I'm onstage with an actual rock band. Except I have no idea what I'm doing and don't play an instrument. This could be a scene out of someone's nightmare. And the person I have a huge crush on is right next to me, about to watch me fail—

"Oh shit!" The words squeak from my mouth. I *do* have a crush!

She chuckles, pointing the mic at me. "Stage fright? This is your doing. I don't feel bad for you at all."

Dan sits behind the plastic drums. "Which song?"

"Sugar, We're Going Down," Nova tells him, winking at me.

My stomach turns a flip.

Dan uses the drum pad's controller to select the song on the big-screen TV facing us, and a memory leaps into my mind—driving with Nova through this same downtown area, singing this song at the top of our lungs. My senior year, Nova's junior. She was one of the few friends I had who I could be myself with and get no judgment. We made up so many stories about our D&D characters...mine who eventually became Awe.

The game clicks off the song's beginning. The guitar track starts, and I'm immediately missing notes. Someone is the audience boos. Crap. I focus harder on the screen with the colored notes. "You put this on too difficult of a setting."

"It's on easy mode." Dan's cheery voice announces from behind the plastic drums, hitting every beat.

"Awe Danamark, you're the bard. Pull it together," Nova whispers in my ear playfully, making me shiver and miss another note. They put a hand on my shoulder, then pull the mic to their mouth. *"Am I more than you bargained for yet?"*

I'm so distracted I miss five more notes in a row when the guitar part comes back in. Her singing voice sounds like I remember—better even. I'm so going down, down.

Three and a half minutes later, the song is over. A few people through the bar—the ones that know Nova, probably—cheer loudly. She's grinning at me, wiping her forehead with the back of her hand. That smile is for me, not Cristy. Not about winning a card game. It feels like sunshine.

The game announces our scores to the entire freaking bar over the giant TV sets. My rank is abysmal. Nova's and Dan's are near perfect.

When Dan stands from the drums, I pass him the plastic guitar controller, cringing. "I think I'm retiring from music."

He chuckles. "Probably for the best."

"Hey, June!" Someone at the table near the stage calls. I don't know them, which means... "I watch your channel. I'm uploading that video right now and tagging you."

"Oh God." I hide behind Nova, putting my forehead on their shoulder blade.

They laugh, looking over their shoulder at me as they hand the mic to the next person. "It's not that bad."

"Liar!" I glare at them.

They turn around. "Aw, your face is as pink as your hair."

I put my hands over my cheeks. "I know! I need a strong drink. But I have to save all my money. Why'd I suggest this?"

"I got ya. Come on." She grabs my hand this time, leading me down from the stage and to the bar. Her cheeks are flushed, too, and her palm is a little sweaty. But she seemed so cool up there.

"Why haven't you sung on stage before? You're perfect." I let her lead me toward the bar.

"I told you why. I don't do stuff in front of people."

But she did for me. And she's on my stream every week, role-playing a character for countless viewers across the internet.

We come to a stop in front of the wooden bar. Retro video game posters are on the wall behind the lines of taps. They only have a few stools here, as the place is mostly set up with tables for seating so people can play games. "You sure about that?"

Nova gives me a crooked smile. "Mm. You're just good at getting past my defenses. It's not fair, really. Your real-life charisma modifier is higher." They hold up two fingers to the bartender, who is wiping down a glass. "Mya, could I get two rainbow nerds, please."

The bartender looks about a decade older than us, with black hair and tattoos on her neck peeking out from her shirt. She nods at Nova. "Sure. Nice job. First time I've heard you sing anything."

Of course, Nova knows her. This is my hometown, too, yet I feel like such an outsider after being away for so many years. I don't know most of the people here anymore, even in specific interests like this.

"Heh. Thanks."

"Rainbow nerds?" I ask, leaning an elbow on the bar as Mya goes to fix the drinks. I look at our hands, still joined.

Nova drops my hand in a hurry, face flushing. Damn, I shouldn't have brought attention to it. They scratch the back of their neck. "It's one of their stronger house drinks. You said you needed one. Nerds, like the candy, you know? And the bar's theme. Mya stacks different colored layers of alcohol and flavors and lines the edge of the glass with the crushed candy like a margarita."

"Sounds way too colorful for you."

"I like colorful." She's looking at my hair when she says it. Her eyes trail down to the top of my light purple dress. Good—I want her to look. It's why I wore this dress, even though it's impractical. That realization smacks me over the head like someone whacked me with the plastic guitar controller. Oh, God. How did I not realize earlier?

I can't help but imagine how it'd be to kiss her. Right here at the bar. Shove her back onto that counter.

Other than goofing around with Nova when we were kids, I've only ever kissed two boys. I don't even know where to start. I could never presume to be any good for her.

Mya brings us the drinks. They're in martini glasses and just as colorful as Nova promised, the liquid starting with red, orange, yellow, green, and blue, lined with rainbow nerds around the rims. Nova pays with a card on the touch-less reader.

They lift theirs and take a drink. "Reminds me of June in a glass. Sweet, sour, bright, and utterly ridiculous."

I pick mine up and take a sip. The taste is thrilling, like being with Nova. I want to be on her mind the way she's always on mine. "Mm, I'll have you know, I taste good." I run my tongue over the candy on the rim of the glass, watching her reaction.

She closes her eyes. "June."

Ooh, she liked that. Maybe it's not fair to try to flirt with her. My life's a mess—surely she could do better.

She leans closer to me.

Oh, my God, please. Kiss me.

Their eyes find mine, and it's like the rest of the crowd disappears. "Want to take these drinks outside? I don't want to go back to the table."

"Yes, *please*. How'd we end up at a bar with our exes, anyway?" I tilt my face toward theirs. Just a few more inches.

They chuckle. "Like all the tricky situations we get into, this one is your doing." They take a long sip of their drink, then take my hand with their other one. "Come on."

Ahh, they're holding my hand again. It feels like butter-flies and cartoon hearts float from my stomach through my body. I want to just live in this moment.

11
NOVA

I'm fucking floating through my morning jog, barely feeling my soles hit the pavement. Maybe I can come up with an excuse to see June again later. The sidewalk of my apartment complex will have to do for today's run so I can get back to work as soon as possible.

My music stops coming through my headset. Dammit, someone is calling me. I glance at my watch. Cristy. Oh, shit. I abandoned her last night with Parker. After June and I ordered our drinks, I took June's hand, and we ducked out the side doors, going for a walk outside. The temperatures dropped, and I put my jacket around her shoulders since I felt warm from the strong drink.

Before I knew it, I spilled all the details about how I'd write the second book after *Curse,* pretending I was planning a fanfiction. I didn't tell her that, as the actual author, I'd already drafted it before the publisher canceled my contract. June listened, enraptured, and then shared all the theories she'd come up with about my characters. Some were probably better ideas than what I'd sketched out so far. It was the best conversation I've ever had about my work. If only I could write what I wanted again and have June as a critique partner...

I slow my pace and hit accept on the phone call, cringing. "Hey, Cristy." She's probably going to chew me out for leaving her with Parker. I know I would if anyone left me with him.

"Well, good morning to you. You out of bed yet? You sound out of breath. Ooh, wait, is June there with you?" Her voice lifts as she teases me.

I imagine June with messy pink hair lying next to me on my pillow, waking up slowly. I'd bring her coffee and trace my fingers along—great, and now I can't get the image out of my head. "No. I'm running. It's not like that. June is just my friend."

She laughs. "Oh, my God, Nova, I'm messing with you. I know she's straight. I talked with Parker last night for several hours and heard all about their relationship."

Right.

I slow my pace. "I'm sorry about that. Did he do anything to bother you? He was a major ass at our D&D session the day before."

"I know. I watch the live video streams, remember?"

Then she sees June and I interact every week as Awe and Hunt. No wonder she's teasing me.

Cristy doesn't miss a beat. "But no, Parker didn't bother me. I actually had fun teaching him how to play Last Imagination. You have to call him on his bullshit a lot, but he's pretty nice and receptive. He's a good listener."

I can't believe I'm hearing this shit. "No. He's not. Did you know he once encouraged June to put space between herself and her friends? That's why she stopped interacting with me! June and I would've been close friends for years if not for him! And she never would've—" I'm raising my voice. I take a few quick breaths. *Calm down.* "He also told her she needed to be a traditional wife. Can you believe that bullshit? That's when she broke up with him."

"Whoa. I touched a nerve."

"Sorry. No. I'm fine." I pick up speed in my jog.

"Hm." There's a rustling over the phone. "Parker said he majorly fucked up in his relationship with June, and he's seeing a therapist to try to be better. You have a crush."

Cristy says it in such a nonchalant way, like it's as easy to see as the color of the sky. I can try to deny it. But what'd be the point? She already figured me out. "Doesn't matter." I grind the words through clenched teeth.

Cristy chuckles. "Despite what Parker thinks, maybe June's not like, straight, straight. Or maybe she just doesn't realize it yet."

"She's only ever dated men."

"So? You shouldn't assume."

"My character Hunt swore an oath to murder Awe Danamark."

"You told me. And? I don't see how fulfilling your game character's oath and dating June are mutually exclusive."

Dating June. Shit, she just said it out loud. "Pretty sure June would feel differently. If she's even into me. Big, massive if." I've been down this road with June before when we were teens. Guess I've really learned nothing.

"Hm, now that you mention it…last night, she pulled you up to the stage and held your haaaand."

I groan, picking up my running pace again. "Don't."

"And after your song, you bought her a rainbow drink, then ran off with her." Cristy's having fun. She knows she's getting under my skin now.

"It's just a drink! And we went outside because I needed a break from how loud and people-y it was in the bar. We were just talking. Like...friends do. It was a regular night out with a regular friend." A friend who I wanted to throw on that bar next to our ridiculous drinks and kiss senseless.

"So defensive. I could give her a call and talk to her if you want. Feel out the situation."

I skid to a stop on the path. "Absolutely not! I swear, if you ever mention this to anyone—"

"You'll take out an oath of vengeance against me?"

I haven't dated anyone since Cristy. She's gone on a few dates here and there, but nothing serious, at least that I know about. This is new territory for us.

"Come on, Nova. I like teasing you, but you have to know I wouldn't say anything. I'm happy you had fun with June, and I'm glad I saw you out again. I mean it. It's been a while. Don't be such a reclusive, serious writer."

"I get out. Remember, I play D&D with a group every week. And I hardly count as a serious writer. My book failed. I'm just a ghostwriter for someone else." I walk along the path, passing parked cars in front of the mani-cured lawns in front of the apartment buildings. I think I've run enough for today. Time to check my mail, head back to my place, and get to work.

"It didn't fail." Cristy's voice isn't teasing anymore. "And it seems like it might get a second life now that there's a buzz going about it. That happens with books sometimes. The publisher could come back and ask you for the second one."

I hadn't even entertained that hope. "It's unlikely. But that's okay." I follow the sidewalk into the clubhouse.

"Stranger things have happened. I heard about this one book that got popular on BookTok..." She continues on about a steamy fantasy romance about a fae prince kidnapping a human woman, and I listen while pulling out my keys and unlocking my mailbox.

Junk mail, advertising flyer, and... What's this? It's from the University of Iowa. Great. My rejection letter, finally. I sigh.

"What is it?" Cristy asks as I tear into the envelope.

"Oh, I got a letter from..." My eyes skim over the printed words.

We're pleased to inform you... Accepted... Fall of 2022... Please respond...

What? The world seems to stop. I read the whole thing. Then read it again.

"From..." Cristy's still waiting for me to answer her.

"I got in."

"To your apartment?"

"To the Writer's Workshop MFA program at the University of Iowa. It's one of the most prestigious creative writing programs in the country. I can't believe this."

There has to be some sort of mistake. All I feel is numb. I've received so many rejection letters, printed and emailed, from agents and publishers. It took getting over one hundred of them to get *Curse* published. There have only been three acceptance letters with my name on them—my undergrad application, when I finally found a literary agent, and when he found a home for *Curse* at D&D's publisher. Now this is number four.

I clutch it to my chest as Cristy lets out a whoop over the phone and congratulates me.

"Thank you," I tell her. "I...gotta go."

I hang up the call and snap a picture of the acceptance letter on my phone, leaning against a pillar in the middle of the clubhouse mailroom.

June is the first person I text. She immediately sends me

back a string of celebrating emojis. My heart lurches with joy tinged slightly with...what is this? Longing?

I don't want to move away from June.

Damn, I'm being silly. She's my friend. Despite what Cristy thinks, there's no real evidence she likes me as anything more. We can be friends from across the country. As long as she's not dating a controlling asshole dude who keeps her from contacting anyone.

This MFA program is what I need right now for anyone to take me seriously. I can't trust people to treat me well without the letters to my name. Writing fantasy is just that—a fantasy. If I want a real career in writing, this is my only path in, no matter what's trending on TikTok.

June

The bell on the coffee shop door chimes as Lyssa enters. I jump up and use my hip to hold it wider for her so she can carry baby Eleanor inside in the heavy plastic detachable car seat. By some miracle, Eleanor is asleep, though she stirs as Lyssa walks into the dimly lit building and out of the sunlight. This building is a hundred years old, with brick exposed through drywall. The walls are covered with regular customers' mugs, local art, and a giant chalkboard depicting the current menu.

I check the time on my phone. Ten-thirty-four. Less than an hour ago, I texted Lyssa, *"SOS! I'm having a full-on gay crisis!"* She sent me a laughing emoji back, then offered to meet me at a local coffee shop.

"I hope it's okay I already ordered." I shake the large

iced coffee in my left hand, sliding my phone back into my dress pocket.

"Ooh, I need one of those. This angel was awake from four to seven this morning if you can believe it." Lyssa steps next to an unoccupied two-top table by the window and sways back and forth with Eleanor's carrier. The baby seems to be settling back down? It's hard for me to tell.

I wince and take a sip of my coffee. "Yet another reason I'm not cut out for motherhood. I can barely take care of myself."

"Will you hold her carrier and kind of dance around like this while I order?" Lyssa keeps gently swaying with the car seat.

I chuckle, setting my cup on the table. "Sure. Speaking of dancing. I need to tell you what I fool I made of myself last night on stage at the bar."

"Ah. This have to do with that gay crisis?"

I groan, taking Eleanor's carrier from Lyssa and trying to mimic her back and forth swaying. "Yes."

She laughs and goes to the counter to order her coffee. The shop is a cute little place on the so-small-it's-almost-nonexistent downtown street of the area where my parents live. This coffee shop, a real estate agency, and a hair salon with elderly clientele are the only three open stores on the block.

The coffee shop is yet another place Nova and I used to come together. I glance up at the upstairs loft with its metal railing. When we were fifteen and sixteen, this shop had different owners. Nova and I would come here, order coffee drinks with way too much sugar while pretending to be real, grown adults, then sit upstairs and chat for hours about our theories on certain anime shows. Or creating D&D characters. Or writing fanfiction about gay men from our favorite manga.

I sigh, still swaying with Eleanor. Part of me wishes I could go back then with what I know now about myself. Maybe I'd have the courage to speak up. Perhaps I would've never dated Parker. And if I'm really shooting for the moon with my dreams...I could be here with Nova right now, watching her sip coffee and write while I work on my computer, sneaking glances at the cute faces I bet she still makes when she's writing.

"You can set Eleanor down now. She looks good and settled." Lyssa slides into one of the chairs. "Right here next to the wall on my side is good."

"Sure." I place Eleanor's car seat next to her mom and flop into the chair in front of my iced coffee.

"Tell me what's going on with you and Nova."

My ears feel a little hot to hear her say it that way. *You and Nova.* I don't think I mentioned Nova by name in my text. "How'd you know it's about Nova?"

"Everyone with eyes or ears knows."

"Ha. It's not that obvious."

Lyssa looks like she's suppressing a laugh. "You two are practically all over each other every session when you're in character."

I have been getting a very high number of comments about Awe and Hunt wanting to do each other. The words "eye-humping" appeared a few times.

"Yeah, but that's just in character. It's not like Drew actually worships Procan—"

"The Storm Lord," Lyssa interrupts in the same dry voice we always do when playing.

I laugh. "Right. It's just his character. I'm pretty sure Nova is just playing her character. And I'm also convinced it's a rouse to get Awe to let her guard down. I don't know what Nova's Hunt is planning exactly, but since reading the book, I have a few guesses."

Lyssa shakes her head. "You can't fake that chemistry. And you found Nova attractive before you started playing D&D with our group. You pointed her out at the party and said she's hot."

I can't deny that. "Yeah. But, like, I'm already twenty-six. I've only been with two men, and let's be honest, the sex wasn't good with either of them. I pretty much had to take care of myself. I'm so far behind—I have no idea if I could satisfy her."

A young man working at the coffee shop brings Lyssa a latte in a large mug. I clamp my mouth shut as he looks at me out of the corner of his eye. I forgot about how Christian this place is—with the praise and worship radio station playing over the speakers and lots of Christian-themed artwork on the walls.

After the guy leaves, Lyssa picks up her coffee and sips it. "None of those things matter. You're not behind, and you're just as valid if you figured it out at sixteen, twenty-six, or eighty-six. If you're with someone you care about, you'll both have fun no matter what."

Nova in my bed. The image flashes into my head before I can stop myself. Their smile. Making them laugh hard like I did last night at the bar, and that time I accidentally sent the gargantuan gold. How they'd feel against my body…

I hold the cup of iced coffee to my face, trying to cool off. "How did it take me so long to figure this out? That I'm bisexual?" I said it out loud. The first time.

Lyssa shrugs. "Conditioning. Heteronormative culture. Your religious parents. A number of reasons, really." She lifts her latte in a toast. "Here's to growing up in the South."

I glance out the window, watching as an older couple crosses the street with their small white dog. "I've been piecing things together in my mind. Last night, I couldn't sleep after drinking rainbow martinis with Nova and chatting with them for hours. They put their jacket around my shoulders when we walked on the square, and I was cold. Then I refused to give it back when I dropped them off because it smelled like them. They tried to wrestle it off of me, which was really fun, but they decided to let me keep it. And then we hugged."

"Oh, June." Lyssa wipes her hand down her face, and I can tell she's trying not to smirk.

"Later, as I was lying in bed awake, I realized that Nova has lots of reasons to be mad at me. Way beyond trashing their favorite book."

"I don't think they're mad about any of it anymore. It sounds like they like you."

"No. Listen." I slam my plastic cup back onto the table. "Here's how clueless I was. Like, possibly the most oblivious person on the entire planet. When we were teenagers, we used to have these spend-the-nights where…we'd hold each other. Like, actually hold each other through the night."

"Aww."

"Other times, I'd tell her she's my heated chair and sit in her lap while we watched anime. Or I'd lay my head in her lap and ask her to play with my hair. I'd go to her cross-country races to cheer her on. After, I'd massage her feet and shoulders, saying that I was her coach and I needed to help keep her muscles from getting sore."

"How is any of this reason for Nova to be mad at you?"

"Because I didn't see it." I lean my forehead on the table next to my cup. "I didn't see how she probably liked me that way. Our D&D characters got married in one of the campaigns we played."

Lyssa laughs. "I remember that. During my high-seas campaign where I was DM. You had a marriage at sea. You stole the enemies' ship, the nicer ship, then the bad guys tried to infiltrate the wedding and set off a mana bomb."

"Yeah, and Nova's swashbuckler human rogue lifted my halfling fighter into her arms and swung away at the last minute. We acted it out. Nova picked me up!"

"Uh-huh. I remember. Aiden and I had bets on when you two would start dating." She sips her mug with a little grin.

I lean forward, spreading my hands on the table. "Wait, what? No one told me!"

"What was there to tell? It was yours to figure out."

"Yeah, but I'm clueless! Someone could've helped me. Nova and I went in couples costumes every year when we went to DragonCon or AnimeWeekendAtlanta. I'd rub my nose on their cheek to make homophobic people uncomfortable."

"Okay, but you know how you feel now, and you're both single. Go tell them. What's the big issue?"

I shake my head. *What's the big issue?* Easy for Lyssa to say. She's had her life figured out. "Who could want to get with someone this clueless?"

"Aw, sweetie." She smirks. "One person has to be the more informed one in the couple."

"Very funny. What about you and Aiden?" Gotcha now.

"We alternate on who's smart and who's clueless that day. Using your brain takes effort. You want someone who will still love you at your most oblivious."

"True." But there's another reason why Nova and I

would be doomed from the start. "You saw Nova's group text about getting into the program at Iowa, right?"

Lyssa sets her mug on the table. "Yeah. I'm happy for them but sad they'll be moving away."

"Iowa. Not even like, to Tennessee or North Carolina or whatever that would be a few hours of a drive. It's twelve hours in the car! I already googled it."

"Aiden and I were long-distance for nearly two years."

Hmm, I didn't realize. It was during the time I barely talked to any friends. "Yeah?"

Lyssa nods. "Remember, we didn't date until after high school. I got into a different college than him. Like, right when we started dating, too. The distance wasn't fun, but we made it work. We talked on the phone a lot, texted each other throughout our days, and played an online game together almost every evening. Then, he surprised me by telling me he was transferring to my school. We got engaged and married shortly after."

"Heh, that part I remember. Thinking y'all were impulsive for getting married at twenty-one."

She smiles, then glances at Eleanor. "Lots of people thought we were, and they have a point that twenty-one is young. But the thing is, we had such a strong friendship years before we even dated, I knew what I was getting into. I was marrying my best friend. Everyone says how the first year of marriage is so hard. But it wasn't, and it's not now, either, because I already knew his heart. Loving Aiden is easy."

"That's so sweet, I'm gonna cry, and my unsweetened coffee is sugary now." I shake it.

"So, if you invited me here to ask my advice, then it's to be Nova's friend. If you have that bond, everything else will work itself out, including the distance."

"Makes it sound so simple."

"While loving him is easy, it's not always simple. Aiden and I fight, too."

"Yeah, I can't picture that."

She laughs. "Really. We argue occasionally."

Being Nova's friend. I can do that. I'm going to spend every bit of time I can with them these next few months. And I'm going to support them as they chase their dreams, even if that takes them hundreds of miles away.

12
JUNE

I shake out my legs. The things I do for videos. Well, that and an excuse to hang out with Nova. "Welcome to paladin training, day one," I say to my phone, which I have sticking out in front of me on a selfie stick. I flex my skinny noodle arm and then point at the phone with my hand not holding the stick. "Someone out there better be doing this with me."

I'm outside doing a live video on the exercise trail Nova sometimes uses. Live videos go over pretty well on my channel. My followers like watching along as I embarrass myself. Hell, the video of my foolishness last weekend at the bar got me a slew of new subscribers. It's one of the things that sets my channel apart from others. Almost nothing is heavily edited or scripted. I have a filter on the camera, which puts fantasy makeup on anyone in the shot. The setting for my face is for a pink orc, but it's close enough to Awe's look.

"I have our resident paladin, Hunt, here to show me the ropes." I tilt the phone over to include Nova in the shot. She gives her best unamused look, the app's filter turning her skin and hair bright blue and giving her fangs. It's super cute.

"You're interrupting my morning prayer time," they say to me, ignoring the phone.

"Oh? Remind me about prayer time?"

"It's how I recharge my spells. I have to spend time every morning deep in prayer."

I pull the camera aside like I'm whispering to it. "I've never seen them pray, not even once, so this is new to me, too." I pan the camera around to look at Nova again.

They cross their arms. "You're going to need both hands for this prayer."

"Ah, gotcha." I flip the selfie stick around into tripod mode and set it up, making sure to keep us both in the shot.

I sit and put my hands together in a prayer position, like what I saw growing up in church. "So, like this?"

Nova laughs. "What kind of prayer is that? I'm talking about pushing prayers." They drop to the ground and start doing pushups. They're wearing a tank top and exercise pants, and wow, they have some nice muscles going on in their shoulders that I never even noticed. They look up at me. "Well? Are you joining me for prayer time or not?"

"Ah, yep! Getting right on that." I kneel and whisper, "Send help," toward the camera. I haven't done a pushup in probably two years. "How many are you doing?"

Nova barely pauses. "I'm only to twenty. Not even halfway there."

I manage five slow pushups. Five. Damn. I lay on the ground, face first.

Nova kneels after finishing fifty, dusting their hands off. "Well? Time for jumping prayers."

"Oh, gods."

Ten minutes later, we've done jumping jacks, squats, lunges, and planks.

I lift the phone and flip the stand back to selfie stick mode. "My constitution score is terrible. Y'all already know this. I'm lucky to still be alive. But at least prayer time seems to be over."

Nova leans over. "That was a good warmup. But time for the real stuff. Running prayers."

I pull the camera closer to my face, whispering to it as we start jogging down the trail. "If you don't hear from me, just assume I've died. If you'd like to contribute to my resurrection spell, you can send a diamond worth at least a thousand gold pieces in the mail, and hopefully, my paladin friend here will rez me. Moral of the story: don't pray with paladins."

I disconnect the video and hit the button to cross-post it on all my accounts, slowing my jog. "Okay, Nova. Great job. We can stop now."

They eye me over their shoulder. "We just started our running prayers, Lady Danamark. It seems you need some additional training in dexterity and constitution."

Oh, so it's going to be like that, is it? I scoff, tucking the cell phone stand under my arm as I attempt to catch up. "This reminds me of gym class. You were better at it than me back then, too."

"I'll massage your feet afterward," they say. "Let's finish one mile. Okay?"

"Fiiinnnne," I whine. "As long as you massage my legs, too."

"Fine."

Oh God, Nova touching my feet and legs. That'll be worth any amount of running. I pick up my pace, loving the way her hair bounces with each step.

Am I being creepy thinking of her this way? These aren't things a friend should be thinking of another. All those times I'd massage her feet after she ran, and her shoulders and back, too, enjoying the feel of her tight muscles as I tried to get them to relax... How the fuck did I not know I was bi?

"What's funny?" she asks. I didn't realize I'd laughed.

"Running prayers," I lie, coming up to run shoulder-to-shoulder with her.

"What? Hunt does those prayers every morning. And their, uh, other prayers." Their cheeks flush slightly pink as they gaze into the trees that line the path.

Other prayers. That one scene in the book...where Hunt tells Lady Danufair that making love to her was the highest form of worship. When I read the book, I imagined Hunt as Nova—I couldn't help it.

"Oh, I remember." I nudge them with my elbow, puffing air as I try to keep pace with them. "I read the book. And reread certain sections several times."

"Heh, yeah."

A sharp pain hits my side. Oof. "Okay, I'm not joking, I need to walk. Side stitch." I hold a hand out and bend halfway over. My fit parents would be so ashamed.

Nova slows, then turns, walking backward as they signal me to keep moving. "Walking's fine. But it'll take us even longer to finish the trail."

Longer with Nova. Maybe I should crawl the trail. But I grin at them as I start walking, then grab their arm and hug it. "Thank you for breaking your vow again to do my video."

"What? I, uh, didn't," they stammer.

I cackle. "Which vow do you think I mean? I'm talking about," I put on my most serious Nova voice, "I don't do stuff in front of people."

She tries to shove me, veering me off the side of the trail toward the pine trees, but even though I almost drop my phone, I hold on tight to her arm and pull her with me.

"I don't sound like that!"

"I'm far too cool with my MFA acceptance letter." I keep doing the voice, teasing her.

"Staaahhp! No one would consider an MFA 'cool.'"

We walk back onto the center of the trail, but I don't let go of her arm.

"Well, I do. It's awesome. Your fanfictions were always my favorite." I squeeze her forearm as I say it, and I mean it —I'm thrilled for her. But I also don't want her to leave me. I push down my selfishness and focus on the good. "I can't wait to see what you're going to come up with year after year."

They drag a hand through their hair. "I know it's silly considering how much I wanted to get out of this town in high school, but I'm a little sad to be moving so far."

"Yeah?" Please. Say it so I don't have to. Say you want to stay with me. But that's incredibly selfish of me to wish.

"I mean, getting a regular D&D group as adults? It's an incredibly rare feat."

True, but not what I wanted to hear. "You *better* be using Zoom or Discord to keep playing. Or else we're all dead."

"Yeah, yeah. Of course, I will. There's just a certain energy in person." She looks at where I'm holding onto her arm.

I don't let go. "That's adulthood, though. Things that you feel like are forever can suddenly change. Your best friend moves across the country. Another has a cute-but-sleepless baby. Breakups. Job changes."

She sighs. "Yeah. I know the program is just two years. But I don't want to miss out on everything while I'm gone."

"You won't. Expect to continue to get a deluge of texts from me. I'll fill you in on everything. And before you leave, we'll hang out every day."

She smiles, and my heart does a flip in my chest. "Yeah. That sounds good."

Nova

I have to squeeze around people to get to my dad's table in the crowded restaurant. It's his lunch break, and I guess the lunch break of half the students and faculty of the University of Georgia. I drove over to Athens to meet up with him and celebrate my acceptance letter in person.

"Hey, kiddo." He still greets me the same as when I was fourteen. "I like the hair."

I chuckle and touch my bangs, which are getting too long and falling in my eyes. In a week or two, I'll have to touch up the roots unless I want them to stand out from the rest. I brush my hair aside. "Thanks. The teal was a friend's idea."

He doesn't watch June's channel. That I know of. Please, no.

I pull out the chair and sit down, glancing at the menu. It's a vegetarian restaurant, and it's kind of nice to see a menu filled with everything I can eat. Athens has more vegetarian options than back in the suburb-to-rural area where I live. Will Iowa City?

Probably. There's a university and a whole city.

Dad clears his throat. "So, congratulations are in order."

I set the menu down. "Thank you."

"Iowa is the best of the best of schools for writing."

"I'm shocked they wanted me, honestly."

He smiles, the skin around his eyes crinkling. "I'm not. You were born to do this. You always had such an imagination. Even when you were tiny. I still remember the intricate stories you'd tell me when you were four and five years old. And you were reading on your own before you could speak properly."

Hyperliteracy is an autism trait, I want to tell him. But I don't, just nodding instead. He and Mom never noticed my struggles with friends and school, but they were dealing with a divorce. And it's not like I talked a lot.

A waitress comes by to take our orders, and I put in an order for water and a Mediterranean sampler plate. Dad orders the same thing.

"How've you been? It feels like forever since we had a chance to actually talk." He's a history professor—sometimes, he gets behind on his responsibilities, just like I do.

"You know. Same old stuff. Writing." Gaming. Falling for a former friend, turned enemy, turned mega-crush.

"I feel you. This semester has dragged on. Just one more week and then finals. We'll try to get together in person a few more times before you move. Those months are going to fly."

Is it really that soon, though? Today is April twenty-first, so most of the month is gone. May, June, July, then on August first, I'll move... Wait. I was thinking it was six months away, and it's more like three. And during the last few weeks, I'll have to take care of things like packing up my stuff, getting my apartment ready to turn back over, and plenty of other tasks. Which means I have more like two months. Which is basically no time!

Dad leans forward. "I think I've set off some kind of anxiety in you, which is normal for a big move. But remember what a great opportunity this is."

I shake myself. I can worry about the timing and move later. "Yes. Of course."

"You'll be able to improve your craft and write another masterpiece. Maybe even teach writing at a university someday."

"Yeah, maybe." I don't think I'd be cut out to be a professor like Dad, though. The thought of seeing hundreds of people every single day... Awful.

"You know, I tried to publish a few historical fiction novels when I was younger. They didn't really sell."

"You told me before." Publishing was so different back then.

"It wasn't until I got my master's and wrote my thesis that I really grasped what I needed to. And now I'm in many publications. I know you don't like talking about...you know. What happened with your release."

Then why are you bringing it up?

"But I really believe you're on the right track with this MFA program."

I force a smile. "Thanks, Dad."

And suddenly, I hate it all. I hate that I'm having to move away from my friends. I hate that I need another piece of paper to validate my worth as a writer. I hate the whole mess. Dad can't understand what it's like for people to target me for existing.

But what else can I do but keep trying? All I wanted to be was a writer, and my career was dead before it took off. In just two years, I'll have proof of my worth.

13
JUNE

I push open the door to the print shop, checking again on my phone to make sure I have the right place. There are two in Gainesville with almost the same name. Nova said this was the good one, to go talk to the owner, and she'd set me up.

"Good morning. Can I help you?"

"Hi." I wave at the woman behind the counter. "My friend, Nova Dawson, referred me here and said you could do a rush order of two hundred shirts in less than a month? I know that's a big ask. But the Atlanta Ren Fair approved my booth, and I could really use the money from selling my merchandise. I have an online gaming channel."

I'm babbling. This woman doesn't need to know my entire story. I only found out two days ago the Atlanta Renaissance Fair accepted my bid to be a vendor. Now I just need the merch to sell.

She smiles. "Ah. June, right?"

I nod.

"We have you on the schedule. We're just waiting for your design."

What a relief. I might have a chance of making my apartment down payment after all. "Oh, good!" I reach into my bag and hand her a printed design and a flash drive with the digital version. "I can also email it to you if you need."

She looks over the paper. "No, this is fine. I'm glad you only used one color. It'll make it easier." She walks over to the computer on the counter and plugs in the flash drive.

"Good," I say again. It's a lot of money to put down—risking a big chunk of my savings—but if I sell all the shirts, I could make up to a thousand dollars in profit. Combined with the money I'm making from the podcast...it'd be enough. Barely. "What else do you need? A credit card?"

She glances away from the computer screen to me. "Oh, no, you're good. Someone already paid for your order."

Someone. "Nova?"

She gives me a slight smile. "An anonymous donor."

I pull my phone out and compose a text to Nova. *"What are you doing paying a thousand dollars for the shop to print my shirts?"*

I see the dots indicating they're writing a response. Then the dots stop. I knew it. They totally did.

"That's way too much money for you to spend!" I add. Should I ask if the print shop can do a refund on what Nova obviously paid?

"I didn't."

"Bullshit. Paladins aren't supposed to lie." I include an angry face emoji.

The dots appear, then stop again, and then I get a selfie of Nova kneeling with a hand over their heart. *"I didn't pay a thousand dollars. On my honor. Procan (the Storm Lord) and Oghma strike me down."*

God, they're cute.

"Yeah, I don't believe you! Who else would?"

"Your friends. You know we like you, right? Fine. Hold on, and I'll send you a screenshot."

I wait for a moment, and three screenshots of a group chat comes through. It's the D&D group, minus myself and Parker.

Nova's question is at the top. *"Hey guys. June got news the renaissance faire gave her a booth, but she needs merch to sell. It's expensive to get t-shirts printed, but she has a really cute design. How about we pitch in to help her?"*

Drew: *"How much do you need?"*

Lyssa: *"we have some extra cash stuffed in a drawer for presents and stuff. Would 200 help?"*

Aiden: *"Oh, so that's where that money went?"* Winking face.

Lyssa: *"Where did you think it went?"*

Aiden: *"Diapers."*

Lyssa: *"Fair"*

Aiden: *"I think it's better spent on awesome t-shirts for June"*

Drew: *"I can do 200 too. Do you do an app to transfer money?"*

Tears prick my eyes. I can't believe this. Real friends who care.

Nova's text pings through. *"That solve your mystery, Lady Danamark? And before you give me any complaints about how that's too much money, don't. I wanted to. We wanted to. We like you."*

I send back the emoji with tears pouring down its face. *"I love you."* I should rein it back. *"I mean, it's so good to have real friends. I love all of you."*

Before I can worry if I said something wrong, I get another picture from Nova with their hands in the shape of a heart. Looks like they balanced the phone on their computer desk to get the picture. Now they're...wearing a t-shirt with a cute anime-style Awe on it. I paid for those shirt designs on a website three years ago. The process was so expensive that I didn't make a lot of money, so I haven't bothered with merchandise for a while. Nova bought one and kept it all this time?

"You're making me cry in the print shop!!!!" I text her. And she is.

She returns with an emoji with its tongue sticking out. *"Want to meet up at my apartment when you're done at the shop? We can watch a show or play a game and make dinner."*

"YES" I return in all caps as fast as my fingers can type.

Nova

June chops onions in the most ridiculous way. I don't want to be a jerk and point it out, but the uneven pieces are going to irritate me if I don't fix it.

Not only is she cutting all wrong, it'll take her forever, and the pot with oil is already heating. We're standing in my apartment kitchen, ingredients for homemade ramen spread out over the counters.

My fingers itch to take the onion and knife. "Can I just..." Walking up behind her, I reach around and hold her hand with the kitchen knife, leaning my chin over her shoulder. Okay, bonus—I get to touch June. She smells good. I want to bend my head to kiss the soft crook of her neck, but that'd be weird. I think. "You have to cut off the ends like this." I position the vegetable and use her hand to make the right cuts. "Then you cut it long way." She lets me guide her hand again. "Then you lay the halves down like this and cut again on the lines. Then dice the other direction. So much easier."

She laughs and bumps me back with her hips. "Thank you, master chef. I thought you hated onions. You used to go on rants about them."

I reluctantly let her go. How many excuses can I come up with tonight to hold her? When she arrived at my apartment, I gave her an inappropriately long hug. "I do hate onions. Raw, at least. They're okay cooked. But we need their flavor in this soup."

June finishes dicing. I pick up the cutting board and use the knife to knock the onions in the pot. They sizzle and pop as they hit the hot oil.

"Do you cook a lot?" She picks up a long-handled spoon and stirs the onions in the pot.

I shrug and begin wiping off mushrooms with a paper towel as the onions sauté. "Yes and no. I go through phases. I'll get creative and make all sorts of recipes. Or decide to grow my own ingredients. Then there was the one time I got really into fermentation. But then I get burnt out and end up eating the same packaged chana and rice for weeks on end."

"Still sounds more stable than what I eat. Lately, a lot of frozen foods, cereal, and peanut butter. I've never been good at organizing recipes and keeping up with ingredients before they go bad. Parker used to complain. Saying my home cooking costs more than going out to restaurants every night."

If Parker were here, I'd hit him with this spatula. Hard.

"Well, fuck him. It never occurred to him *he* could be the one cooking dinner?"

She sighs and leans on the counter, looking at the container of miso. "He works full time."

"So do you." I know she puts in overtime hours with all the content she creates. So many videos over the years. And her talent only gets better and better.

"Doesn't count as a real job. Ask my parents."

Well, fuck them too. But I don't say that. "It's absolutely a real job. Your channel is amazing and growing every day. I don't care what Parker makes—at this rate, you'll out-earn him soon. I improved my role-playing skills so much while watching your videos."

"What? Really? I remember you being good at it even in high school."

I shake my head, picking up the paring knife to slice the mushrooms. "Nah, I was awkward as hell. I still loved it and had fun." I cut a mushroom into thin slices. "But when you started posting the videos that let viewers practice their conversations with NPCs, it really let me work past my insecurities."

"Aw, Nova." She gives me a quick hug around the waist, sending butterflies through me.

I have to focus hard not to cut my fingers. "So yeah, your career is legitimate. And I bet way more legitimate than whatever bullshit Parker does." I don't even know what he does for a living, but based on his attitude, it can't be anything difficult. Or else he'd have more respect for other humans.

"He's a quality control manager for his dad's sunglasses company. I don't know how he managed to move here, honestly. The company is based in Charleston."

After cutting the rest of the mushrooms, I put them in

the pot and give the mixture a good stir. "Why did it matter to you so much if Parker was happy? He never cared about making you happy. I...used to watch those videos too. Where you talked about your relationship and shared little bits of your lives together." The things he'd say to put her down. It was supposed to be cute, relatable couple stuff, but... "All it ever made me want to do was punch him."

"Ah. Yeah. I got that comment several times from viewers. Hearing from them was one of the things that got me rethinking my relationship. After so many years, Parker became a given in my life. We were engaged for so long. My parents liked him. My brothers liked him."

I tilt a tiny bowl of garlic and ginger, which I chopped earlier, into the pot. "Well, I never liked him. He treated you like garbage." I wish she'd tell him to get the hell out of our group. We'll have to deal with his bullshit tomorrow night during the game session.

"I don't think I liked him for a long time when we finally broke up." She leans on the counter, facing me. "You know what's funny? Every time I cried after we broke up, I never once thought, 'I miss Parker.' It should've been a clue I was only with him because it felt as though that was what I was supposed to do. What they taught me at church. Like, when you're with someone like that, it's lonelier being with them than actually being alone."

"What made you cry, then?" I stir the vegetables, the flavors and aromas sautéing together.

"Thinking about all the years of my life I wasted. How everyone was going to see me as a fuck up. I should've had times with my friends—with you. Road trips. Inside jokes. D&D games. Instead, I spent my wild, young college years pretending to be someone else and not in the fun gaming way. Pretending to be the good, responsible girl my parents still want me to be."

"I like the real you. Exactly as you are. Quirks and all."

She nods and blinks like she's trying not to cry. "Nobody's ever said they like me for me. Not, like, out loud, at least."

I put the spatula down on the rest and step close to her, trapping her between me and the counter. She doubts herself because of insecure people like Parker and her family, but she's amazing. I want to hold her, to reassure her. "I mean it, you know." Our eyes meet, and I lean in closer. If I kissed her here, what would she do? She's so beautiful, standing in my kitchen.

She hits me on the shoulder, covering her face with one hand.

"Ow, what was that for?" I grin. It didn't hurt at all.

She peeks through her fingers. "Making me blush."

Oh my God, I want to kiss her so bad. She's so cute, and her body feels so good against mine as I press her against the counter. Just like it used to. I want to make dinner with her like this every night, play-fight over video games, snuggle on the couch, bring her coffee in bed... Totally normal friend stuff. Ugh.

June is straight. I know this—I've been down this path before, and it hurts.

I take a breath and step back, then pick up the spatula and stir the veggies again.

We shift to lighter topics as we finish cooking the ramen. It turns out to be the most delicious I've ever made, and God, watching June's eyes light up when she eats it is the best. After we eat, we play a round of Mario Kart, and she puts her legs across my lap on the couch.

On the last lap around the track, when I go over a ramp,

I mess up the landing, crashing Luigi's car into a lake instead of crossing the finish line.

"Haha! It's-a-me! I'm the winner!" June laughs.

I want to grab her and tickle her like we used to do, but instead, I take a deep breath. I'm letting myself get carried away with this. If I don't stop, I'm going to crash our friendship worse than Mario Kart.

14
JUNE

I nudge Nova's foot with mine under the table. She doesn't break her intense stare with Parker. This is just how it's going to be at tonight's session, I guess. It's our second hour of playing, and the whole fucking time has been awkward, all thanks to my fucking ex.

Parker laughs, then continues speaking in the ridiculous voice and accent he gives his character. "Well, it's a good thing I'm here. This group would be dead many times over without my sword."

"I disagree. If we die, you'll be the reason," Nova replies as Hunt. They're so intense when they role-play sometimes. They're wearing the tiefling horns I brought for them, and I'm wearing mine. I made cloaks for the entire party, and everyone but Parker is wearing theirs. I also brought Parker a white wig for his character, but he said wearing it would be pushing him out of his comfort zone. Which is fine. But I wish he'd stop pushing everyone else out of theirs with this utter bullshit.

Lyssa and Drew glance at each other. Both are wearing their embroidered cloaks with the hoods pulled on. I'm slowly winning this table over with costumes, and I love it. Even Aiden is wearing a black hood, a costume I recycled from attending the midnight release of Star Wars a few years back. I'm in my pink cloak, with a brown leather bodice and glitter makeup that tints my skin slightly pink like Awe's.

"Friends." I put one hand on Nova's shoulder and one on Parker's. Awe can solve this with diplomacy. "We're on the same side. Come on. No one is going to die today."

"Not true. A man did. Needlessly. You killed him." Nova glares at Parker. Jerald just finished murdering a non-player character Hunt was trying to question.

I try to catch her eye, but she's way too invested in this altercation with Parker's character. I've had so much fun with Nova this week. We even made two more videos in character earlier today before we met at Aiden's house. Maybe after this awkward session is over, I can convince her to go to the Awful Waffle with me.

Parker scoffs. "Uh, yeah. The man attacked us. He's part of Yhallister's forces."

"Yes." Nova grinds out through their teeth. "And I subdued him. We were about to get information from him. Information which could've been the difference between our lives and deaths. You know Yhallister doesn't play around. If we were able to spare this man, then we were supposed to. The entire party could end up dead because we didn't get this info!"

Parker looks over at Aiden and gestures at the grid where our characters' figures are. "I wipe my sword off on the dead loser's shirt. And I spit on him."

Nova makes a growling sound under their breath. "He yielded to us willingly. This is an insult to honor I can't ignore." They glance at Aiden. "Hunt draws their sword and aims it at Jerald. I challenge you. Single combat."

Parker puts up a hand. "Jerald doesn't take up his sword. Yet." He switches voices back to Jerald's. "Heh, seems you're a bit on edge, Hunt. Maybe you're waving that thing around because you're jealous that you don't have a 'sword,'" he makes air quotes, "where it counts?"

"Parker," Aiden warns. He rarely breaks our role-play.

But I agree. This is getting out of hand. Baby Eleanor is sleeping right now. Lyssa is reclined back in her chair, her feet in Aiden's lap, sipping a beer. This was supposed to be a fun time. Parker needs to cut it out.

"What?" Parker shrugs, going back to his real voice. "No offense, Nova. I don't have anything against you. I'm just trying to role-play my character the way I created him. It's not me; it's how Jerald would act."

Maybe don't create your character to be an absolute asshole, then?

Nova narrows her eyes. Why'd I decide to sit between them? I should've sat on the other side of Nova and let her get into it with Parker directly. "There's no reason to stop playing."

"See?" Parker gestures to the board again. He clears his throat and speaks again in his Jerald voice. "You speak of honor? I was the one acting honorably. I killed that man because he threatened Awe."

"Who can take care of herself," I say, pointing at myself.

"I'm sorry, Awe. Hunt lowers their sword and sheathes it." Nova leans around me to point at Parker. "You heard her. Awe doesn't need anyone to protect her. She can protect herself. And even if she wanted a protector, the fact that you're so worried about your supposed manliness all the time means you're a failure."

"Jerald isn't worried about this scenario." Parker grins. "Please. Since I've joined up with your hapless group, Awe's been flirting with me nonstop. She knows the whole party would be dead without me. She's biding her time before she can get me alone. It's the effect I have on women. It's in my backstory."

I meet Lyssa's eyes across the table, and she snickers, probably at the disgusted, panicked look on my face.

"I roll to kiss Awe." Parker rolls his d20.

"Wait a second," Aiden says. "That's not how that works."

"And I'd like to take a swing at Jerald with my fist." Nova doesn't roll their dice yet.

Technically, you're not supposed to roll until the DM calls for it.

I clear my throat. "Whoa, there." I hold up my hands to press each of them back. "You two do remember where we are, right? We're in a hidden chamber, stuck in the middle of two very deadly scenarios in the most lethal place in the entire realm. We need to use our brains to get out of this. We can't be wasting our resources and our health with this infighting. Hunt. Come on. Listen to me. Tiefling to tiefling." I plead, looking Nova in the eye. Let's just get back to the game scenario.

"He's going to get us killed!" she retorts. She's really worked up. Maybe I should ask for a time-out and take a walk with her for a breather.

"It's a seventeen, by the way." Parker smirks. "Does this mean I get to kiss June—er, I mean Awe?"

I roll my eyes. "Give it a rest."

"No," Nova says. "You don't."

"And why's that?" Parker keeps using that same irritating character voice. This is beyond annoying. Why is he so worried about sounding cool? Why did I even let him join? I'm such a fool for trying to please everyone around me all the time.

"Because I have the higher initiative." Nova grabs me by my cloak and yanks me—Awe?—over to her. Their lips are on mine, and all functional thought is gone from my brain. Oh my God. They're kissing me! Nova is kissing me. This is really happening!

I want to grab her and kiss her back, but I'm so stunned, and suddenly the moment is over.

They pull back, hazel eyes so wide I can see the whites all the way around them. They release my cloak. "Shit!"

I touch my fingers to my lips. It was so fast—I want to do it again. Take our time.

Their face is crimson as they stand and run from the table, going out Aiden's front door.

Oh crap, the cameras! I pull my phone from my pocket and use the remote function to cut the stream. Aiden gives a low whistle, and Lyssa chuckles the way she does when she's nervous.

Drew seems unfazed, stacking his dice in a tower.

What just happened? Did Nova get so into role-playing she forgot we were on a stream?

Parker snorts laughter. "That was wild! This some kind of method acting shit? Maybe I should try it."

"Parker, shut the fuck up!" I yell, my chair falling backward and clattering to the floor as I stand, running in the direction Nova did.

Please, don't leave. I hurry through the kitchen, cloak trailing behind me, and out the front door. It feels like much longer, but I'm only a few seconds behind her. "Nova!" I call, running toward the driveway and looking around in all directions. It's cool out tonight after the nighttime temperature snapped back again to the fifties.

I catch a glimpse of them standing around the corner of Aiden and Lyssa's house, their back to the wall facing the woods, and their hands covering their face. They've pulled off the tiefling horns and cloak from their costume and are standing in a t-shirt.

I run to them. "Hey!"

"Oh my God. I'm so sorry. I just assaulted you. I'm worse than Parker." Their voice is muffled through her hands.

Nova doesn't realize. I thought I've been the most obvious person in the world with my crush on her. I laugh, moving closer and putting a hand on her elbow. "Nova. It's okay."

She doesn't move her hands. "No, it's not! I can't believe I did that! In front of everyone—and the cameras!"

I pull on her arms, trying to see her face.

"Please. Don't make me look at you. I wish I could just fucking sink into the earth right here. Let it swallow me whole."

They're so embarrassed. As if I didn't like it. As if I haven't been dreaming of it constantly. I want to kiss them again. And again. As many times as they'll have me. If they want to, and it isn't just what they feel like our characters would do.

I reach up, taking her hands in mine as I pull them down, and her face is flushed so red I can tell even in the near darkness. Her eyes are squeezed tight. Still so pretty.

"That's not why I need you to move your hands." My heart hammers in my chest. *This is it.* I have to take this chance. Be brave. I press my body against Nova's, pushing her against the house, and she gasps. It feels powerful—*I* feel powerful. I love it. I stand on my toes and kiss her.

Her lips are soft and yielding against mine, letting me take the lead. I taste the hint of the one beer she had earlier during the D&D session and smell the mint from the color conditioner I gave her to keep the teal bright.

Oh, this is so good—the heat between our bodies in the cold night, the electric feel of her lips on mine. I wrap my arms around her shoulders and kiss her deeper, wanting to make her feel how wild she's been making me. I tease my tongue into the entrance of her mouth. She wants me—it's almost too good to be true.

"June," she moans against my lips, her hands gripping my hips, holding tight. Not Awe. June.

I love role-playing with her, but hearing her moan my name... It's a brand-new thrill.

We break, and I'm breathless, still pushing her against the house. "I like that."

"What? Kissing?" Her eyes search my face, a wide smile breaking across hers. "Yeah, me too."

I have to be grinning like a fool. "My name on your lips." It sounds so cheesy I laugh. "And my lips on your lips!"

"June." She kisses me again, making my head spin. "June." She kisses me deeply this time before breaking off and giggling. "June."

She's such a dork in the best way. Like me. I laugh and swat her shoulder. "Don't ruin it!" Not that she could. I had nothing but water to drink at our session, but I'm dizzy like I had a giant mead at the Renaissance Fair on an empty stomach.

Nova's eyes go wide. "Oh my God, I still can't believe I did that in front of all our friends. And the live stream!" She puts her arms around my waist, hugging me to her again and hiding her face in my hair.

I'm trying to be sensitive to her embarrassment, but I love this contact so much I can't stop grinning. I want to drag her home with me and make out on my couch...or bed. Even though I have no idea what I'm doing. I could figure it out with Nova. Show her my collection of dragon dicks, as she once called them.

She pulls back to look at me, grimacing. "I'm so sorry! You'll have to deal with homophobic trolls about this!"

I push the tip of my nose to hers. "Pfft. If they come out of their holes, I'll smite them with the ban hammer. I'm a pro at wielding it. Someone once even drew a cartoon of Awe holding a ban hammer. No being sorry—not for this. Most of my viewers are nice. They're other nerds like us. The stream will be a hit. Hell, I want to go rewatch that part. It was super-hot."

She groans. "No, please."

"Natural twenty on your seduction roll." I dare to snake my hand in between us, running it under her shirt and over her body. Touching her belly, the edges of her bra, her cleavage, her collarbone... I want to explore all of her. Slowly. Taking in every detail.

Her breathing is ragged as she leans her head back against the house. "Oh, June—"

"Let's get our stuff and go back to my place," I interrupt, pulling my hand out of her shirt. I don't want to play any more D&D tonight. I can't wait. Even though I'm staying with my parents, the basement apartment is private. And even if I don't fully know what I'm doing in bed, I feel confident I can wield one of my vibrators in a way that'll make her feel good.

"Yes, to going to your place. Oh my God, yes. But I can't

go back in Aiden and Lyssa's house. In fact, I don't think I can face our friends or the internet ever again."

I raise an eyebrow at her. She can't possibly mean that. "Your character sheets are in there. And your keys."

She shakes her head, pressing her lips together tightly. "No, you'll have to get them for me. Tell everyone I died!"

I laugh. "Awe casts 'Raise Dead.'"

"Tell them I died and moved to Moscow, then."

"No." I kiss her again. Mm, it's so good. I twirl my fingers through the short hair on the back of her head. "But I'll get your stuff for you."

15
NOVA

O f all the impulsive, embarrassing moments of my life... Who does something like that? I've had the ten-minute drive to June's parents' house to ruminate and replay every single moment.

But wasn't making out with June worth it? Hard to argue with my brain on that one. June ran inside and quickly came back out with my keys, bag, and D&D stuff, then grabbed my hand as we ran up the hill to our cars.

My car tires crunch gravel as I pull down June's parents' side driveway to the basement entrance. I've been here before—years ago. We even had a few sleepovers. During which I was berating myself for thinking inappropriate thoughts about my friend. Am I...sleeping over tonight? Nerves shoot through me. What does it all mean for us now?

I pull my car in behind June's. I never asked if she got the leak fixed.

She gets out of her car. She's taken off the tiefling horns but still wears the rest of her Awe costume. "Hey." She nods and waves at me as I get out of my car.

"Hi." I bite the inside of my cheek. She had time to think on her drive over, too. Maybe she realized what a mistake she made. What if the only reason she kissed me was to make me feel better after such a colossal fuck up?

"Ahh, who am I kidding? I have zero chill." June runs to me and throws her arms around my neck and shoulders.

The embrace is like a balm to my worries. June. Warm. So cute. I wrap my arms around her waist like before. She's so perfect to hold.

She kisses me on the lips—again and again. Each melts my anxiety.

"Mmm," she says against my mouth. "Let's go inside! Fair warning, besides the area I film, the basement apartment is a wreck." She pulls me by the hand toward the door. The house sits on a hill, so there's a ground-floor entrance to the apartment. And it has windows, feeling more like another piece of the house than a subterranean dungeon.

"I absolutely never would've suspected that with you. I'm shook," I deadpan.

She turns and opens her mouth in faux offense.

"It's not like I knew you as a teenager or anything." Back then, her room was almost as messy as mine. I've managed to combat my own natural messiness by owning as few things as possible.

"My bed is clean. Mostly. Isn't that the place that matters? I'll take you straight there."

Straight to her bed. Oh, God. "What—" I choke on the words.

June cackles. "You've been in my bed before. What's your issue now?"

I tackle her against the door, pinning her hands above her head, and she makes an 'eep' sound. I've wanted to do this for so long, and it's even better than I imagined. "My issue is you've been driving me fucking wild on purpose! In the game and outside of it."

"Ooh. What are you going to do about it?" she teases.

What am I going to do? Everything.

A light comes on from the room above us. June's parents.

"Shit, let's get inside," June hisses.

I release her and let her unlock the door—hurrying inside with her before Mr. and Mrs. Bishop decide to stick their heads out the window. It's pretty funny to be sneaking around like this as grown-ass adults.

The place...is a wreck. June was right. There are tons of boxes stacked around the living room area, some opened and some unopened. It looks like she didn't fully move in, which I guess makes sense since she's only here a short time, and her folks are moving in two months. I slide my boots off by the door, and June does the same.

"Just ignore all of this." June puts a hand over my eyes, then grabs my hand with her other one, leading me forward through the path between the boxes.

"If you do that, then I'm going to trip over all your mountains of junk."

She makes a fake offended sound. "Good Ser Wygarthe, I am trying to lead you to my bed. You can be nice to me!"

"I know where your bed is. And I'm going to be very nice to you." I scoop her up in my arms and carry her. She moves her hand from my eyes and clings to my shoulders. Damn, I love holding her. We go through the small kitchenette. Past the storage room to the right. She moved down here her senior year of high school before she left for college the next year.

Maybe I did die of embarrassment earlier. My brain keeps arguing with me. *This can't be real.*

But we're in her bedroom, and there's June's bed with the dragon-printed comforter I've seen in her videos. I toss her onto it, covering her with my body, pinning her. My God, her smeared makeup, her adorable surprised look. I never want to forget any of this. I touch her face, brushing away strands of pink hair. Her expression falters a bit.

Was I overexuberant in carrying her in and tossing her onto the bed? This has to be all new to her. "I'm sorry. Is this okay?"

June nods quickly. "Yes. More than okay."

The agreement seemed too quick to me. I don't want to pressure her when she's not ready. "You're nervous." I never want to be like Parker, where she feels like she needs to appease me.

"Well, yeah. Of course, I am."

Nice going. Basically assault her twice in a day by not getting permission. I roll off her.

"Wait, no, come back and crush me with your larger body!"

I laugh. "Wait a minute. Are you calling me big?"

She pulls on me, trying to roll me on top of her again. I climb on, and she sighs contentedly. "Only in the best way. I like how you feel. It's...comforting."

"You like this?" I grind my body against hers, putting all my weight on her. We're not that different in size—I'm a head or so taller, but I'm not super muscled or anything. I'm not worried about hurting her.

"Yes," June groans, her eyes fluttering shut.

Okay. I can work with this. "Can I kiss you?" I'm going to make sure to get express permission from here on out.

She could've experienced all sorts of awfulness in bed

with Parker that I don't know about. Considering the words he says to her...how he acts entitled to her body and her life. I can't make her feel those ways. I won't.

"Yes." She's breathless already, keeping her eyes closed. I love that I have this effect on her.

I take in the sight of her again. Under me in the dim glow of the stringed lights that illuminate her small room. Tangles of pink hair fanned across the pillow. The scent of her shampoo and the leather corset of the costume she's still wearing. The weight of it all hits me—I have a real-life fantasy girl under me.

Slowly and tenderly this time, I lower my lips to hers. Like I'm Aragorn kissing Arwen or Wesley kissing Buttercup. She's so soft. It's utter bliss. Everything about her captivates me—I can see why she's so popular online. Who could take their eyes off her? Watching her get more and more confident with each video.

Over the past few weeks, I went back and watched every single one. All of the videos on her main channel and on her OnlyFans—which were pretty tame for that site and mostly contained down-to-earth talk about fantasy-themed sex toys. Didn't stop me from losing my mind over them. Didn't stop me from pleasuring myself to them.

I'm all-out obsessed with this girl, and somehow, by some miracle, she invited me into her room and bed. To hold her and kiss her. To taste her.

I drop my jaw, beckoning her mouth open to give me access to more of it. I use my tongue to tickle her lips. *I can do this to you in other places,* I try to signal with its movements. Worship her like the goddess she is.

She lets me, moaning into my mouth. I hope her mind is on the same things mine is.

I cool the kiss, then break off, staring at her face. "I

should've thought about this earlier, but do you have a dental dam, gloves, or anything you want me to use?" I thought I could say it with a straight face, but even mentioning those things has my cheeks burning. Something about the name dental dam. Am I assuming too much that we'll have sex? I mean, she brought me to her room. "I hate to ask you to take my word for it, but I see the doctor every year. They run a full STD panel, and I just went last month."

Her eyes are wide, panicked. "Oh, shit. No, I don't have anything like that. I didn't think I'd have sex again for a long time, and I'm living with my parents. But...I'm...well." She cringes. "I went to the doctor after Parker and had a full check, you know, 'cause he's such a douche."

I cup her face, smiling. "Hey, it's okay. We don't have to do anything you're not comfortable with. We can just cuddle all night. Like old times."

"I...want more than cuddling. Way more. But Nova, I have to be honest. Despite what my videos imply, I'm not any good at sex. I've only been with Parker and my one other shitty high school boyfriend."

"Brett. Yeah." I roll my eyes. Another douche. "I remember. I was jealous."

Amusement plays across her face. "You were?"

"Oh God, so jealous. Burning up with it." I lean on my elbows, one on either side of her. "But I couldn't tell you. I thought you were straight."

June runs a hand under my t-shirt again, like she did outside at Aiden's house, this time touching my back. It makes me groan and shiver. I want her hands everywhere.

"I thought I was straight, too, even though I'd look for excuses to touch you. And watch you run. And role-play with you. Our characters were even married in-game at one point. How did I not see it?"

I laugh. "I was still in the closet and terrified to put how I felt into words. I didn't even go on a date until college. And it's not like I'm a pro. I've only had three partners." Two shitty hookups and Cristy. Well, hookup, Cristy, break up, hookup, then Cristy again when I moved in with her. But I don't want to talk about all of that.

"But you know, like, what to do and all."

"Okay. It's hilarious to me that you think I'm some sort of sex expert, considering I'm about the most awkward person in the entire world, and you make videos on sex toys. But yeah, I know what I like. And I know what usually makes others feel good. Do you want me to touch you?"

"Yes." She answered so quick—as soon as the question crossed my lips.

I smirk. "Do you want me to fuck you?"

"Christ, Nova. Yes!"

Satisfied with her exuberant confirmation, I sit back. "I'm going to take your clothes off now, Lady Danamark."

Will she like role-playing? Should I not? The lines aren't just blurred between us but absolutely erased at this point. Friends and lovers. Real and fantasy.

"Please, Hunt. I can't wait any longer. I don't care if this is our last night alive and we're stuck hiding away in this dungeon."

Guess that answers my question.

I undo the clasp on the wool cloak around her neck. Hm. This leather corset thing seems trickier, though.

She sits up, sweeping the cloak off the bed, and turns around, showing me her back. "Loosen the laces."

My fingers are shaking as I undo the tie and pull on the laces.

She turns to face me. "Now, pull it together to unlatch here." She points to her front, where the corset is clasped.

I pull the clasps together, and then it falls off. She's wearing a linen dress underneath—no bra. I can see the peaks of her nipples through the light fabric. She shakes her shoulders, and the dress falls down.

"June." My throat is dry. She's perfect—her pink nipples and wide areolas standing out against her pale skin in the dim room. "You're gorgeous."

She smiles, sliding the rest of her dress down and off her body, tossing it aside with the cloak. "You want to take these off?" She hooks a thumb inside the elastic of her underwear—a skimpy bikini with lace around the edges.

"Uh-huh." I can barely form words.

She lays on her back again.

What would she like the best? God, suddenly, I'm nervous. I lean down and kiss where the fabric meets skin, pulling her panties down. *Yes. June. Can't believe I'm here. June, June, June.* My mind won't shut up.

I pause from my kissing. "You'd speak up if I'm making you uncomfortable, right?"

"Nova. I'm telling you to fuck me. Your fingers, your mouth, your hands—I don't care what. Hell, I have a bunch of toys you can use tucked in a box under the bed. Just, please."

I grin at the desperation in her voice. Sometimes, a bit of frustration really does enhance the pleasure, though, so...

I pull her underwear down and completely off, then kiss her thighs and nudge them open wider with my face. Her legs fall open like a book. Flexible. I kiss the soft, light brown hair that curls at the ends. She lifts her hips up, inviting me to do more.

"So impatient," I tell her cunt.

"I'm going to shove your face there, so help me."

"I think you'll find I'm quite talented if you have patience and let me attend to you, thank you very much."

She groans, sinking her head back on the pillow.

I breathe her in, savoring her smell, then bring my hand up to trace and tease her entrance.

She shivers and breathes faster.

"A finger okay?" I glance up to study her face.

"Mm." She nods, eyes closed.

I slide the digit in. So hot. And wet. "Lady Danamark, you're this soaked for me?"

"Nova." Her voice takes on a desperate note now.

No more teasing. I just want to make her feel all the good things she deserves. I lower my mouth to her clit, holding still for a moment while letting her feel the warmth and get used to the sensation. My finger strokes a gentle rhythm.

She groans and grips the comforter.

"Mmm," I hum into her, hoping the vibrations add to the sensations. I add one more finger and dip my tongue to lick her clit.

She gives a sharp intake of breath. Has she been with anyone who was attentive to her? Parker is such an ass. Maybe he never treated her well. Whatever happens between us, I'm going to give her this.

She deserves the world.

Damn, she tastes so good. I flick her with my tongue a few times before I shift to sucking on her while my fingers stroke her on the inside.

"Fuck, Nova. I'm already about to—"

She comes undone in my mouth, on my fingers, my tongue. So quick. What a compliment. I love it—though I'd do this to her all night if she wanted. I let her ride out the sensation, then slowly remove my mouth and fingers.

"That... You..." She's breathless. The best compliment.

I crawl on top of her again since she seemed to like it earlier, smirking and crossing my hands on the top of her chest. "Yes?"

"I've never... I mean. It always takes me forever to come with a partner. If I can do it at all."

I'm fucking bursting with pride right now but decide to try to play it cool. "I'm happy to be in your service, my dear lady."

She laughs. "And no one has ever wanted to role-play with me in bed."

"If you thought I wouldn't want to, then you've greatly underestimated my nerdiness."

"I want to do you next. But I don't know if I know how to do...all of that."

"You can do anything you want. We can go to sleep right now, and I'm fully satisfied. I'm walking on the moon." After pleasuring her, feeling her climax on my face, I feel like I'd probably come from a single touch from her. I'm not sure I've ever been this aroused before.

"Can I...use a toy on you? I guess I feel more comfortable starting there since that's how I usually pleasure myself."

"As long as it's not the gargantuan gold."

She laughs. "You still have that one in your apartment's inventory, remember? Take your clothes off. I have an idea."

I sit up, yank off my shirt and stretchy bra, toss them both, and shuck off my jeans and undies in one fell swoop.

June blinks, her eyes wide as they roam up and down my body. "Wow."

I don't think anyone has said "wow" about me. I laugh —surely, she's just being nice.

She puts a hand on my chest, feeling my right breast. "Nova, I realize this will sound silly, but I'm, like, really into boobs. Yours specifically. Your whole body, really. Everything you have going on. I can't believe I didn't realize it sooner."

"Congrats," I say dryly, climbing under the comforter, now a little self-conscious.

"You felt how aroused I am."

My heart softens. "Yeah, I know. I believe you."

"Good. I never want you to think you're some rebound experiment or curiosity or whatever ridiculous shit people say."

"I trust you." With my whole self, my whole heart, my whole body.

June smirks. "Good. Lay back and close your eyes."

I do, heart pounding in my ears as I stretch my hands behind my head. She's rummaging through something under the bed. The toys she mentioned... I've seen her explain some of their functions on her channel. But I've never really got into sex toys. I own a single vibrator, and it's the boring kind I bought at a drugstore. "June?" I crack an eye open to peek at her, trying to get a clue on what she's about to do.

I glimpse only her pale, exposed chest and messy pink hair as she puts a soft hand over my eyes. "No peeking."

She pulls down the comforter, making me shiver at the sudden chill. Then her mouth is on my nipple, sucking it, and it's good but utterly overwhelming.

"Ah, stop!" The words fly out.

She does, pulling back immediately.

I open my eyes to see her eyebrows knit in concern. Ah, shit. I hope I didn't kill her confidence. She's so nervous already. "Hey, it's okay." I cup her cheek. "Sorry, it's just too much for me if you start like that. I have some sensory... stuff going on. Start by touching me with your hands." I guide her hand up to cup my breast. "And then move your thumb..." I gasp as she runs it over my nipple.

"Sorry for being over-exuberant. I just want to please and—"

"God, June, everything about you pleases me." I can barely speak through the sensations. "Try to be confident in yourself. Be Awe for me." I close my eyes again. "You know, horny bard-level confidence."

"Fine. You asked for it." I love the playful tone in her voice. She throws a leg over me, climbing on as she moves her hand from my chest. Her breasts brush mine, and I feel her reach to pick up something from the floor. There's a low buzz sound. Must be that toy. "Okay, Hunt. I'm going to use my favorite *special* magic wand on you. Don't worry. I'll start on a low setting. Then I'll slowly level you up. How often do you use vibration toys?"

I open my mouth, but no sound comes out. Oh, my God, Awe. June. I want her to touch me so bad. Words. I should use words.

"Well, then. I'll have to find out myself." She leans in to whisper in my ear. "This is okay, right, Nova?"

I manage a frantic nod, opening my eyes to see her face framed by her hair. *Yes. Anything, goddess.*

She smiles and shows me the toy. Damn, it really *is* a wand. It's styled like something from a magical girl anime show—lit up yellow and pink and a silicone purple rose in the center. She sits back on my thighs and puts her mouth to the rose, running her tongue on it. "I added this part to the toy. For texture. Now I'm going to use this vibrating rose right here"—she lowers it to the front of me—"and see what happens."

Even on this so-called low setting, and even though she hasn't even parted me yet, it makes me about come off the bed. I arch my back, lifting her on my thighs. "Oh, fuck."

She giggles, pressing the toy harder onto me. "Yes, Hunt. I'm doing that to you right now."

I'm going to be done even faster than she was. Like, no way to even hold it back.

"Awe. June." I feel untethered from my voice, like I'm listening to a voiceover. "Put your fingers in me while you use that." I grab her hand and shove it between my legs.

She laughs, parting me and dipping a finger inside with the hand not holding the toy. "Like this? Damn, you feel nice."

"Mmmh." All I can do is make a strangled sound while she touches me.

She angles the toy a little different. "I like to rub this toy against my clit like this."

Pleasure shoots through me, building even higher. And suddenly, the texture of the silicone attachment June added makes sense. I both want to grab at her hands to be in control and simultaneously want to let her do anything she wants. I hold her hand, pushing her fingers into me, grasping for something, anything, as the wave crests and overwhelms me.

As it passes, the sensitivity gets too much, and I laugh, yanking the toy away. I push buttons on it until it turns off. June draws her hand back, and I pull her onto my chest, holding her tight.

"Was I okay at it?"

She has to ask? "Okay?" *Words, Nova.* I grip her shoulders. "You were incredible! A freaking sex-demon-goddess. I'm like putty in your hands. My whole body is still like a live wire."

She laughs. "I don't think I really did much."

How does she not know? I roll her to the side so we're facing each other on the pillow. I kiss her slowly now that I feel in control of myself again. "You did."

"You tired?" she asks when we break.

"No." I feel alive, on fire, even.

"Me neither."

My freaking phone keeps buzzing from the floor where it fell last night. I crack my eyes. There are no windows in my room, so I have no idea what time it is. It's doubtful my room in my parents' basement technically counts as a bedroom, as far as legal floor plans go.

"Oh, hi." Nova is already awake, leaning on her side, watching me. Her phone is in her other hand. How long has she been up?

I blink. I have to look like a mess, especially after not washing my face or brushing my teeth last night. Hell, I didn't even turn off the string lights in my room. The sight of Nova in my bed is thrilling, their messy teal hair sticking up at odd angles, the circles under their eyes making them look a little sleepy. They're adorable.

I smile. "Hey."

"You're so cute I can't stand it." They pull me in for a hug.

"Well. I'm relieved that absolute hot garbage seems to do it for you."

Nova laughs, rubbing my back. "Hot is right. Not garbage. Can I borrow a toothbrush? Or have a toothbrush? Not that I want to use your toothbrush because that would be weird. I think."

"Considering the places your mouth was last night and then where mine was, no, I don't think it would," I tease. "But I do have a fresh toothbrush you can have, still in the freebie pack from the dentist. I tossed it in the cabinet under the sink."

She kisses my forehead, lingering there for a moment. "I'll be back."

She climbs out of bed, still naked, and heads to the little bathroom. Nova, naked in my room. Wow. After she shuts the door, I find my phone on the floor and check the time. Seven-ten in the morning. Why are we up so early? Ugh, so many messages. There are texts from Lyssa and about ten more friends and acquaintances who must've watched the game stream last night. I'm not awake enough to deal with that.

Either my mom or my dad pounds on the door above the stairs to the basement, jolting me. I'm not awake enough for this, either. I sigh and pick up Nova's t-shirt from the floor, pulling it over my head, and snag a pair of lounge shorts I'd left draped over my dresser yesterday. I trudge out of my room and up the wooden stairs. Dad is waiting when I unlock the door at the top and yank it open.

He shifts his weight from one foot to another. "Sorry to knock so loud, Junie. I know you sleep really hard on Sunday morning."

"You could've texted me," I mutter, blinking at the bright light that floods the main floor of the house. If I were a cartoon character, I'd hiss at it like a vampire.

"I did." He frowns, looking uncomfortable. "Look, I

know you're an adult, and I don't want to get in your business, but when you moved in, you agreed you weren't in a good place for anything, you know, with guys. You promised you wouldn't have any of them spend the night. And I couldn't help but notice the car parked in front of the basement."

Oh, for fucks sake. "It's Nova's car. No guys involved."

He lets out a sigh, visibly relaxing. "Oh, okay! That makes sense. Goodness, I'm sorry. I didn't mean to embarrass you. Gaming night and a sleepover like old times, then?"

"Um, sort of." Fuck, I want to go back to bed.

"Well, tell her we'll have breakfast in an hour after your mom and I go for a run. I'll be making my buckwheat pancakes she used to like with agave-blueberry syrup."

"Mm-hm. I'll pass that info along." I freaking hate mornings. Nothing good happens before eight A.M.

I close the door, lock it again, and shuffle back down the stairs.

Nova is at the bottom, shirtless, arms crossed over her chest. "Hello, thief. You stole my shirt."

I look down at it. "Heh, I was just putting on something quick to speak to my dad. And it wasn't like I was going to put the corset back on."

She points at me. "I sure as hell won't be wearing the corset, so I'm gonna need that back."

"Do you really?" I squint at her. "I think you have a good look going on." She's in her jeans again and nothing else.

She grabs me, crushing my body against hers, then pulls on the bottom of the shirt. "If you admire it so much, then join me." She yanks it over my head.

A squeak escapes from my mouth. "I haven't even brushed my teeth yet or used the bathroom!"

"Fine." She spins me toward the bathroom, shoving me down the hall. "But hurry up."

When I come out of the bathroom, Nova kisses me and steers me to the bed.

Turns out some good things do happen before eight in the morning.

After, we lay in my bed facing each other, still breathing hard. Wide awake. Maybe I do like exercise in the mornings.

"What kind of paladin prayers were those?" I tease. "Fucking prayers?"

She kisses me on the lips. "The best kind."

"Have you checked your phone for messages? I'm sure people are bombarding you, too."

She scrunches her face. "I've been ignoring them and reading books on my phone when I couldn't sleep. I didn't dare look at your channel. And I already told you yesterday. I died. You'll have to tell everyone else the sad news."

I laugh, brushing my fingers through her messy hair. "This again? Well, too late. Dad already saw that you were spending the night and invited you to breakfast."

Her face goes pale. "He doesn't watch your stream, does he?"

"Fuck, no. He and Mom are health nuts and in bed by nine every night. He still owns the vitamin shop."

Nova pauses like they're thinking about it. "Well, I guess breakfast would be fine, then. Eventually." They smile, cupping my face with their hand.

I close my eyes and lean into their touch. I want to just linger here in this moment. No messages. No one moving to Iowa or having to find a new apartment. Just us in my bed on a Sunday morning.

But Nova's phone starts buzzing. They glance at the screen and groan. "Cristy."

"She watched the live stream."

"Yeah, I'm sure." Nova sits up, then shoves the phone at me, putting their face in their hands. "Now's your chance. Answer and inform her of my death."

"You're really that committed, huh? Fine." I sit up and slide the bar to answer. "Hello?"

"I can't believe you actually answered that!" Nova hisses.

"You told me to!" I whisper back, shielding the phone speaker.

"Yeah, but I didn't think you would!"

"Hello?" Cristy's voice. "Oh my God, is this June?"

"Hang up!" Nova climbs on top of me, trying to grab the phone.

"Hey," I try to sound casual, rolling around the opposite way to dodge Nova's grasp. "Good morning. Situation normal. How're you?"

Nova slaps a hand to her forehead, grabbing at me with her other. "June, I swear."

"Ooh, you're both there! Put me on speaker! I need all the deets!" Cristy sounds thrilled.

"Sure, hold on," I tell her.

Nova manages to wrest the phone from my grip. "Bye, Cristy." They hang up, then toss it aside. "You'll pay for that."

"I look forward to it." I lay back on the bed, stretching my arms behind my head.

That was a miscalculation because Nova takes the opportunity to tickle my sides.

"Agh, stop!" I squeeze my arms to my sides, squirming under her.

Now my phone starts buzzing. What now? Nova relents, and I manage to find it and squint at the screen.

"Oh, shit, this is Geoff at NerdyPodCasts calling!"

Nova jumps off me, and I sit up, trying to think my most professional thoughts.

I slide the bar on my phone. "Hello?"

"Hey, June? This is Geoff at NPC."

"Hi, yes, I remember! What can I do for you?" I sit up, feet brushing the soft carpet beside my bed. Still naked. Nova sits behind me, pressing their breasts against my back and kissing my neck, sending shivers through me. Damn them. I guess they did swear I'd pay.

I put the phone on speaker so I don't have to hold it up to my ear.

"Oh, I'm just checking in."

"Great! Yeah, I think the live stream is going pretty well. We're getting good views." I fight to keep my voice level despite the sensations running down my spine. "I have a great group overall. And I think the little hiccups we're having with Parker's character, Jerald, will be relatable to plenty of groups dealing with new players. He'll learn, or he'll figure out no one wants to play with him."

"That's just great." He sounds insincere. What's this call really about if it's not about Parker? "I just wanted to make sure we were on the same page. We consider this podcast to be family-friendly, and there are some themes that've come up lately which I'm not sure will be what our company wants to publish—and though we agreed to pay for the rights to publish your sessions, it's in your contract they have to be the quality of content NPC wants."

Oh, shit. Ice shoots through me. If I lose the money from this contract, I'm sunk.

Nova stops her ministrations.

"Oh, geez. I mean..." I swallow. "I'm sorry." *Shit, shit, shit.* "Even though certain family-friendly mainstream shows have brought D&D to bigger audiences, the game includes mature themes such as violence, gore, and other trauma. The main conflict of this campaign is defeating an undead wizard who has, in essence, taken an entire city as his prisoners. It gets pretty dark—I thought I was clear about the content rating weeks ago. And as far as the foul language my friends and I sometimes use, I thought we discussed that also. If you need us to tone it down, I can talk with them, but I can't guarantee a word won't slip by. The game itself is rated mature, including all the game supplements. My channel's target audience ranges from sixteen to forty-five, with the vast majority being in their mid to late twenties."

I'm babbling. What am I going to do if they refuse to publish it?

"June, June, relax. It's fine. I didn't mean to worry you. I wasn't talking about that stuff. And it's nothing we can't fix in editing. I want to make sure going forward, we're putting together a family-friendly podcast."

What the hell does he mean, then? I look back at Nova. She's frowning, pointing at herself. "Tell him you'll make sure that happens," she whispers.

"I'll, um, make sure that happens. No problem." But I don't feel sure about it.

"Great," he says again. "Thanks." The call ends.

I throw the phone against the pile of clothes on my chair. No more calls, please. "What the hell do you think that was about?"

"Me. Of course, it's me." Nova pulls her legs up to her chest. "My very existence is considered 'shoving sexuality in people's faces.'" They make air quotes, then hug their legs. "This is why I was so upset with myself yesterday. I opened you up to this kind of transphobic, homophobic bullshit before you even realized whether or not you want to be out."

"If I get to be with you, then I'm way, way out." I lean into them, lifting their chin with my hand and kissing their lips. "I don't care about what people think."

Her eyes meet mine. I love her eyes so much. But they look sad now. "You should think and consider what you want to do. People will treat you differently. Professionally. Personally. And we're not even sure what we're doing with this." She gestures between us. "I'm moving across the country in a few months."

I sigh, standing up and plucking her shirt from the ground again. "I didn't want to think about all of this." I pull it on over my head. "I'm your friend, first and foremost. No matter what else happens, we're *never* going back to not speaking, okay?" I pick up the 'magic wand' we used last night from the nightstand and aim it at her. "Or else I'm zapping you with a spell."

She gives me a half-smile. "What's your spell? Tasha's Irresistible Orgasm?"

"Yeah. That's right. Level nine. You can't resist."

"If you're stealing my shirt, hand me one of yours." She holds a hand out.

I dig through the pile of clean-ish laundry on my dresser.

"I think we should keep things quiet for now," Nova says. "Just until you're a bit more used to the idea of being out. And because I don't want NPC to pull your show."

It feels extra shitty, but what she's saying makes sense. Can't I just hide with her under the covers from all of this?

I have an idea of a shirt she might like and dig through clothes, looking for its maroon color. "Yeah. I hate it, but I'm counting on the money from NPC. Please, don't worry about me. You've certainly done enough for my financial situation by paying for those shirts I'm selling." The worry eats at the bottom of my stomach, even as I say it. No, I don't have a real plan past my attempts at promoting and making money through my channel. But I don't want to sound like the utter fool I am.

Ah, here it is. My t-shirt printed with a skull wearing aviator sunglasses and the words 'One Flesh, One End' from one of my favorite book series involving lesbian necromancers in space. Nova reads the books too—we sent each other a bunch of memes about it over texts the past week. "Here you go, my cavalier primary."

She laughs as I toss the shirt to her, then spreads it, looking at the print. She shakes her head as she slides it on. "How did I ever think you were straight?"

I have absolutely no answer for her.

I always forget how awkward it is to talk with people who haven't seen me in years.

"Nova," June's dad, George, starts again. "June says you still run like you did in high school."

"Mm." I swallow my bite of pancake. "Yes, sir." Sun is streaming in through the dining room windows. I feel self-conscious here in the bright light of day, wearing June's t-shirt and no bra, sitting at June's parents' table—like I used to do as a teen. Both everything and nothing has changed. Same buckwheat pancakes, non-dairy spread, and organic blueberry syrup made by Mr. Bishop. Same table. Same sleepy, gorgeous girl next to me.

June's parents exchange a glance. Her dad continues, "Well, maybe you can convince June to finally make fitness a priority. It's really important as she gets closer to thirty."

June sighs, leaning an elbow on the table and resting her forehead on her palm. She's sitting at the end of the table next to me. "I'm twenty-six. Twenty-six. And Nova, tell him I work out." A smirk forms in the corner of her mouth. "Like, just this morning, after I spoke with you, Dad, Nova had me working out. Left me breathless."

I try to nod noncommittally and pick up my cooled cup of mushroom-based "coffee" June's dad made with breakfast. Even drinking that is better than having to participate in this conversation. I set my cup down and pull my phone from my jeans pocket to text June under the table. *"Don't push your luck."*

Her phone buzzes next to her plate, and she picks it up, holding it under the table to respond.

"Can't help it." She adds a winking face emoji with its tongue out. Then she sends me the hot face, sparkles, and the water drop.

Ridiculous. I'll make her pay later. I put my phone in my pocket.

"Well, good for Nova, then. Hope it helps you stick with it." June's mom, Nancy, smiles.

"Yep! She's good for helping me stick things—"

I kick June under the table, glaring at her.

But her parents don't seem to notice. Her dad whispers something to her mom, who nods.

"We needed to tell you something this morning, and it'll affect your immediate plans, so it can't really wait."

"Did you need me to go?" I stand and go to reach for my plate to take it to the sink.

"No, it's okay." June grabs my hand, pulling me back down to sit. Under the table, she keeps hold of it.

I run my thumb over the back of her hand. It's obvious this conversation is going to get even worse.

Nancy fiddles with the edge of her napkin. "The realtor found us a buyer for the house."

June smiles, but I can tell it's a fake one as it doesn't touch her eyes. "That's great! So quick."

I remember some of the mixed feelings I had when my dad sold his house the year I moved out to college. It made sense he found a smaller house closer to his job at the university, but it still felt...bad. Like a piece of my childhood was gone. I drove by the old place when I was back in town, but it wasn't the same. It felt like all the pieces of me it held had scattered.

June's dad cuts a piece of pancake. "Our area has a hot market and a low inventory, so we even got over the asking price."

Her mom smiles. "The family who bought it will take great care of the place. I know it matters to you to have someone keep the trees in the backyard. And they have kids that'll enjoy it."

June nods.

I squeeze her hand. Her treehouse. Even though we were too old to really play in it when we hung out in high school, we still spent time laying back there on the wooden platform, looking up at the tree canopy and talking about our D&D characters.

June's mom frowns. "But of course, there's a catch. They need us out in two weeks so they can install new flooring down in the basement and new counters up here."

Her dad leans forward. "We've been reminding you for weeks, but do you have somewhere lined up?"

"Uh..." June's mouth hangs open. She doesn't. I know she doesn't.

I squeeze her hand again, trying to reassure her as much as I can.

She shrugs. "I'll figure it out, of course. I got my first advance check from the podcast the other day. If I have to, I'll rent a cheap Airbnb or something for a few weeks while I set a lease going."

"Ah, that's a relief." June's mom smiles. "I told your dad that you'd have a plan."

June nods, brows knit.

I might be pushing her way past her comfort zone if I ask...but would it be so bad if she came and stayed with me? I'm not in town for long, so it wouldn't be forever. But it seems ridiculous she'd need to pay to find a temporary place when my bed is available. And God knows I want her in it.

I give her hand one more squeeze before I drop it and stand. "Um, June, can I speak with you downstairs for a minute?"

She nods at me. "Sure."

When we're back down the stairs, I hug June and she sighs into the embrace. She fits so nice.

She squeezes me tighter. "I'm sorry. I shouldn't have agreed for us to have breakfast with them. Kind of puts a damper on the day, huh?"

I cup her face. "It doesn't. Come stay with me. Move in until you get your own place."

"*What?* Nova, you can't be serious."

Did that sound creepy or overbearing? Or like that cliché joke about sapphics moving in together after the first date? "I don't mean to come on too strong. I just mean...stay with me as a friend." I cringe at the wording. "I'd offer it even if you didn't just blow my mind last night. And this morning. I'd offer it to you if you never liked me the way I do you."

"But..." She gestures to her boxes and items scattered through the basement. "You have a one-room apartment, and I have too much stuff. And a shitty sleep schedule. And you're moving soon. What if I drive you away, and then you break up with me when we're not even, like, officially dating and then—"

I cut her off with a kiss. "I don't care about any of that. Really. I'll help you find a cheap storage building for your stuff and help you move into your new place when you find it."

She touches her lips while staring through the floor the way she does when she's thinking. "Are we official?"

There are so many expectations that come with a label. She's worried about driving me away, but I'm way more likely to push a girlfriend away—just like I did with Cristy. I've never had what I'd consider a successful relationship.

"Am I officially smitten with you? Yes. Of course, I am. But there are few things..." I drag a hand through my hair. I didn't sleep more than two hours last night, and combined with not taking my med this morning, my brain isn't powering up the way I need it to. "Can we cuddle while we talk about this? I feel like we should."

"Oh, is this your excuse to drag me back to bed for more 'exercise'?" June makes air quotes.

I laugh. "Maybe." Of course, I want to touch her again. As many times as she'll have me.

She leads me to her room, and we lay over the covers facing each other, propped up on our sides.

I trace a finger down her arm, starting below my t-shirt sleeve. God, I love how she looks wearing my shirt. "If we say we're official or whatever, then there are, you know, expectations. Like me being able to properly open up all the time. Or you'll be worried about my opinions and feelings before you make important decisions. And we're both in the middle of difficult life transitions right now, you know?"

She frowns but nods. "I guess that makes sense."

I want to ask for more. But it's not fair to her. Too fast.

"Be my friend, June. No matter how far we move from each other. Even if you meet someone else you'd rather date or if I fuck up and say something rude. I agree with what you were saying earlier—I never again want to go years without talking to you. I need your friendship in my life."

June gives me a sad smile. "Lyssa gave me similar advice, telling me to be your friend and it'll all work out. I don't want to lose our friendship either, no matter what the future holds. That was the biggest realization I came to the day I had my big gay crisis."

I bust out laughing. "Big what now?" She said it so nonchalantly in this serious conversation it caught me off guard.

"Oh, you know, the day after we went to the bar." She winks at me, then does a fake gasp. "I bet it's because you gave me that rainbow drink! I should've realized it was contagious."

I push myself over onto her, rolling her to her back and pinning her wrists beside her head. She feels amazing under me. "I'm afraid you have a terminal case. No cure."

"Is that so?"

"Mm-hm." I touch my nose to hers. "So come stay in my apartment with me. No pressure. Let's just spend as much time together as we can." I touch my lips to hers, teasing with feather-light kisses.

Before I leave for two years. But I can't think about that now.

"Let me see if I'm getting this right." She wiggles her wrists, but I hold her tight. "You want me to freaking *move in* with you on the day after we get together, yet I still have to keep this a secret from my channel and parents?"

"I mean, I guess you can tell your parents we're having a sleepover again."

She chuckles. "Fine. Okay." A big smile breaks across her face. "Yes. I'd love to stay with you."

My brain is sending me warnings. This is going to hurt so bad when I leave. When she eventually finds someone else who can treat her the proper way she deserves, who talks about their feelings. I haven't even been able to admit to her that I wrote *Curse*. But I can't help myself. I want all the June I can get.

June

I hit the button to start the recording on my phone. This is just my simple set-up for my YouTube channel where I check-in with my audience. I haven't showered, but the filter fixes my makeup well enough for a quick check-in video. Later this week, I'll do a detailed cosplay walk-through with a project I've been working on. For now, I want to make this fast and get over to Nova's.

"Hiya, friends. Just wanted to have our usual post-game Sunday chat." I do finger guns at the camera. Nova and I made sure to clear all questionable items from the bed and nightstand—I checked the shot three times before starting my live video. "I'll be taking your questions from time to time during this video, so be sure to write in."

"So...interesting night last night. Such big. Much drama." I pull out my real lute, which I'd set slightly off-camera before beginning the recording. I lack the skills to make anything musical come out of the instrument, but it makes a good prop. "I think my song of friendship worked a little too well, if you know what I mean." I give an overexaggerated wink to the camera. "Maybe some of you song-writers can get on writing a real one for me. If you haven't seen the session, you can go check that out right now. I just glanced at the views, and they're, like, super high, so you guys are clearly just as horny as Awe is for the teal-haired demon-born paladin."

I lean in slightly like I'm speaking to a close friend. "And speaking of, just to make sure we're perfectly clear, there's nothing going on outside the game between Nova and me other than friendship."

I guess that's the truth. That's what they told me they wanted. Of course, then they tackled me, kissed me, and made me come two more times. So confusing. I guess these are the usual steps to dating now? I'm so out of the loop. Not that I ever really practiced since Parker and I got together so quickly out of high school.

"She's a great role-player, and sometimes I, too, totally get lost in thinking she's Hunt, but she's not. We totally planned that kiss last night, and I think it really brought some drama to the session and upped the tension between Awe and Hunt." It's a lie, and I hate lying, but I want to save Nova from feeling so embarrassed. I hold a hand up. "Will they kiss each other?" Then I lift the other hand. "Will they come to blows when the real truths of their pasts are revealed? You'll have to watch and see."

I lower my hands. "But please, y'all. Being serious. Don't go harass Nova over this. They're a really awesome D&D player, and I want them to continue coming to the sessions. We're not actually dating, and there are no secrets you can find by attempting to contact them. They like their privacy, so let's respect that. And I'm going to have to come down hard with the ban hammer if anyone tries to bother them or uses any remotely transphobic or bigoted language in the comments. Cool? Cool."

I smile, pulling out my computer so I can check the comment feed. "Speaking of, let's hear from some of you."

Oh God, there's like a hundred comments already. Some people are having an entirely separate conversation with each other.

Friends. Right. I kiss my table buds all the time. Platonically.
U wish u could
June we all knew already!
Do you like boys are girls
June. Pls.
Best special friends!
This is sus
Wut nothing going on like do u think were dum

"'Peg the paladin?'" I read, "I don't really understand this comment I keep seeing pop up. Her real name is Nova, and you know her character, Hunt—" It hits me. "Oh. Oh! Not cool! Y'all are deviants!"

So am I, but not going to admit that out loud.

I read another. "'If five hundred of us say it, will you do it?' What? No!" The replies are ticking up faster by the second now that they know I'm reading them. "How many of you are watching this?" The chat is coming in so fast. I shake my head, picking another to read. "'I wrote a smutfic about Awe and Hunt after last night. Will you read it?'" I point at the camera. "Yes, I will." More comments pop into the box. Like I figured, a lot of them are quite positive. Some very intrusive but nonetheless positive.

I read another. "'Yesterday was a big day for me.' Me too, swordart4hire24, me too. 'I have a whole art Tumblr blog dedicated to you guys, please check it out. I stan you so hard.' Okay, I'll go look."

I click the link, scanning the anime-style sketched images. They're...Nova and me. No costumes. My heart beats faster. People were watching and hoping we'd get together? I...need to finish this video and look deeper.

More comments fly into the box.

She's totally wearing Nova's shirt! Look at the design in the corner.

I look down at Nova's shirt. It's a dark grey t-shirt with an open book spilling out fantasy staples like swords, dragons, and more down from the shoulder and across the front. But Nova had on a cloak last night when they were on camera. Is it really noticeable? The conversation ticks by. Shit. Shit! I should've showered and changed clothes.

OMFG it is. Look at the book in the corner same as what Nova had on. They totally fucked

Whaaat? What a waste

It's happening! Everyone, stay calm.

Parker ruined her for our team.

My gf and I tried this and no one believed us either

June come back to meeee I'll treat u right

U wish loser

June pls put Nova on your OnlyFans its what the people want.

This is spinning out of control. "Y'all! You're looking too deep into the shirt." How can I come up with a way to stop them from creating wild rumors? "Nova came over after the ending of the session, which again, we totally planned, and then we worked on some character ideas with me. Then, in the morning, I just picked up their shirt from the floor and borrowed it. Situation normal."

The same ridiculous thing I said to Cristy, only then, I wanted her to know Nova and I were together. Oh God, with every sentence I'm making it worse and worse. Tons of lols and emojis and comments like *I knew it!* pop into the box.

"Your comments aren't helping my case! She's going to wake up from her nap, and I'm going to have to explain that y'all are ridiculous."

Wait, why are they napping?

"'Why aren't you with her?'" I read, then gesture to the empty bed behind me. "Sorry to disappoint. There's no story to be found here. And it's normal for someone to nap after I keep them up all night."

Bahhahaha!

Dead.

Lololol

I open and close my mouth. "I mean up all night playing D&D! I am saying a lot of things. Okay. I think I'm going to call this chat a wrap for now. Thanks for watching."

Just say you're official already!

I would if I could, hot4dicemaster.

I wave at the camera and end the stream. Fuck, Nova is not going to be happy with this. The comment section is still on fire. I can't believe at least a few of them are "shipping" us in real life. And have an art account about it.

Someone types in a slur, and I breathe in quickly through my nose. That's what Nova was afraid of. The people in the comment section jump on them immediately, but still, I hit the button to delete the comment and ban them. My moderators and I are going to have to pay attention and watch for comments like that.

The last thing I want is for Nova to regret getting involved with me. She loves her privacy.

I flip over to the tap I opened and scroll down the fan's Tumblr. It's...cute. And yeah, a bit flattering. They have a whole timeline of our supposed relationship that goes all the way back to before session one. Funny. My followers think I have way more game than I do.

Oh, shit. My heart about stops as I read on. Some of them are even speculating that Nova is the author of *Curse* and that's why she's playing a character so similar to the main character. It's all part of their timeline. I can put that rumor to rest by emailing *Curse*'s real author and perhaps getting an interview with them. If they'll speak with me.

But even if I clear Nova of that rumor, she'll still have online people speculating about her, and I know how much she hates that sort of attention. Have I shoved her into a spotlight she never wanted by getting involved with her?

18
NOVA

Someone knocks on my apartment door. *June.* Nerves flutter in my stomach like I didn't just do the most intimate things of my life with her last night and this morning. I shove the vacuum in the closet and close the door.

I glance at my bed, made with clean sheets for the first time in two weeks. I've been cleaning up like she'd care—as if I could impress her that way. She's coming here tonight, then we'll get to work on packing her things from her parents' house in the morning. I'm doing well enough with my word count I can take half a day off tomorrow. *June in my apartment.* Or I can take off the whole day.

I jog through the small hall, past the dining area and living room, and pull the door open. "Hey."

She kisses me immediately, pushing me backward as she comes inside. Warmth floods me—like yesterday after I was overthinking everything on the way to her house. I could get used to this kind of greeting. I slide the duffle bag off her shoulder, not breaking the kiss, and set it down inside the door. She's carrying a bag from the pho place in her other hand. Aww. I didn't even think about dinner yet.

We break, and I don't know what I want to do first. Where do I start? My freaking dream girl living in my apartment, and she's going to stay with me for the time we have left together before my move.

Ugh. The move.

She lifts the takeout bag. "I think this is my apology go-to meal."

I take it from her, carrying it to the little table. "Heh, stop apologizing." I don't want her to feel bad about staying with me. It's not pity—I want her with me. Every second of June I can have. I shrug, trying to act nonchalant about it. "Like I said, think of it as an extended sleepover. It's no trouble."

She sits down at the table and puts a hand on mine, golden brown eyes staring up at me. "Wait. Sit down, and let me tell you what happened."

Oh, no. What could've gone wrong in the few hours we were apart? I do as she says—sitting down in the other chair, quiet.

"I did the follow-up video to yesterday's session." She cringes. "You're not going to be happy. I found out in the comments that there's...a group of superfans who watch my channel that've been rooting for us to get together. Like, our characters, but also us in real life."

I laugh. After all, I'm one of them. "Why are you sorry for what online people do?"

Her shoulders droop as she looks away. "They can be... intense. And they think you're the author of *Curse of the Dragon's Gate* since you've been playing Hunt."

I sit back in my chair, letting the information wash over me. It's not a surprise. I knew people would make that connection eventually when June made the video talking about my book. But...does June know?

She sneaks a glance at me. "God, wouldn't that be a living nightmare for me if I'd trashed *your* book? It's bad enough *Curse* was one of your favorites. Don't worry, I'll send an email to the author, and if I can, I'll get them to answer some questions or, better yet, do a video interview with me."

I'd be a fool to be mad at her about it. Because of the spark her video lit, people have been sharing about my book on TikTok. I've never been able to use TikTok. And yesterday, my old agent sent me an email informing me that I earned out my advance, so I'd get a royalty deposit at the end of the quarter. It also included an offer to represent me again, which I'll reply to tomorrow.

"It's fine." I smile, chuckling a little.

She cringes. "There's more."

June thinks I'm going to blame her for what other people say? It hits me—in a way, I did, even if she doesn't realize it yet. Yeah, she shared a video stirring the controversy up, but the damage was done by that interviewer, homophobes, transphobes, and bored people on the internet. Whether June made a video about it or not.

"You know with that one conversation this morning when I said we should have it on the bed to make it better? I think we should have this one with you on my lap." I open my arms to invite her.

She laughs. "Why should it be me on your lap just because I'm smaller? You could come sit on mine."

"You don't think I will? Fine." I get up and drape myself around her, hugging her face to my chest and kissing the top of her head. Mmm, she smells good. Mint conditioner.

Her lavender lotion. And the indescribable smell that's all June.

"People think we fucked because I was wearing your shirt in the video I made earlier," she says against the fabric of my shirt.

"Um. They'd be right."

"But you said we should keep it a secret! I know you like your privacy, and this is pretty invasive. And unfortunately, being with me means constant invasions of your privacy."

I lean back to look at her. "Even if that were true, you're worth it."

"But...are you sure?" She tilts her head. "You're leaving in a few weeks. And people are weird. Stuff like this could follow you, or worse, make it difficult for you to succeed professionally when you do get your books published."

"Yes, I'm sure." I used a pen name for a few reasons. A big one being because my agent felt like initials would sell better than the name Nova. But I kind of wish I didn't. "No matter how I present myself, hateful people are going to find ways to attempt to make me miserable and want to hide. But that doesn't mean I should."

She nods. "But you think we should keep us secret still. Well. If not secret, quiet."

I laugh, running my fingers through her soft hair, swiping it back from her face. She didn't curl it or style it today, and it falls a little below her shoulder blades. "That's for your sake, you dork. You're the one with people obsessed with you. And a kinda conservative family. I mean, they go to church at least. Does owning the hippie vitamin shop cancel that out?"

She shakes her head, giving me a half-smile. "I don't know. Maybe?"

"I want you to get a chance to tell them and the rest of

the world when you're ready. Not because I messed up and kissed you on camera." Still can't believe I did that.

"I hadn't really thought about how they'd react, to be honest. I'm enough of a disappointment already. Hard to imagine it'd faze them."

I kiss her cheek and down her neck where I moved away her hair. She leans back in the chair, giving me better access.

"You're amazing." I mean it from my soul. "Don't say that about yourself. If anyone is disappointed by who you are, the fault is in them, not you. You left a man who was trying to keep you boxed in when everything in your life conditioned you to stay with him. That's not easy to do. You're one of the top cosplayers and content creators in D&D. You're good at this." I couldn't have imagined getting this level of word-of-mouth for my book on my own. Promotion is a completely separate skill set from writing.

She sighs. "Weeks ago, I applied to that D&D reality show I mentioned earlier. Crickets. Not sure when they'll start filming. I think your assessment's a tad biased."

I reach under her shirt, dipping my fingers under her bra to cup her breast. "I'm absolutely biased. But it doesn't mean I'm wrong."

She swallows and takes a ragged breath as I tease her nipple. "Our soup will get cold."

"I have a magical item for that. A microwave." I kiss away any further protests.

June

I stretch a piece of packing tape across a box, hip-deep in more boxes in my parents' basement. "Why do I have so much stuff? I don't need all this. I don't know how to say no when people try to give me things."

Lyssa carries a bag of light pillows, Eleanor strapped to her chest in a front-facing baby carrier. "You can always give it away."

"But then I'd have to go through it."

"If you don't know what's even in the boxes, do you really need it?"

"I don't know. Maybe. Nova says they keep minimal stuff so they don't have to clean as often. I'm trying to take up as little space as possible while I'm staying with them, but I already feel bad for making their place cluttered."

Lyssa puts the bag in the pile by the door. "I doubt she minds."

"Yeah, and that's confusing!" I walk across the room to look inside a few boxes I haven't taped yet. Most of this stuff is going straight to storage.

Lyssa follows me, and Eleanor makes a coo. "Weren't you just angsting the other day about whether or not you could get with her?"

"Fair burn, Lys. And yes. Every moment I spend with her is wonderful, but I'm even more confused. I mean, not about if I'm bi or not. I figured that out. I'm like, super mega gay."

Lyssa laughs. "I already knew."

I'm glad I can amuse others with my cluelessness.

This box has some old kitchen stuff from my apartment with Parker. Definitely not going to need it at Nova's. I pull the roll of tape from my pocket. "I'm confused because, on one hand, she's asking me to move in with her. Kinda. At least stay with her. And the other, she's telling me we're just friends!"

"Sounds like you guys do a lot of things I wouldn't with someone I was"—Lyssa makes air quotes—"'just friends' with."

"But, like, isn't friends with benefits a thing? Is that what she wants from me?" It doesn't feel like that's the correct label for our relationship.

"Nova feels things really deep. I don't think she's trying to hurt you. If anything, I think she's trying to take the pressure off you."

"Well, her taking the pressure off sure is stressful!" I carry the box of kitchen stuff and set it by the door with the rest of the things I don't need right now. My phone rings from my other pocket. Great. Probably the podcast dude again complaining about my terrible video. I answer without looking.

"Hello."

"Hey! This June? It's Cristy. Nova's friend."

I swallow. Nova is at her apartment working. After she took all day yesterday to help me move and…do other things, I insisted she not skip additional writing days to help me pack; that way, we could have the evenings off to do fun stuff.

"Ah, hey there."

"Who is it?" Lyssa mouths, peaking around a stack of boxes.

I hit mute on the call. "Nova's gorgeous ex."

Lyssa pulls in air through her teeth.

"Got a few minutes to chat?" Christy asks. "I'm on break from work, and I had an idea for you. Hope it's okay I got your number from Nova."

I unmute the phone. "Yeah, of course!"

"So, first, I'm gonna be nosy. I tried to ask Nova, but they were like a locked chest you can't access without end-game abilities. Are you two together?"

"Ah… I mean, not right now. They're at work, and I'm packing more of my stuff from my parents' basement. We're special friends! That's how my followers put it, at least."

Lyssa covers her mouth, trying to silence her laughter.

"Wait, packing? Are you moving in with Nova? Ah-ha, that's why she was so cagey! Damn. Might be the quickest I've ever heard. That on-camera kiss was y'all's first, right?"

"I didn't say that! It's not like we're in a relationship and living together. My parents are selling their house and got an offer quicker than they thought, and I was living in their basement, and I'm still looking for a place of my own, but it's damn expensive and hard to come up with that much money so quick." I'm rambling. I take a breath, trying to steady my words. "Nova said, and I quote, 'Think of it like a sleepover.' They don't want to date me, you know, 'cause they're moving to Iowa so soon. So, we're friends. Officially. They're so amazing to help me out. Please don't embarrass them over it."

Cristy laughs. "I'm skipping Nova and calling you directly next time I need information. Girl. If Nova's the high-level chest, you're the one at the beginning of the game that the character spawns right next to."

I'm really terrible at keeping secrets. How long is it going to take Nova to get annoyed with that? They have such a great poker face. I have endless tells. Maybe the next character I cosplay should have a literal mask on. And be mute.

But before I can think of any type of rebuttal, Cristy continues. "It's okay. It's a relief, actually. I saw the video you posted after the session. Another reason I called was to make sure that you weren't secretly trying to hurt Nova or use them for views or something. You know, after that book review video a few months ago. But they're correct on your alignment, from what I can tell. Chaotic good."

Ugh. Chaotic foolish, maybe. I'm blushing so hard I'm sweating.

Wait, why would the book review have anything to do with Nova? "What else did you want to ask about?" I need to get back to packing and off the phone before I make a bigger fool of myself.

"Oh! I know you're somewhat of a celebrity and probably get people asking you this all the time, but I thought since I'm local, it might be okay. Can I join your D&D table? I know the game rules, and I have a great idea for a character who can help you keep Parker from being so annoying."

"Um." I'm not sure what I expected her to say on this call, but it wasn't this. "I'll have to talk to the group."

"Yeah, of course! I played Last Imagination with him, you know, the last two Sundays."

I didn't know Parker went back to the bar without me. Interesting. And a relief—I don't want to be the center of his social life anymore.

"Cool! I'm glad he went back." I wander around boxes to the window and lean my forehead against it.

"Yeah, he seems decent. In some ways. But he's such an ass at your table. You need backup. And despite that squeeze orc toy you feature in several of your channel's videos, your party is orc-free."

Oh, geez. She's seen a lot of my videos.

Both of our big exes playing in the same D&D group? Am I asking for trouble by even considering this? But Parker's been irritating. At the very least, Cristy coming might put him on better behavior.

"However," she continues, "I can't guarantee Jerald's safety if he acts like he did on Saturday."

I laugh. "Yeah, I can't either. I'll ask our group and make sure Aiden can adjust the encounters, but it sounds good to me."

"Cool. Save my number, and we'll talk soon."

We say goodbye, and I end the call. I take a deep breath and let it out.

Did I just make a decision that'll affect Nova without talking to her about it? She said she didn't want me to have to consider her opinions before making decisions, but at the same time, no matter what we label our relationship status, when I make a call like this, it'll affect her too.

19
NOVA

The soft brush of June's toes on my knee makes me look at her again. I'm trying to be good while these cameras are on, but she's making it so damn difficult. She's sitting across the table from me tonight since I suggested we put some physical space between us, trying to be less...obvious. Can her internet viewers tell I'm imagining taking off her cape and corset again? I helped her weave flowers into her one-sided braid before we came here, and seeing them brings back the memory of her smell, kissing her neck... No, I'm going to keep my mind on the game. Our party is debating on whether to activate a scroll to return to the Orc Market after clearing out a section of the dungeon.

"Aren't we wanted for something important at that market...y'know, murder? Thanks a lot, Jerald," Lyssa, as Solla, mutters under her breath. Rose whines and puts her fluffy head in Lyssa's lap.

Parker scoffs. "I was protecting our party. You're welcome."

Cristy came tonight, and she's sitting in between June and Parker. Drew is at my right side, stacking a dice tower.

June shakes her head. "Our party is hurting. I know, nothing new. We have to risk it. It's the only portal we have. Unless you have a better spell to refresh our supplies, Solla."

Lyssa sighs. "No. We're down to our last rations. And I could use the chance to resupply spell components. I can't be caught without a Fireball."

Drew starts in his nasally Nam voice. "That's because you pretty much cast it on reflex. You see, one of my favorite things about Procan—"

"The Storm Lord," June and I deadpan at the same time as Lyssa. June grins at me, catching my eye at the inside joke. Maybe it can't hurt to tease her a little too. It's not like our characters are at the center of the conversation right now. I slide a foot out of one of my boots.

"—god of the wind and sea, is that he's an easy patron to work for. All I need is saltwater to power my spells. I can get that from the massive amount of sweat Hunt gives off every morning during prayers. Solla, perhaps you should consider joining the church of Procan."

I drag my sock-covered toes lightly up June's calf. She lifts a brow at me.

"Pass," Lyssa says.

I love tickling June's legs. God, when we were in high school, we sometimes got into epic tickle wars. I thought my interest was one-sided. And now I get to have her in my bed. I push my foot closer into her lap.

"Hunt, what's your specialization anyway?" Drew continues as Nam. "You're a holy person, but I never see your symbol or hear you evoke the name of who you're devoted to. Might I offer a shift in allegiance to Procan?"

Oh, shit. I pull my foot back and sit up, trying to get into character. What would Hunt say to that? It's complicated for them—this world is a land where gods sometimes walk on the ground, but none are worthy of trust. "Devotion is a strong word. I serve Oghma, god of knowledge, as a hand of vengeance. My desire for justice is what powers my smites. No components needed."

"Justice for what?" June blinks at me from across the table. Fake innocence.

I narrow my eyes. At this point, she has to have a clue as to what. I take a breath. "The life of a scholar, taken early. Someone robbed the world of living knowledge."

"Someone…hm," she says. "I pull out my lute and start strumming a song to ease painful memories. Bardic Inspiration in case I need to persuade Hunt to tell me more."

That would be better used on the guards when we inevitably run into trouble at the market. I glare at her harder as she pantomimes playing a lute. Her real one is in storage with most of her things. I swear, the way she's moving her fingers is suggestive.

"Solla, my vote is to activate that scroll and take us back to the market. With any luck, we'll find beds to get proper rest."

"Awe, you can share with me. I'll protect you all night long." Parker tries to lean around Cristy to look at June, but Cristy manages to block him while at the same time looking like she's just stretching. That's my wing-woman.

June doesn't seem like she even notices Parker. She scoots closer to the table, and I feel her toes on my knee again, trying to reach further like how I did to her. Heh, her short legs.

"*Just wait,*" Cristy whispers to me and puts a fist in her

other hand like she's ready to punch something. Aiden knows what she's planning, but none of the rest of us do.

"No, thanks, Jerald," June answers in a cheery voice, still miming playing the lute, grinning, and poking my knee with her toes. "Hunt, are you part elf? Your ears are so long and perky. I wonder because elves need less sleep per night than many other denizens of this land. And I find myself sometimes bored in the middle of the night."

"My lady, I don't know what you mean." *Stop looking at her fingers.* I cough. Goddammit, we're going to be so obvious to every single person watching the stream. "Solla, the scroll?" My voice cracks.

"Sure."

Aiden draws a circle in the air with a finger. "A portal appears in front of your group, and you see the familiar outline of the Orc Market."

"Awe puts her lute away and snakes her hand through Hunt's elbow. Shall we?"

I grab her foot under the table and tickle the arch. She yanks it back.

Our party moves through the portal and into the market, and Aiden gives the rundown of the scene. The same market we visited before, though suspiciously bereft of shoppers. As soon as Jerald steps through the portal, twenty orcs emerge from behind carts and walls, axes, swords, and staves raised. Great.

Aiden's trying to hide a smirk—that annoying DM kind, where we can guess that things are about to go upside down in a hurry.

Lyssa and June groan. They're down to almost no spell slots as our party hasn't gotten proper rest in a while. This'll be tough.

"The largest orc steps forward. Cristy, you can describe your character." Aiden gestures to Cristy.

Cristy slams a mini figure at the center of the table. "The big lady orc is over seven feet tall, green skin, with long black hair and bulging muscles. Despite her girth, she wears fine, brilliantly dyed clothing that appears custom-made. She adjusts her monocle and stares down at the dirty, white-haired man. 'Jerald of Rivera, your reckoning is at hand.'"

I snort a small laugh. Christy used the most ridiculous attempt at a British accent.

She points at me. "Is something funny, tin can?"

I shrug. "It's mithril, but no, ma'am."

"That's right." Cristy taps her chest. "Show some respect. This man's reputation as a murderous, honor-less miscreant has spread through the land, and it's time for that to end. You may choose one of two outcomes. Either you will repent of your ways, or I will become angry. And you won't like me when I'm angry." Cristy crosses her arms.

The Hulk reference. She must be playing a barbarian.

Parker picks up a d20. "Jerald pulls his sword."

"Croga removes her jacket and monocle, then rolls up her sleeves and cracks her knuckles. Her demeanor changes immediately—into fury. This means I'd like to rage."

I catch June's eye. Whatever's going on, this is going to be hilarious.

"Roll initiative, Jerald," Aiden says. "Anyone else joining in this battle?"

I hold my hands up. "No. And I signal the rest of the group to take a step back."

"Yeah, we all listen to the paladin," Lyssa adds.

"Heh, cowards." Parker rolls his d20.

Aiden picks up his pencil. "Initiative total, Jerald?"

"Fourteen."

Aiden scribbles something down. "Croga?"

Cristy flexes. "Twenty-two. Unarmored, baby. Makes me faster. I heard a rumor of some dirty, white-haired man bragging about his armor. Let's see how it turns out for him."

Aiden points his pencil at Cristy. "You're first, Croga. What would you like to do?"

"Croga yells as she charges and grapples him, attempting to force him to the ground."

"Okay. Athletics checks," Aiden says.

"Feh, strength's my best stat." Parker rolls his d20 again.

June was brilliant to invite Cristy. Cristy loves messing with insecure men. I always admired that about her.

"Croga, you get an additional advantage roll on any strength checks since you're using barbarian rage. So that's two rolls for you. Take the best. One for Jerald."

Cristy's two d20s clatter to the table. "Look at that. Nat twenty. And I'm adding five from my strength score. What about the little man?" She leans in to look at Parker's dice.

"Um. Eleven."

"Perfect. I sit on his head. I'm going to keep pinning him until he relents."

"Sit on my head? Wait, guys!" he protests. "I'm not into this!"

Cristy glares at him. "Through Croga's terrifying yells of rage, you make out her saying, 'You killed innocent orcs at the Orc Market unprovoked! You'll repent of these egregious actions against the realm and use your money to fund every person's resurrection, or I'll start slinging you against the ground like the puny man you are!'"

Another Hulk reference.

"Oh my God," June mouths to me, poking me under the table with her toes again. She looks like she could bust out laughing.

Parker's had this coming for a while. And this could be a great distraction away from Awe and Hunt.

I raise my hand. "I'd like to ask Croga a question. My lady, are the rest of us free to go to the market?"

"Yeah, I need to restock my scrolls and components." Lyssa takes a sip of her water. That could take some time. Perfect.

"Croga doesn't seem to notice the rest of you anymore and is solely focused on pinning and embarrassing the shit out of the little man. You know," she grins at Parker, "despite the fact Croga is a diplomat with impeccable fashion taste, her nickname is 'the Crusher.' Wanna see firsthand all the things she's good at crushing? Or are you ready to give up now?"

"Wait, this isn't over! I don't concede!" Parker protests.

Aiden sighs. "We'll finish the fight with Jerald and Croga, then do the component and scroll shopping, okay?"

Lyssa always takes forever to finish haggling with Aiden's NPCs, and Drew likes to take a look in every corner of the market, looking for side chests like he's in a video game. June and I have some time...if we can sneak off successfully.

I slide my boot back on, then stand and walk off camera. June's eyes are following me the whole time. I love that I have her attention.

I beckon her with my hand.

"Excuse me." She stands and practically runs out of the range of the cameras, still barefoot, skipping up to stand by me. God, so cute.

"Parker, what's Jerald's next turn?" Aiden asks.

Good. They can play this part without us. I don't even have a plan here—I just want June alone. "I think I have a problem, Lady Danamark," I whisper to her.

"Hm. Might I be able to assist you?"

"Perhaps."

She takes my elbow like we're walking through a real market, and we walk through the kitchen to the front door. I pull her outside, shutting the door behind us. The night air is warm—May already. I don't want it to be summer yet. Summer means we're headed to August, which means going to Iowa. And I just want to live in June. The person.

She giggles as I pin her to the outside wall, reaching under her cloak to run my hands down her body. "Why Hunt, you just can't help yourself? Taking advantage of a lady in view of the market rather than dragging her back to your room?"

"Mm." I reach down, trying to find the bottom of her skirt so I can touch her under it, but there's way too much fabric.

She's faster than me and slips her hand into the front of my jeans. "Might we go to your carriage, good paladin, before someone comes to check on us and we give them an eyeful?"

I groan as her fingers brush me, grinding my hips into her hand. "What is wrong with me? I've never been one for PDA."

"I've invaded your brain. And your pants."

"Ugh." She has. It's like every thought is June. I've never wanted to be touched this bad. And to touch her.

"I'm really good at being in your pants." She rubs her hand against me, and I'm losing my mind. I need her. The backseat of my car will have to do.

I pull her hand out of my jeans and yank her up the hill

toward my car. "You are the most ridiculous bard I've ever met. And that's saying a lot."

She laughs as we run over the grass through the cool night air. It feels like freedom.

I've never shown myself to a person like this before. Never felt this deeply about another. Not with my family, not even with Cristy.

It's like all the love I had for June when we were kids just grew and grew inside me until we were able to be together. She's worth it—all those frustrated one-sided feelings I had for so many years. The car's unlocked, so I open the backseat door of my sedan and shove June, her ridiculous cloak, horns, dress, and all, inside. I get in and close the door behind me.

I climb on her and cover her with kisses. Her lips, her face, her neck, moving down while I push her cloak away. God, she's so gorgeous.

She laughs and shoves my shoulders back. "Hunt. Nova. Me first this time."

"Like I would ever *not* take care of you first!" I want her to feel how much I want her. How much I love her.

Fuck. I love her. I *love* her. Maybe I never stopped acting socially inappropriately with her—it's only been a week since we kissed. Since we first made love. Since I asked her to stay with me as long as she could before I have to leave. We haven't been together enough time for me to be feeling these sorts of things—and we both agreed on friendship only. But it's inevitable as the sun rising: June is my favorite person in the world, and I love her.

"No, I mean I want to take care of you first." She tilts her chin up and kisses me.

I can't tell her. I'd be pushing her too hard, and not fair

to her to put that pressure on her. She hasn't even realized her own sexuality for more than a few weeks.

Her hands fumble on my jeans, trying to unbutton them, but there's too much fabric in the way between her costume and my cloak in the tight backseat of the car. I unlatch my cloak, release it behind me, then let her flip me over.

June

Nova laughs as she reclines across the backseat of her car.

I love the sound of her laugh, seeing her open up. "What's so funny, my good paladin?" I feign seriousness as I sit on her legs and unbutton her jeans.

"I've never had sex in a car."

"A carriage," I correct, pointing to my tiefling horns.

"Yes, my lady. I've never had sex in a carriage."

"I'm happy to assist in your corruption." I grin as I yank her jeans and underwear down. What do I want to do to her first? It's only been a week since our first time, but damn, I've never felt so confident in bed. Or in the car, I guess.

She grabs at me, pulling me close, kissing my neck. She's really into grabbing me and kissing me there, and every time she does it, it sends shivers all the way down my body. Her hands reach to cup my ass, urging me up. "Sit on my mouth, and I'll worship you like the demon-goddess you are."

Instead, I sit back again. "You have no loyalty to Oghma, then?" I tease.

"The only heaven I'm interested in is this. Take me to church."

I cackle at her song reference. "I'm going to take you, all right." I reach between her legs as I lean over her—so warm and wet for me. "Wow, Hunt. What thoughts have been going through your head while navigating a scary dungeon?"

She gasps as I stroke her. "Really perverted ones. You should feel lucky I have the self-control—" Her words cut off, squeaking an octave higher as I press my thumb in exactly the right place and rub.

I know how to touch her now. And every time we're together, it's better and better.

"As a bard, my fingers are very talented," I murmur in their ear, kissing along its helix at the same time I rub their clit. It makes them shiver and gasp.

I've been collecting Nova's buttons over the past week. There are a lot of them.

"June...you're so good. It feels so good."

Her appreciation—every single time—makes my heart leap. She sets no expectations on me when we make love, like there were in both my previous relationships.

I lean my shoulder into hers to balance myself as I try to put my other hand down there...and almost fall off the seat.

She catches me, rolling me back over her, but I have to use my left hand to steady myself. One-handed, it is.

"Do you know how sexy you are, running your toes up my leg under the table? It tickles, and then I look across to see you with that ridiculously sharp jaw and intense eyes on me and my God, I just wanted to drag you away." I kiss her to punctuate what I'm saying, increasing pressure and intensity with my hand now that she's a bit warmed up.

She moans into my mouth—I can tell she's almost there.

"That's right. Come for me." I let my lips brush against hers as I command her. "God, you're so hot in the backseat under me. I'm never going to be able to ride in this car without thinking of you like this."

And she's undone, her body pulsing under my hand. I look at her face. Stunning. Mine. Nova's so closed off to most of the world, but I get to see her like this—without inhibitions or shame. It's the most beautiful thing I've ever seen.

After a moment, she catches her breath and grabs my ass again. "Awe. Get up here. Now. Let me taste you."

I hold onto the oh-shit handle above the left side of the car so I don't lose balance again as she pulls my hips up to her face and shoves my skirts back.

"Ugh, June...you're not wearing any underwear. Why do you do this to me?"

I love doing everything to her. I wiggle my hips. "Can't blame me for being hopeful." I let go of the handle with one hand, run it through her hair, and knock her costume horns off her forehead. I'm going to have to fix everything we're wearing after this anyway.

She inhales through her nose. "You smell so good."

I love that she likes my smell, whatever soap I use or don't use. Freaking Parker used to complain on the days I forgot deodorant or sweated at all. "You know, Parker is inside that house right now and has no idea what you're doing to me. Heh, both our exes are. Cristy, too."

"Cristy probably has an idea." Nova uses her fingers to part me and dips her tongue in to lick my clit.

Oh, so good... I grind my hips into her face and hands.

"What, you guys used to sneak off like this, then?" I don't know if I'm more jealous or turned on.

"No." Her voice is muffled into me and under my skirt. I love it. "She knows I used to watch all your videos."

"Mmm. Did you now?" Sex is so different with Nova. I'm not on a timer to get off before my partner loses interest. I don't have to pretend to orgasm to appease her ego like I had to with Parker.

"Mm-hm," she hums into me, tongue flickering across my clit. The vibrations send flutters through my body. She removes her mouth, holding my hips back in her hands. "She used to tease me about having a crush on you. Still teases me about it. Eh, I guess I'm pretty into you." She dips two fingers inside me.

I gasp. "You guess?" The car windows are fogged up. It's a super quiet cul-de-sac, a dark night, and the rest of the neighbors went to sleep hours ago.

She rubs her thumb across where her tongue was, making me squirm in anticipation. She's teasing me, the jerk. "Okay, I might have a little more than a crush. I might be a tad obsessed."

"Nova—stop talking." I command. "Use your mouth for better things than teasing me."

"Yes, goddess." She pulls my hips forward, and I have to grab tighter on the handle. Her tongue is on my clit, her fingers stroking inside me. She finds a rhythm, and I meld to her touch and her mouth as the sensation builds in my core.

I shove my skirt back to look in her eyes. They're intense, anchored on me, and it's the hottest thing I've ever seen in my life, kneeling over her like this. "I'm going to come on your face," I manage to breathe out.

She moans into me, and it pushes me over the edge, the

intense waves of pleasure making me grip the handle for dear life.

She releases me gently with her mouth, sliding her fingers out at the same time. I'm floating, pleasure still zinging through my body. Nova sits up and catches me in her lap, and I realize how tight I'd gripped that handle. I bet my bicep on that arm will be sore tomorrow.

Nova holds me against her chest as she leans on the door, both of us still breathing hard.

I kiss her lips. "You taste like me."

She smiles into my mouth. "You were right at the bar when you said you taste good."

I run my hand through her messy hair. "We have to get dressed and sneak into the bathroom to wash and freshen up."

"Shit. If we leave, your viewers are going to know, aren't they?"

"I think that ship has sailed. Remember, they knew before we did." It might've taken me a while to figure this out, but damn. It feels like, for the first time in my life I finally know who I am and what I want.

20

JUNE

I hit the button to make Kirby fly into the air. This new couch smells bad, and the TV is on the floor of my parents' new place, but the game set-up works well enough.

"Check this out," I tell my nephew, Liam, and make my pink puffball character turn into an angry brick and crash down on Nova's character, sending her sword-wielding green-shirted knight flying.

She hits the jump button and manages to make Link recover. "You'll pay for that."

My parents aren't fully set up in their new place yet, but they wanted my brothers and me to see it.

Since my nephew was coming, I brought my Switch to play on the TV—and at least make the gathering somewhat bearable. And I brought Nova. Which automatically makes everything better.

"Harmon, come on and join us. I have an open controller, and this round's about over. Let me show Liam how I used to kick your a—uh, butt," I call to my younger brother, who's chatting with Mom and Dad in the kitchen. I keep Kirby away from Nova's sword as her character chases mine. Ha.

"Heh, gotta pass on that one, Junie," Harmon calls back.

The whole place echoes with its open floor plan, wood floors, and high ceilings. Harmon is a little less than two years younger than me and bought a house in this neighborhood a few months back.

I still can't figure out why both he and my parents wanted to buy a house crammed in with other homes in a neighborhood in the middle of the country with no trees around it. And it's a farther drive from my dad's store. But that's another subject I don't bother arguing about.

Sage, my older brother and Liam's dad, walks in, looking at his watch. He has a very respectable wardrobe and a beard and could pass for someone ten years older than me, not four. I have hair the same color as Kirby and look like an overgrown kid in a blue blouse covered with clouds with smiley faces.

"Okay, Liam. Your screentime is up for the day."

Nova glances at me, eyebrow raised. I shrug. We've played games with this kid for less than thirty minutes. Liam's only seven, but still. I used to love playing games with my brothers while we were growing up. It's like I missed the memo of when to become a serious adult. Or they missed the memo that it's still okay to have fun sometimes.

Liam groans but hands the controller to me.

I hit pause. "Hey, Sage. Wanna play Smash Bros?"

He smiles at me but shakes his head. "I'm sorry, I haven't had time to play video games in a while."

"Well, that's okay." I hold a controller out. "You don't have to be good to play this one."

But Sage doesn't take it and escorts Liam away, saying "No thanks."

Dammit. I'm always feeling rejected by my freaking family, even in little things like this.

"You don't have to be good at this game to win? This how you console yourself when I beat you?" Nova says.

I turn to them with fake offense, grateful for the teasing distraction. "How dare?"

They give me a sad smile. "My family's complicated, too. They love me, but I never feel like I fit in." Nova drops their voice low, glancing around, probably to see if anyone is nearby. They put an arm around me, squeeze me in a side hug, and drop a quick kiss on my forehead.

It's such a little gesture. But the absolute relief at someone understanding me...

She sits back and nudges me with her elbow. "Now, unpause it so I can knock your fluffy pink butt off the screen."

"Okay. That's it. I was going easy on you 'cause I didn't want to embarrass you in front of my nephew. But no more!"

We both focus on the game. I am, actually, very good at Smash Bros. I've played in online tournaments. I'm eight kills ahead of her when the timer ends.

Nova groans and leans back on the couch.

I put my hands in the air. "Bam! Take that. Kirby for the win."

"If we were alone, let me tell you what I'd do to your pink..." She whispers a string of absolutely not family-appropriate things she plans to do to me.

My laugh rings out louder than I mean to across the mostly empty home.

"Must be a good game," Harmon calls. I hear Mom's nervous chuckle.

I look down, self-conscious now. Why do I care so much what they think? I should just grab Nova by the shirt, kiss her in front of my family, and declare we're together. And if they don't like it, too bad.

But we're not really together. Despite how I feel about her, we agreed we weren't a real couple.

And then afterward, I'd probably have to deal with subtle jabs about being a bad influence on Liam or that people "nowadays" like to force their lifestyle on everyone else. I've heard them say similar things about others.

"Why do I care so much about pleasing them?" I ask in a small voice, looking down at the perfectly shiny wood floor in front of the couch. "Why do I care so much about pleasing *everyone*?"

Nova glances back at my family, gathered in the kitchen and chatting. I look, too. They can't see our hands with how we're sitting, so I take Nova's.

They give mine a little squeeze. "Because you care about everyone. But that doesn't mean you owe them."

I nod. "Exactly. It's a bad habit. I don't even know when I started. I can blame Parker all I want, but I'm the one who decided to put my life on hold in order to please him."

"Pft. I *do* blame Parker. He should've never encouraged you to do that."

"But the problem is with me, you know? I constantly try to please everyone around me. My family, my boyfriends, my friends, my viewers, now this podcast company... I'm thinking about it, and even my character is a bard. A support class who specializes in persuasion and charisma. Everything I do revolves around pleasing others."

"Hey, you take that back about Awe. She's got big main character energy."

"I wish."

She strokes the back of my hand with her thumb. "If you want to change classes, you can. You can do anything. Think about your channel. You're *good* at what you do. You've brought so many new players to D&D, and eventually, Wizards is going to see that and hire you for something big, like that reality show. Or you'll make your own company if that's what you want. Or you'll create an entirely different path I can't even see. But you're good at this. People love the real you."

I close my eyes and let her words sink into my brain, playing with them like dice. "My views are up, and I just got the biggest royalties deposit in my life. NPC backed the fuck off on complaining about content. But I still have a long way to go before I could ever make enough to, you know"— I gesture around—"buy a house."

"You don't have to compare yourself to the rest of your family or to anyone else."

I lay my head on their shoulder. I don't care if my parents see. "Let's get out of here. I made an appearance. Good enough."

Another squeeze of my hand. "Of course. I'll put the Switch and controllers in the car."

"And I'll go tell my folks we're heading out. Teamwork!" I stand and stretch.

When we arrived, we ate an awkward meal of salad and pizza—I know they wanted us to share some dessert Mom picked up from a gluten and dairy-free bakery near her work, but I don't want to hear any more subtle and not-so-subtle reasons why I'm a failure.

I walk around the couch, through the mostly empty

house, and into the kitchen, where my parents and brothers are standing around the large kitchen island. "I'm going to head back."

"Mom said you're staying with your friend." Sage gestures to where Nova is carrying the box of video game stuff, walking to the front door.

"Yep. Just for a few weeks. Nova is moving to Iowa to go to grad school in August. I've got an apartment lined up." Sort of. They wouldn't officially reserve it for me until I have the massive amount of down payment money in the bank, but they assured me there were plenty of units available.

And I'm still doing the people-pleasing thing. Why do I feel the need to justify everything?

"Bye, guys." I wave.

"Wait, June." Dad holds a hand up. "I didn't get a chance to tell you."

"Tell me what?"

Dad nods at both of my brothers. "Harmon did some checking for me, and we have a lead on a job for you."

Great. As if this wasn't awkward enough. "Really, there's no need—"

"Our church needs a new social media lead, and the pay is solid. I told them your degree was in marketing, and they want to interview you." Harmon sips his water.

I laugh before getting control of myself and covering my mouth. "I don't think they'll want me for that job. Have they seen my channel?"

"Don't dismiss the opportunity," Mom says. "Harmon says it pays almost as well as his job there and has benefits."

Ugh. Benefits are almost unheard of. But still... I don't want to do something like that. "I really appreciate it,

Harmon. However, I can say with certainty I'm not going to be the brand they're looking for."

Harmon shrugs. "No one cares about what you wear, if you play games, or what color your hair is. It's a cool church."

"I think if they even take a second glance at my channel, they absolutely will care."

"You'd be behind the scenes. I'm sure it won't be a problem."

Gah. What am I supposed to say? "Okay. Maybe? I'm pretty busy with my channel, and I have a few things lined up to try to make that apartment down payment. I'm selling merchandise at the ren fair next weekend."

"I think a job with benefits is worth looking into." Dad taps his fist on the granite countertop. "That's a lot more stable of a future than selling t-shirts."

I fake a smile. "Yeah, I'll look at it. Thanks. I gotta go."

I wave at them and hurry out the front door. Goddammit. I just did the people-pleasing thing again. I clench my fists as I speed walk to Nova's car, which is parked alongside the road.

I get in the passenger side, sighing as I lower myself inside. "I'm a fool."

Nova looks me up and down. "What happened?"

"I agreed to take some interview for a job at their church." I click my seatbelt into place.

"I'm guessing you don't want this job."

"Of course not. They were talking about benefits and responsibility, and I just—"

Nova leans over and kisses me on the mouth. "Shh. You're not a fool. Your family sucks." Their lips hover over mine as they try to soothe me.

God, this thing we're doing... It's so confusing. She

makes me feel so good—she believes in me. But she's leaving me. She won't even say we're dating.

I push her back. "What am I going to do? What if they're right?"

"About?"

"How much of a loser I am!"

Their eyes narrow. "They seriously called you a loser?" They clench their jaw. "I will go inside that house right now and tell them all off."

I put my palms over my eyes. "No, not directly. If they did, then it'd be a lot easier to not care what they say. I just feel like one every time I talk with them."

"You can always talk with them less."

"Then I'll have no one!"

"That's not true."

"It is because you're leaving me." And there it is.

We sit in silence for a moment.

Nova starts the car. "I... it's not like that. I didn't want to make you—" she swallows. "I mean. I don't want. I can't."

She's not making much sense. We drive down the back roads. Mom and Dad moved here, away from their work, to get closer to my brothers, but I can't see them ever moving closer to me. No matter where I live.

But my family is all I have. I failed in my relationship with Parker, which I invested over seven years into.

I lean on my elbow against the car window ledge. How can I not feel like a loser? Nova obviously doesn't feel the same as I do—and it's probably pity that drives her to try to help me.

I'm not being fair to her, telling her she's leaving me. We agreed to friendship. But just once, I'd like to be someone's first choice.

Nova

I pull into a parking space at the grocery store and turn off the car. I glance at June, who's still looking out the window of the car. Her shitty family. I want to slap them all. I hate condescending people, especially because I'm not going to be able to convince June that they're the ones in the wrong.

How can I write entire books and still have not have the right words to help my partner? A few days ago, my publisher offered me a contract on the sequel, so I must have some skill with words, but why are characters much easier to help than real people I love?

"What are we doing here?" she asks.

I'm not actually sure. "Um, food." A useless answer. It's been less than two hours since we ate.

She sighs. "Okay."

I remember this look in her eyes. Back when she was a teen, she tried so hard, so fucking hard, to do everything right in her parents' eyes. Her grades. Her positive attitude. Her perfect daughter image—conservative dresses and long light-brown hair. And inevitably, when it wasn't enough, she'd shut down like this.

Why is it so hard to break out of old roles, even as full-grown adults?

We get out of the car and walk into the store. It's pretty busy, people getting off work and picking up groceries, some pushing those big green carts to hold young children. I snag a basket and head for the freezer aisle, June trailing behind me, rubbing her arms in the air-conditioning.

I know her favorites—cherry, strawberry, chocolate. Anything pink or red plus anything chocolate.

Back when we were in high school and I'd buy a pack of fruit-flavored candy, I used to split up the pieces and give her all my cherry and strawberry ones. She said she didn't like the lemon, lime, and orange, and therefore, there wasn't a point in her buying the candy.

I never told her, but the pink and red ones were my favorites, too. Even sweeter than eating them was making her smile.

I open the freezer and pick out a few pints: chocolate-covered cherry, double chocolate brownie, and strawberry, dropping them in my basket.

"Any other flavors you like recently? This evening definitely calls for ice cream." I gesture to the freezer.

Out of nowhere, she hugs me tight, right here in the freezer aisle. "I'm sorry. I shouldn't have said that about you leaving me. That wasn't fair. I know we agreed. My family... Ugh."

I relax into her embrace, setting the basket down and wrapping both arms around her. "It's okay. Really."

I wish I could transfer my thoughts to her brain. There's so much I want to say, and I have no idea how to start.

The thought of moving away from her makes me want to cry. All I can do is shove it back and pretend it's not happening. Then she says something like she did in the car, and I just can't. How am I going to be able to do it? But it's also not fair of me to ask her to date me long distance after this short of a time. And I can't ask her to come with me, right? That'd be like something Parker would do. Make her move to the middle of nowhere to chase my dreams.

Situations like this prove I'm not a good partner. Being with June is amazing, but long term, she's going to want someone warm, with all the right words, who can comfort her and open up.

I swallow back the lump in my throat as we break. "Someone needs to tell your brothers avoiding fun isn't a personality trait."

She chuckles. "Right?"

I loop my arm through hers, picking up the basket and pulling her toward check out. "Come on. Let's go home. Ice cream and a show. Something fun. Maybe with some Jedi knights."

I just said 'let's go home' like we're really living together. Like a real couple.

Damn, how I want that to be true.

To: n.h.davidauthor@gmail.com

From: Junethesparkling@gmail.com

Dear N.H.,

First of all, I want to say that I'm a big fan of your work. And I apologize for what I have to confess next. Once, months ago, I contributed to an online pile-on of *Curse of the Dragon's Gate* before I read your work. But now that I've finished the book, I have to say it's one of the best fantasy books I've ever read.

My friends and I are big fans, and my partner loves Hunt so much that she made a D&D character inspired by them.

I have a semi-popular online presence, particularly on YouTube (follower count enclosed at the end of this email), and I'd be beyond thrilled if you could find the time to do an interview with me, preferably over video. I think it could help rightfully clear your name and promote your story. More apologies, but some of my followers seem to think that my partner and you are one in the same because she's playing a character inspired by yours, and I'd just like to clear that up for both your sakes.

Your loyal fan,

June Bishop, AKA Awe Danamark the Sparkling

P.S. any information you could give me on the sequel, which I hear was unfairly canceled, would be wonderful. My partner has some amazing fanfiction ideas, and I want to know how close she got to guessing the next part of the story.

Reply:

Dear June,

As an avid follower of yours, I'm aware of your videos, both the negative and the positive. Nothing could've made my heart soar more than hearing what you thought of my book after you read it. For that honest and true love of my work alone, I could've gone through all the hate of the world ten times over.

You may be pleased to hear that *Curse of the Dragon's Gate*'s publisher has offered me a contract on the sequel, which will be releasing in May of next year, with the official announcement coming soon.

As far as a video interview, though I'm honored by the offer, I'm afraid doing a video for the internet breaks my personal oath against being observed by others. However, I'd be thrilled to donate a few signed copies of the book for your channel giveaways and any fundraising you'd like to do.

Sincerely,

Awe's biggest fan, N.H.

Reply:

Are you KIDDING ME?!? Omg, thank you so much!!

Both me and my followers are going to be over-the-moon to read the sequel!

You'd get along with my partner as they have the same personal code! I think their direct quote was "my gender is don't perceive me" lol. She's an author too, and I'm sure she'd fault me for using too many exclamation marks in this email, but I'm not going to delete them because this is the most amazing reply I've ever received!!!

I can't wait to read your sequel, and you can bet that I'll be promoting the hell out of it from now to release!

21
NOVA

Normally, being in a crowd like this would be completely overwhelming, but I make an exception for the Renaissance Fair. Hot weather and all. At least there's a breeze today, and we're in the shade. I nod at a man in pirate clothing browsing in June's tent.

The tent is set up in the artist's alley, and she's splitting it with another artist who sells D&D keychains. June has prints of Awe, which she drew and printed on cardstock. She's in her full Awe costume and is selling and signing the prints for five dollars. I donated about thirty signed copies of my book for her to sell, which I retrieved from storage, and June assumed I got out of the mail. I keep dropping hints, but eventually, I'm going to have to tell her and hope she's not too mad at me. Hopefully, between the books, prints, and the t-shirts—which turned out adorable—she can make enough for her apartment down payment.

Cristy and I stand behind June's table, playing the parts of her guards today—both of us in costume. I can't believe June was able to come up with costumes like this.

I'm wearing thin foam armor June spraypainted and

then hand painted to look like mithril. It's the most detailed costume I've ever worn. The armor wouldn't stop a real blade, but I feel like a real knight. I even have a sword.

Cristy's costume uses some green prosthetic muscles on her arms and legs that June got from a Hulk costume from Goodwill. She has orc teeth on her lower teeth, sticking out over her lips. June was able to get her what looks like what renaissance nobility would wear, even borrowing a real monocle. A kick-ass costume for basically no money and little time.

The man in pirate gear leans forward to say something to June. She laughs that big sparkling laugh, glancing at me.

I smile at her. She's in her element here. Her warmth is infectious to all the fair-goers who stop by—adults and children. And she's so dang cute in that costume with the horns. We have a speaker set up with a playlist of lute music going and a fan that sprays a cooling mist. June hung a sign underneath that says 'Curing Mist.'

"Hunt, come here for a sec." She hooks a finger in my direction, and I step next to her. "Look right here."

I start to lean over the table to look at the print she's pointing at, but as I do, she grabs the back of my head and kisses me. Our costume demon horns knock together. Mm, June. I can taste the dragonfruit mead on her lips.

I hear the shutter sound of the man's phone camera. We break, and I raise an eyebrow at her. Before the fair, we spoke about how any photos of us could—and probably will—end up online. I told her I was comfortable appearing with her as a couple and the rest would be up to her. She's smart and so good at running her channel. She doesn't need me being overprotective about online bigots.

June shrugs, grinning while still looking into my eyes.

The guy in the pirate costume chuckles. "Thank you. Oh

man, my partner is going to be so excited. We love your stream."

"Have you read this book I'm obsessed with?" June turns and picks up a hardback copy of my book, waving it.

"Oh! *Curse of the Dragon's Gate.*" He takes it from her as she passes it to him. "I keep meaning to. This is the one with Hunt, yeah?"

"Mm-hm. Did you know there's gonna be a sequel? I need y'all's help figuring out what this mysterious author is going to do next." She grins at me.

Mysterious. Ha. Yeah, I'd like to know what happens at the end, too. The vengeance-filled sequel I drafted seems to not fit anymore—at least not all the details. I've been editing it like crazy to meet the upcoming deadline.

June chats with the guy for a few minutes. Looks like he's buying a book, a print, and two t-shirts. I can't keep my eyes off her. She's incredible at this. Charisma score off the charts. How could she doubt herself?

Cristy nudges me with her elbow. "Wow, Nova, I really have to say, you have some talent."

I glare at her. I've practiced, gotten better at detecting tone, and she's being mega sarcastic. "What?"

"I mean..." Cristy looks me up and down. "You done fucked up."

I scoff. "I didn't do anything wrong by letting June kiss me for a fan's picture. That's her choice."

She blinks at me slowly. "Uh-huh. That's not what I'm talking about. Look at you. You're absolutely smitten."

"So?" Of course I am.

"So? What the hell are you doing? What's with all this 'we're just special friends' shit? Good grief. Take a page from what Croga would do—take charge and kidnap her. Take her with you to Iowa!"

June throws a peace sign and winks at the camera as another fan poses for a picture with her.

I imagine scooping her up and carrying her off. Hiding her in the little apartment I reserved in Iowa. "Of course, I want to! Believe me, there's nothing I want more. But I can't. Then I'd be like Parker."

"Not the same. Have you even asked her if she'd want to go?"

"No. Look, her coming with me isn't going to work out, and I don't want to waste the time June and I have left talking, or worse, arguing about it. That's why we're focusing on our friendship."

Cristy shakes her head. "Ugh. Your issues aren't my problem anymore, thank God, but damn, I don't think I've ever met a person more talented at dodging confrontations. You're literally avoiding conflict in two different worlds. Both the real one and in our game. You're not letting Awe and Hunt work things out, either."

In the last three sessions, I managed to swerve June and my role-playing to focus on Yhallister's mega dungeon and traps, even though June keeps trying to bring up Hunt's oath.

I lower my voice to be extra sure June can't hear. "You should know why. Hunt swore an Oath of Vengeance, but I can't kill Awe now! And I don't even want to tell June about it."

"Have you told her about your pen name yet? I thought surely she knew, but either y'all are role-playing something and she's good at pretending, or she actually has no idea."

"I... No. I emailed her from my pen name, but there hasn't been a good time to tell her. I don't want to make things weird."

Cristy crosses her green, fake-muscled arms. "How's that working out for you?"

I give her a strained smile. "It's fine. We're good."

June stands and stretches. "I need another of those meads. You guys want one? I made a trade with the mead guys for a print and a t-shirt, and they gave me like ten of them. Usually, I can barely afford one."

Cristy holds out a hand. "Croga never turns down mead."

"Here ya go." June passes Cristy a tall can from the cooler, then opens one for herself.

They're like ten dollars each, but probably double the volume of a normal can. "How many of those have you had?" I ask.

"Psh, not that many." June waves me off, taking a long sip of her mead. "Look at this! I think we only have twenty shirts left. Can ya believe it?"

"If you've had more than one of those, and I know you haven't had a meal today, then you've had too many. You're tiny."

June pokes me on the chest plate. "Ha! What are you, the fun police?"

"They *are* a paladin," Cristy comments in a dry voice.

"Paladins are fun!" I hold up a hand. "Okay. Maybe some of those old lawful good paladins were stuffy and zero fun. But new rules say we can be any alignment. I'm a true neutral vengeance paladin with an oath to maintain."

"Oh, and what is that oath exactly?" June slings an arm around my shoulders.

Cristy cackles, opening her can.

Shit. "I'd...need at least three more meads to discuss that," I counter, leaning my face close to June's.

"Well, luckily, I have pleeenty!" June shoves the one

she's holding into my hand and almost falls over as she goes to reach for the cooler again.

I steady her. "Okay, well, call me the fun police if you want, but you're going to eat a turkey leg, a funnel cake, or something else hearty right now. No falling out mid-fair. Cristy, can you run the booth for a bit?"

"Croga is on it." Cristy salutes, sliding into the chair June was in earlier. "Hunt. Remember. WWCD—What would Croga do?" She points at me. "Your new motto."

Take a page from what Croga would do and kidnap her. Take her with you to Iowa.

I put an arm around June and lead her out of the tent, walking in the direction of the concession area, open mead still in my other hand.

"So. What would Croga do?" June grins up at me in the sunshine.

I stop walking and kiss her deeply on the lips, ignoring the crowds ambling around us. "This. And probably lots of activities not safe for the public."

June laughs and lets me lead her to the food. Of course, every place with turkey legs and funnel cakes has a line a mile long.

I sigh. "Ugh. Come on. Let's go to my favorite—the only stand that sells vegetarian stuff."

We walk through the fair, holding hands, and the simple joy of it has me floating. No one here takes a second glance at us.

We wait through the line to get mediocre veggie wraps while June chats excitedly about the different fans of her channel she met today and how she's doing better than she thought when selling her items. I order us two wraps, chocolate-covered strawberries, and water, and when they give it to me, I carry it all to a small table under an umbrella. The eating area is so crowded. There's only room for one of us to sit at the table.

"Nova. Sit down."

"Absolutely not. You get the seat."

She sighs and shoves me from behind until I do what she wants—sit down on the bench. Then she plops herself onto my lap.

Oh. This is a good idea. Between the lunch crowd and the minstrel music on a nearby stage, it's so loud that no one is really paying attention to us.

I watch June take a few bites of her wrap. She reaches for the mead, and I put the water bottle in her hand instead.

"Cristy thinks I should kidnap you. That's what she meant by 'what would Croga do?'"

A drip of water rolls down her chin as she brings the bottle back down. "What?"

"You know. When I move. Uh, and I would. Kidnap you, that is, if I thought you'd be happy. If I thought living in Iowa was what you wanted. I'd take you with me anywhere. But no matter how much I try to convince myself of that, I can't. You have your own life and your own areas where you're brilliant. If I kidnapped you, I'd deprive you and the whole world of them."

She tilts her head, blinking at me. "Wait. What?"

This is terrible timing. Goddammit, I'm so bad at this. I shield my eyes and look down. "I'm not making sense, and you're past tipsy. Off a moderate alcohol beer." I wrap my arms around her and give her a squeeze while leaning my face into her shoulder. "That shouldn't even be possible." She's so cute—and fits so perfectly in my lap like this.

She laughs and pinches her fingers together. "I'm not. Just a little tipsy."

"I love you, June." It rushes out of my mouth, unbidden. Bad timing—critical fail on my diplomacy roll. And I don't have the excuse of being tipsy on mead. We're sitting at a crowded table in the middle of the fair, sweating in our costumes. I should be telling her this somewhere romantic. The beach. Breakfast in bed. Roses in a bath. She deserves that from a partner. She deserves the world.

"Nova!" She hugs me around the neck so suddenly, I almost tumble backward off the bench. Lettuce and hummus fall in my hair from the veggie wrap she's still holding. I don't care. She presses her forehead to mine, our horns knocking together again. "I love you, too."

She kisses me, and I forget everything else.

22

JUNE

The fair is winding down in less than an hour, but tons of people still crowd the seating area in front of the jousting zone. "Come on, Hunt." I yank Nova's hand as we dodge around the fair attendees. "The actors need us backstage before the show begins."

Nova laughs, and I love the sound. "I can't believe I'm doing this. You know you're making me an oathbreaker again on my vow not to get in front of people. Oathbreaker on more than one level." She mutters the last sentence.

"Oh, what was that?" I turn, grinning up at her. My mead has mostly worn off, but I still feel tipsy from the joy today holds.

"Er, nothing, Lady Danamark." She rubs the back of her neck. Mmm, she looks so good in that armor standing in the afternoon sunshine. Like a real knight. Strong, handsome, and striking.

I'm going to have such a good time getting the truth out of her in-character in the coming sessions. But for now, Awe and Hunt are going to have a good time watching the joust—from the coveted royal box.

We walk up to the fence, and I send a text to Paul, my fair contact, that we're here waiting. I think I was twelve the first time I convinced my parents to take me to this Renaissance Fair, and I was hooked. It was magical, and I remember looking at the costumes, touching the crafts, and being in utter awe of the whole thing. I knew one day I'd go in costume, but I had no idea that I could do something like this, something that'd get me VIP seats.

I had no idea I could build an online community that enjoys me being me and that they'd show up like this.

I blew my money goal out of the water. The t-shirts sold out, as did most of the donated books, but the goods that surprised me the most were the signed art prints I made. I could've sold just those, and between that, the podcast money and my increased channel revenue from monetized views over the past four weeks made enough to cover the down payment.

The gate in the wooden fence swings open, and Paul waves at me. "Hey, June! And Nova, right? I've seen you on her show."

I've met Paul a few times in the process of signing up to be a vendor. I wanted to come last year and even went through the process of applying, but I backed out when Parker didn't want me to do it. Why did I ever listen to him?

Nova nods and squeezes my hand. I love this. Being out with her.

"Do we need to do anything special other than wave when the actors tell us to?" I ask. The other 'celebrity' guest they had for today ended up needing to leave before the last jousting show at five, and Paul was kind enough to work me—and Nova—in.

"Nope, that's it! The fair wins because you promote it on your channel, and hopefully, you get to have some fun too." We follow him around the wooden fence that surrounds the fairgrounds and up to the stairs that lead to the high stage above the jousting area.

I bounce from one foot to another, still holding Nova's hand as we follow him. "Yay, I'm excited! I've never been up there before."

A group of costumed fair cast members waves at us as we reach the top of the stairs. Two are dressed like a king and queen, and the rest are either knights or royal nobles. A dad and his child with a "birthday boy" shirt wait with them—the fair sells special tickets for that.

After a few minutes, the announcer starts calling the royal group out, followed by the family, then us.

"We have, from a tabletop far, far away, tiefling bard, Awe Danamark the Sparkling."

Paul urges me to walk out, and I stride confidently into the sunlight, giving an elaborate bow. The crowd cheers. I hear my character's name—this is incredible. It surprises me every time that there are actual, real-life people who know Awe. And willing to buy my merchandise.

"And her...special friend," some people in the crowd laugh as the announcer pauses, "Paladin of Oghma, Hunt Wygarthe."

Nova walks out after me and waves as the fair attendees clap, then when she reaches my side, she grips my hand firmly in hers again. Guilt has an even firmer grip on my heart—I know how she hates crowds. But when I offered to do this appearance on my own, she insisted on appearing together.

We take our seats on the bench under the fabric tent, which is styled to look like the royal box of an actual medieval joust.

I sit up, peering down into the round area where the

announcer is calling the "knights" out one at a time. "I can't believe this," I whisper to Nova, and my face hurts from smiling.

She rubs my hand. "It's pretty cool. I come to the fair every year, but I've never been up here. I usually don't bother to watch the joust."

"That's 'cause it's where all the crowds are." I kiss her cheek.

"Yeah." She's blushing and smiling. Ah, so cute.

I pull my definitely-not-time-period-appropriate phone out of my pocket and put it in selfie mode, leaning my head in with Nova's. I snap a few, including one where I'm kissing her cheek again. I love every picture. We look so happy.

"Can I post this?" I show her. "I'm done worrying about whether I can be public with you or not. The podcast company already backed off, but regardless, they'd be foolish to fire me. I ran the numbers, and I've increased traffic on all their podcasts way more than they've increased mine."

She kisses me on the lips—a quick brush. "You're brilliant at this. You post what you're comfortable with."

"I made enough money for the down payment. More, actually."

"That's amazing. I knew you could."

"I've been thinking, though. I don't think I'm going to go with the apartment complex I talked with."

"Yeah?" she asks, watching the first two jousters run at each other. It's a planned match—they're using real horses and jousting poles, but it's scripted.

"I actually need your opinion."

"Hm?" She's still watching the knights as they circle their horses around, getting their lances ready again.

I lean my chin on her shoulder. "What's the story on the best place to stay in Iowa City? Like, right near the university."

She turns, frowning. "Wait, what? No, earlier, I was saying you shouldn't go!"

I jerk back. That wasn't what I was expecting her to say. "You don't want me to come with you?" Maybe I misjudged what she was saying—maybe she needs space.

"God, no." She puts her hand over her face. "Shit. No, that's not what I meant." She takes my hands. "June, I want you to come with me. More than anything. These weeks we've been together… I've never been so happy."

I was tipsy on mead when I sat in her lap at lunch, but I heard every word she said. When she told me she loved me, I felt like I was flying. "Me too. I love you. Let me come with you."

She blinks quickly—is she going to cry? "I love you too. Yes. If that's what you want, yes. I just don't want to take you away from your family and friends, and Iowa probably sucks—"

"If we're together, I don't care where we live. I can run my channel anywhere, and we can figure out a way to keep the campaign going via Zoom and cameras. I can show Aiden how to set the cameras and mics up and even buy some decent equipment for him."

Nova nods, still blinking. "I can't believe this. I'm so happy."

"But you look like you're going to cry." I reach up to touch her face. Her ears are bright red, along with her cheeks.

She squeezes her eyes shut. "I'm trying not to cry in front of this whole crowd!"

I laugh. "Sorry, Hunt. Guess I'm going to ruin your tough paladin image."

Nova pulls me into a tight hug. I don't know if anyone from the stands can see us, sitting back on these benches, or if anyone is even paying attention over the joust.

"I don't care if it's early in our relationship, and I'm shit at what's socially appropriate or whatever, but don't get a different apartment. Live with me."

Now I'm crying, probably making my makeup run. "Yes."

We hold hands as we watch the joust and give our opinions when the announcer calls on us. They let the ultimate judgment of the winner fall to the birthday kid.

When the joust is over, we clean up our tent with Cristy, and it's twenty minutes after the fair closes to the public by the time we get back to Nova's car. I collapse into the passenger seat, exhausted but so fucking happy.

I pull off my boots while Nova sticks the table in the trunk. I should post some of the cute pictures I took on a few social media. Later, I'll do a longer video post about it and reply to anyone who tagged me.

Oh, I have a high-priority email—I set up a special notification for certain addresses.

Wait. It's the official response for the D&D reality show. Oh God. My heart jackhammers in my chest as I read it. I'm accepted. They want me to come to Seattle. Filming begins at the start of August.

Shit. They want me to come to Seattle!

Nova slides into the driver's seat in a t-shirt and shorts, no longer wearing her armor and horns. "Phew, hope you don't mind that I put the costume in the trunk. I'm sweating buckets."

I can't make my mouth say the words. I should tell her. This opportunity... I won't get another like it. If I do well on the show and people like me, it could catapult my channel into international attention. But doing the show would mean I couldn't come to Iowa. It's a six-month commitment in Seattle. And the very worst part, the part I knew signing up for it...

If I'm going to participate in the show, I have to appear single.

"June, you okay, love?" Nova tilts her head, regarding me.

Love.

I fake a big smile. "Yep." Oh, who am I kidding? I can't hide things like this—she's going to able to tell. I sigh. "No. Here." I hand her my phone, showing her the email.

She reads it, face blank. "Fuck."

23
NOVA

I let the hot water wash over my face and body, sobbing. I managed to keep it together until we got back to my place, but here in the shower, June can't see me get upset.

She has to take the job. It'd be foolish for her not to. I'm so proud of her. I have to support and encourage her.

But goddammit, the universe hates me. It's like the moment I let my guard down and feel true happiness, life has to snatch away what I love the most.

After a few minutes of letting myself utterly wallow, I take deep breaths, in and out to the count of four. Okay. I can do this. I turn off the shower, wipe my face, hair, and body with a towel, then wrap it around me.

"June, if you need to use the shower to wash off your makeup, I'm done—"

She's sitting crisscross on my bed, wearing one of my t-shirts, and looking intently at her laptop. Her sparkly makeup made tracks down her cheeks where her tears fell, but her face is dry now.

"What are you working on?"

"An email." Her lips are in a flat line.

I walk up and peek over her shoulder. "What's this?"

"I'm telling them no."

"What? You can't."

"Why not? I don't need to do their show. I'm doing fine. My channel's making money."

I shake my head. "You can't be serious. It's less than six months. You have to do this show—it's a miracle they're making one at all. You've been talking about it for weeks. Being on the show could mean endless opportunities, more jobs with Wizards, and make your audience explode."

"But what's the point of any of that if I can't be with the person I love?"

"It's six months or less. It's not forever. You think I can't wait six months?"

She fixes a typo in the email while she shakes her head. "A lot can change in six months."

I sit next to her on the bed and take her hand. "Not this. I've loved you since we were kids. Whatever happens, I'll love you all my life."

"Good. I love you, too. I intend to spend that life with you, which is why I'm saying no." She pulls her hand from mine and goes back to focusing on the screen.

"Don't be stubborn."

"Nova. You couldn't speak basically all the way home. You got here and were crying in the shower. I can't do it."

I was trying to hide those emotions. The last thing I want is for her to make a rash decision based on my feelings. Or for her to think I'm trying to manipulate her by feeling them. "I didn't... I mean, of course I'm upset. It's like the universe conspires to take away what I love the most. I should've expected this the moment a miracle happened, and you said you loved me too. It's easier for me to be alone."

She lifts her eyes to mine, and I feel like I've stabbed a puppy. I said too much.

She shakes her head. "That's not true."

"I shouldn't have said that. And it's not about how I feel."

"Yes, what you feel matters. You can talk to me."

I take a deep breath. "It's just how things go. Happiness is fleeting for me, and whenever I find it, the universe likes to take it away. I had some professional troubles when I started writing..." I swallow. I can't tell June about losing the book deal now—she'd feel too guilty, and it's not like that would help. "Or like in my relationship with Cristy... After a while, she couldn't stand dealing with my...issues." I sit back on the bed, leaning against the headboard, closing my eyes. "But the absolute worst was when I connected with this amazing girl in high school, she became my best friend in the whole world, and then a boy took her away and she disappeared."

"I'm so sorry."

I hate bringing up things she can't fix. "Please, you don't have to apologize. It's in the past, and I understand why it happened. I'm not mad at you or upset with you. I'm just upset in general. I'm not so selfish I'd ask you not to take that job. It's a dream opportunity. You have to do it."

"You're not asking not to take it—I'm telling you I'm not taking it. Now let me finish sending this email so we can plan where we're staying together in Iowa."

"You're not coming with me."

"You're retracting your offer?"

"No!" I stand, pacing across the room, clutching the towel so it doesn't fall off. "I'm just scared, okay? I hate admitting this. I hate having to be raw like this." My brain feels like it's buzzing, and my chest feels wound tight. I don't want to explode at her.

June's computer closes with a click. "Nova."

I walk to the bedroom doorway, leaning my forehead on the frame. How can I even describe this fear that grips my heart like a vice?

"You probably don't even remember." That's the worst part. She was my whole world, and she just forgot about me. "When we talked at your graduation, you said, *'you'll be in college with me in less than a year,'* and *'I bet we can go to the same college,'* and *'we'll always be friends,'* and at the end of that summer, you were gone. I sent you so many messages, and you'd either give a short answer or not at all. I tried to keep in touch on social media, and you didn't see or didn't reply. I tried to...call you. You know how I hate phone calls. Eventually, I gave up."

I hear her soft steps as she walks up behind me.

"I'm so sorry." She puts a hand on my shoulder. "I... actually remember seeing your number come up on my phone during a fight Parker and I were having. I said to myself I'd call you back the next day. Then the next. Then a week, and I felt bad trying to call you back at all. And before I knew it, it'd been a year. God. I really am an asshole."

I take her hand from my shoulder and kiss the back of it. "No—I didn't mean for you to feel bad. It was forever ago. And you're here with me now. I don't blame you for taking time to break out of the mindset in which your family and this whole fucking Bible Belt raised you. I don't blame you for needing time to figure out your sexuality."

It's not fair. I can't believe I have her right here. She loves me, she wants to live with me, and I'm still going to have to let her go.

"Like, real life isn't D&D. Sometimes there's not a reward, the universe isn't kind, and doing the right thing doesn't give you ten times the gold or experience points you would've got from doing the easy thing. But I still want to do the right thing—what lets the woman I love take the opportunity to do what she's brilliant at."

June's face looks resolute again. "I'm going to send that email. The right thing is us being together. Fuck that show and their requirement to be single." She turns and walks toward her computer.

"No!" I grab her from behind and tackle her onto the bed before she can open the computer. What's my plan here? I don't even know.

"What are you doing?"

"Keeping you from doing something you'll regret."

She wiggles under me. "This isn't fair, you know. You're crushing me with your large body! In a towel!"

"And it's falling off. I'm not letting you send that email. I know you've been wanting that show to choose you."

"It's different now!" She tries to push me off, but I have her pinned.

If she asks me to move, I will, but she's said how much she loves it when I do this. How it's comforting. "Forget about 'what would Croga do?'—I know what Hunt would do. They'd believe in the one they love. In Awe. And trust her."

"I don't want to pretend to be single just to be on a show." She says into the blanket, voice muffled.

"Come on." I kiss her neck. "It'll be a little fun to sneak around."

"No, it won't! You know I'm bad at it!"

"Exactly." I gather her hair in my hand and pull it back, kissing her on the nape of the neck. "No one will believe us.

All your viewers will eat it up. And the showrunners can't legally ask you to disclose your private life, only that you appear single."

She wiggles under me again. I let go of her hair and push my body up so she can turn over. Then I take her wrists and pin them next to her head, pressing my forehead to hers. Deep breath. We're here together now. Whatever the future holds, I have June pinned under me, and she loves me. It's enough.

"I'll...think about it," she says, voice strained.

"Don't just think about it. Join that show and win."

Sometimes doing the right thing really, really sucks.

June

I push the door to Dad's vitamin store open, and the bell chimes.

"Hey, Junie," Dad looks up from a book and waves at me from behind the counter at the vitamin shop. "What are you doing here in the middle of the day?"

Regaining my dignity. I put my sunglasses on my head and lift the takeout bag. "Brought you some salad from your favorite Greek place near Mom's work." I check the time on my phone—one-twenty-eight. Timed it about perfect for Dad's lunch break. I just finished talking to Mom and texting my brothers. It went...reasonably well.

"Well, I'm not going to argue with that. Sure beats the third day in a row of leftover chicken quinoa casserole." He grins, then walks to the door and flips the open sign to the "be back soon" side, locking the front door.

I follow him to the break room, hand him the bag, and sit down while he pulls it out. "I wanted to tell you and Mom thank you. You know, for letting me come home for a few months."

Dad smiles, a piece of his thinning salt-and-pepper hair falling over his forehead. "Of course. You know our door is always open to any of you kids."

I nod. "I really appreciate it."

Dad unwraps the set of plasticware the restaurant put in the bag with the salad. "So, how'd your sale go over the weekend? Oh, and did you have a chance to talk to Mitch over at the church? He was interested in doing that interview this week."

I give my most diplomatic smile. *Come on, charisma check.* "My sale went excellent. I also wanted to come tell you about some news regarding my business."

I've been practicing saying 'business,' not 'channel' or 'stream' or anything else that could give people a reason to look down on me.

"Well, lay it on me." Dad holds a hand out for me to continue.

"I got an offer to be on a web-based reality show in Seattle. It starts filming in August." It's been three days. I can almost talk about it without wanting to cry. I can't believe I'm going through with it.

"Huh. How about that?"

I swallow. "Yeah. It's an amazing opportunity, and afterwards, I'll be eligible to apply to several other jobs."

I can tell by the look on his face he has no idea what I'm talking about.

"It's like getting an opportunity to be on a D&D pro-sports team. They're serious—if your character dies in the show, you can't use them in anything else unless you can get someone to bring them back to life legally by the game rules. The winner of the show gets to be in the D&D movie sequel that'll start filming next year. Imagine if you saw me on the big screen."

He smiles, the skin around his eyes crinkling. "That's great, Junie."

I've got this. "So no, I won't be interviewing for the church job."

He looks like he's about to protest, so I hold a hand up.

"And also about that...I'm not a Christian. I don't want to go back to church. Don't suggest me for jobs like that again, please. Or any job. I know you're trying to help, but I'm fine. My success hasn't been traditional, but I'm finding it in my own way."

Dad pauses for a moment. "Yeah, I hear you." He laughs and opens the container of salad, dumping the Greek dressing over it. "Did you know your grandpa thought I was foolish trying to open this shop? Being a parent comes with a lot of worry. I told myself years ago I wasn't going to let fear run my life, but I probably let it influence how I talk to all my kids. Tell me more about this show."

Warmth spreads in my chest. I've been so nervous to stand up to my parents about anything at all, but they've both surprised me with their empathy.

I give him more of the details, at least all the stuff I know. How even though it's a great opportunity, it was still a hard choice to say yes. Moving to Seattle from August to December and possibly staying even longer if I do well enough to win.

Each word feels like a lead weight in my heart. But I can do this. Nova believes in me. I believe in me. It's only a few months.

"I did, actually, go check your channel out."

"Er, you did?" Shit. Mom didn't mention that. I wonder how much he watched and when he did. What's even on my channel recently? Making out with Nova at the Ren Fair...

Dad spears a piece of lettuce and points it at me. "Sleepovers with no guys involved?" He shakes his head. "Actually, don't tell me the details. Are you happy?"

I nod quickly. "Yes. Very." Tears well behind my eyes. I'm not sad, so why do I feel like I'll cry?

"Well, that's good enough for me."

This is going...surprisingly well. I breathe in the feeling, letting myself revel in the relief his acceptance is bringing me. Maybe none of the worst-case scenarios I've imagined about coming out to my folks will come true.

"So, is she moving with ya?" he asks.

I swallow back a sigh. "No. I told you before, she's starting a master's degree in Iowa. I...was going to move with her until I got accepted into the show."

"Well, you know, with computers these days, you can talk to people and it can feel like they're in the room with you."

"Yeah." And I'm glad Nova and I will get to talk and text, but it won't be the same. How am I going to spend months apart from her?

He pauses. "That probably sounded ridiculous to suggest it's the same."

I chuckle. "Well, yes."

"Oof, not going to let me off easy on that one?"

"Eat your salad, Dad."

He dips a tomato into the dressing. "I know a few months seems like a long time when you're twenty-something, but you'll blink, and you'll be fifty."

"Uh, thanks?" He likes to get on this subject about time

passing quickly. I'm not sure if it's supposed to be comforting or not.

"Nova seems nice, you've seemed happy recently, and you always had fun together when you were kids. I figure it's most important to spend your life with someone you like. I'm trying to say those months will go by, and you two will figure things out."

"Thanks, Dad."

It might seem easy to him to wait, but the thought of moving across the country from Nova has me wanting to pretend summer will last forever.

24
JUNE

Awe draws her sword and faces the person she cares about more than anyone else in the entire realm. She can't believe it's come to this. Winds swirl around her and Hunt as they stand on the platform, which hovers twenty feet in the air. Yhallister himself smirks from a portal—watching them. His cold eyes hold something akin to glee as he rubs his long, scraggly gray beard. The party can't reach him from here. All they can do is hope to get through his challenges so he'll grant them access to his sanctum. The party members who survive, that is.

"I knew it. Admit it. Admit you've been trying to get my guard down in order to kill me."

Hunt looks at the ground. "Why are you so determined for this to happen? Things have...changed between us since we met."

"Did you or did you not make an oath to kill me? You can't avoid this forever! And we can't cross this portal without clearing all old promises!"

So it's come to this.

Nova glares at me from across the table, and I rub my d20 between my hands. I blow them a kiss, which seems to piss them off even more. I'm entertained already. We have our figures set up on the board after walking right into Yhallister's trap. The rest of the party can't interfere.

The session and combat are somewhat planned. This is my last night with the group. I'm trying not to think about it—to just enjoy the game. That's all I can do. Enjoy the ride, and trust that Nova will still love me when this is over. Even though in fifth edition, our characters don't technically die when they go down to zero hit points, we're playing as if that counts as a kill for the purposes of this duel. And if Nova manages to win, someone will have to resurrect Awe so she can go on the show.

"Initiatives." Aiden gestures to the table for us to roll.

Eleanor is sitting in her mom's lap tonight, holding an unpainted plastic dragon figure. Lyssa kisses her hair. "Ahoo," she coos.

Nova throws their die against the table.

A two. I smirk.

"So slow." I roll mine. "That's thirteen total."

I press my fingers together, cracking my knuckles. Everyone always underestimates the bard. Heck, even I do sometimes. But I'm going to make my last show with this group a good one. Poor Hunt. "I summon Bigby's Hand and use it to shove Hunt off the platform. Opposing strength check. You vs. my hand." I wiggle my right hand in the air.

We both roll, and I'm up by two.

"Bye, Hunt." I wave. "You fall off the ledge."

Aiden rolls two dice behind his screen. "That's six fall damage."

Nova rolls her eyes, smirking. "Fine. You want to be that way? I cast Misty Step as my bonus action. That gets me back on the platform and next to Awe. For my action, I'm going to attack." She rolls to hit, scoring much higher than my armor class. "I'm going to make that a Smite."

"Boo!" Drew and Cristy throw a few pieces of popcorn at her.

"What? Awe started this fight."

"We know to cheer for the healer." Cristy puts a hand on my shoulder, then turns to Parker. "Right, Jer? Say I'm right or else."

"Yes, ma'am. You're right."

What in the world? I don't know what kind of real-life magic Cristy is pulling to make Parker easier to deal with in and out of the game. I don't trust him, but I'm not complaining.

"Pfft, I'm a healer too." Nova shakes her head.

"You're a paladin. You might cure something inconsequential—"

"Like the Creeping Death trap you walked into last session?" Nova interrupts.

Cristy waves Nova off. "Yeah, whatever. We're still cheering for Awe down here." Yhallister is forcing the rest of the characters to watch as Awe and Hunt have their single combat.

Nova's second attack misses. Concentration check time. Shit, this is the one part of the plan that could go sideways quick. I need to keep Bigby's Hand to get rid of some of Hunt's hit points before I pull out the big spells.

You got this, pinky. I roll my die and hold my breath. Seventeen. Phew. "Okay. My turn. For my bonus action, I'm going to grapple the paladin with the hand and squeeze them." I pantomime doing that with my hand.

We roll, and I succeed. Nova's face is neutral, but she betrays her annoyance by running her tongue over her teeth. Heh.

"I cast Lightning Bolt. Dex save at disadvantage." I make a finger gun at her. "Kapow."

Nova rolls their eyes as Hunt takes more damage. "That's it." This is even more fun than I thought it'd be. "For my turn, I cast Command."

Command isn't a damage spell, and they can only give a one-word command to my character. I smile. "I don't even try to resist."

Nova stands, then points downward. "Grovel."

Cristy snickers.

"Awkward," Lyssa whispers.

"You're prone, and you lose your turn." Nova's smiling, enjoying this. Gotta play this up to really embarrass them.

I take a step back and kneel in front of the table. "Oh, Hunt. You look so gloriously handsome. Please, I'm begging of you. Let me do to you what I did last night. I'm in the perfect position."

Nova has that adorable, flustered look on her face. "That damn hand is gone, right? Surely, she lost her concentration."

Aiden flips a page in the player's guide. "Command is only a level one spell, and that's not in the description. But Awe does lose her turn and is considered prone."

"Fine," Nova says. "That makes it my turn again. First, I cast Misty Step to get out of that grapple. Hunt readies their sword. This is the most painful moment of their journey, but a necessary one. I'm sorry, Awe. Level four Smite." They roll their dice.

Shit. I might've miscalculated.

I do a little prayer to the fickle gods of numbers while I'm still kneeling. If the damage rolls go too high, or if Hunt gets a critical hit, Awe might be dead. My heart hammers in my chest.

Nova counts up the numbers. She points at me. "You're damn lucky, but it doesn't matter. You only have one hit point left. And just in case you forgot, I'm a tiefling, too. I have Hellish Rebuke that I can use when you hit me next turn. I hope you're planning some sort of elaborate escape. Oh, Aiden, make her roll a concentration check for that damn hand."

Phew. I smirk at Nova. They were actually going to do it —actually going to kill me. Well, we'll see how they like it now. "I drop concentration on the hand. And why would I escape? Hunt, you just made a critical error. You ended your turn in melee with me."

Nova scowls. "I'm a melee class. And I have plenty of health left."

"As a lore bard, I have access to wizard spells. And since I've had a hunch this faceoff was coming, I've chosen one with you in mind for my level seven slot. Finger of Death." I make an upward gesture with my first two fingers. "Make a con save."

Nova rolls. Twelve total—not enough.

I stand, count out seven d8, and shake them across the table, counting the result. "Thirty-seven, plus an additional *thirty* necrotic damage. You're unconscious. And..." I slide my spell card over to Nova. I like having the printed deck for exactly this reason. "Read the last part out loud."

Nova sits back in her chair. "A humanoid killed by this spell rises as a zombie that is permanently under your command." She sounds *pissed.* This is glorious.

"We agreed we'd have to play with some of those spell meanings because they aren't designed for player versus player. Are you wanting to actually take Hunt's hit points low enough to kill them?" Aiden asks.

"Nope." I walk around to Nova's side of the table, smirking. "Awe gives the paladin a kiss"—I punctuate that by leaning down and giving Nova one on the mouth. Ah, sweet victory—"and casts Healing Word, preventing them from becoming her zombie minion. Although, that would've been pretty fun." I wink at Nova and plop myself in her lap.

"You got damn lucky!" she growls.

I grab their chin. "Well, not yet."

We have a mini-going away party for Nova and me after the session. Soft rock music plays through a small speaker in Lyssa and Aiden's kitchen. I unwrap a lemon cupcake Aiden made and lean back against the kitchen counter. I feel inside like this dessert tastes—sweet and sour. Happy and sad.

I'm thrilled for more people to meet Awe. It's a dream job. But...

Nova. My thoughts return back to her, and I swallow a lump in my throat. She's outside, taking Rose for a little stroll. It's been hard on her too. So many times, it's felt like she has more to say about the move, but she holds back.

"Hey, Junie." Parker walks up to me, picking up a cupcake. "Cool fight."

I nod. "Thanks."

"I have something I need to say to you before you leave."

I cringe. "No, I think we're good."

"You were right. I moved out here to try to get back together with you. So, I have to ask: will you go out with me?"

He has to be shitting me with this.

"Are you kidding? No." If I'm not careful, I'm going to end up yelling at him. "First of all, I'm not single. Surely, anyone with eyes at tonight's session could see that. Like, every one of my viewers figured out Nova and I are together even when we were trying to sneak around."

He reminds me of one of those cartoons where a light-bulb comes on over the character's head. "Oh! Er, wait..." And the confusion is back.

I roll my eyes. "Good grief. What?"

"You were attracted to me when we were together, right?"

"Goddammit, bisexuality exists! Why is this so hard for people to understand?"

"Okay." He puts his hands up. "I see how that was offensive, and I apologize!"

"Let me make this very clear to you. Even if I wasn't dating Nova, there is not a single scenario where you and I would *ever* get back together. Understand?"

"Yeah." He smiles. Weird. "I expected you to turn me down; I just felt like I had to shoot my shot. It's not like I was going to follow you to California."

"Seattle."

"Seattle's in California."

"No, it isn't. It's in Washington."

"With the presidents?"

Cristy clears her throat from around the corner. "Don't worry. I'm already making notes on what I'll coach him on next time. US Geography is now on that list." Guess she was listening in.

Parker nods. "I'm paying Cristy to be my life coach. And I'm attending regular therapy."

"Great." I wish him the best, but geez. He can go away now.

"I want you to know—" he points to me—"that I know" —he points to himself—"that you know—" back to me— "that I was a dick." He accentuates it by putting his thumb on his own chest.

"That was a few extra knows."

"Well, whatever. You get what I'm trying to say. I know it was creepy of me to move to try to get back with you. However, I think since I've been here, I've discovered a few things about myself. I don't want to be the type of person that keeps their girlfriend from having friends."

"I'm...glad for you?"

Nova walks in the back door, spotting me through the pass-through window to the kitchen. She speed-walks to where I am, puts an arm around my shoulders, and kisses my forehead. "Is everything okay?" she whispers. She doesn't have to ask aloud if Parker is bothering me.

I lean into her embrace. "It's great. Parker asked me out in what I sincerely hope was a joke." I shoot a glare his way.

He chuckles, rubbing the back of his neck.

"And then he told me that he's doing life-coaching with Cristy."

"It's been good for my wallet. And my entertainment," Cristy announces.

First, my closure with my parents, now with Parker. Things are going surprisingly well. Maybe I should trust Nova that everything really is going to be okay.

"Ready to head home?" They smile at me.

Every time they grin like that, it still makes my breath hitch. "So ready."

25
NOVA

All the way home, June is smirking in that mega-irritating way she does when she wins a game. I can't believe I lost. But even though my character should be devastated, I can't feel anything but pride for June. I could play games with her for hundreds of years and never get tired of it.

We pull into a parking spot in front of our apartment, and she chuckles to herself.

"What?" I ask dryly.

She tries to compose herself. "It's just that...I fingered you in front of all our friends. And it was so good you *died!*" She cackles, laughing so hard she's almost crying.

My ears feel hot. This insult will not stand.

I slam the shifter into Park and cut the car off. "Okay, that's factually untrue. Victory has made your already huge bardic ego absolutely insufferable." I point at her. "Rematch. Inside. Right now."

"I mean, we can, but the result will be the same." She wiggles her fingers.

I catch her fingers and bring them to my lips, kissing their tips. "I'm going to make you grovel for multiple turns."

She's so sexy when she's looking at me like this. I'm pretending that I'm mad, but I'm so aroused by our whole game I almost can't stand it.

She lifts her eyebrows. "Are you, now?"

"Yeah, among other things. After I prove I'm the real winner of the fight. You got lucky when I rolled low damage."

"Mm-hm. Just keep telling yourself that, Hunt."

Let's just keep playing together—all the games. Then nothing else exists. No master's degree program, no reality show, no moves across the country.

We race up the apartment building's stairs and inside, carrying our bags. We're both wearing our costumes still—though I didn't wear the armor to D&D night, just the cloak and horns.

"Okay." I hurry to the table and take off my backpack. "Set it up like at Aiden's. Grid. Dice. Character figures."

She laughs. "This fight isn't canon, right?"

"No cameras. No canon."

She shrugs. "Good. Then I won't have to worry about resurrecting your ass when I vaporize you."

"You mean you won't have to worry about *finding* a resurrection spell so that Awe can appear on her big show?"

"No, that's not a worry."

I narrow my eyes. "That's it."

We set the stuff up on the table, sitting next to each other in front of the grid.

Five minutes later, I have her on the rocks—and after last time, I'm smart enough to end my turn away so she can't use her Finger of Death.

"What now, Lady Danamark?"

"Again, we agree this isn't canon? Because Awe wouldn't actually do this to poor Hunt."

"Bring it." I'm just waiting until I can finish her off. Although that was the same position I was in earlier at Aiden's... Nah, I ended my turn in the air on Yhallister's platform. She can't actually get to me.

"I cast Disintegrate. It's a dex save. But seeing as you're slow as fuck..."

I roll a d20, and it's not good. "Eh, whatever. Tell me the damage."

She starts adding the numbers. Ah, crap.

I sweep the figures, grid, and her dice to the side with my arm. Obviously, this is the mature response.

"Nova! What the—"

I kiss June hard on the mouth as I lift her by the cloak, pinning her to the table. God, I love doing that. If I can't win in D&D, I'm going to win in real life.

"You absolutely ridiculous bard. You know what?" I growl into her mouth. "Since this isn't canon, I want to go back to my turn. I cast Command."

She's laughing under me. "You totally lost again. If anything, I should get to command you."

"Why don't you try it?"

"Ooh, you're really bothered. It's super-hot." She smirks, wrinkling her nose. "Command: take me to the bedroom."

"Actually, that's a good idea." I climb off her, and she sits up. I lean into her, grab her under the ass, and toss her over my shoulder. She squeals in the most delightful way as I carry her through the apartment. Those pushing prayers were useful for something, at least.

I plop her onto my bed.

As soon as her ass hits the mattress, she's scrambling to take off pieces of her costume. "Command, come into the closet, find my box of sex toys, and take your pick of something to use on me."

"You need to return to magic school. Command can only be applied to one word." But even as I complain, I'm already doing as she says, walking into the closet and pushing aside June's hanging clothes to where I know she keeps her box of toys. Like she'd have to force me. "But I'll follow your command to come."

I've never had a partner who was this into sex toys, especially nerdy sex toys. I kneel and look through the plastic bin. Some of these things seem...confusing. I lift a long, navy blue phallic object and turn it over in my hand. How would you even use a two-sided dildo in a mutually satisfying way? I put it back. Ooh, a dick that looks like a lightsaber. I press a button on it, and it lights up, vibrates, and makes a noise. Hmm, maybe not.

"If you take too long, I'm taking care of myself," she teases in a sing-song voice. "I have a wand in the drawer next to your bed..."

"No! Not without letting me watch." Shit, I better hurry. The "Gargantuan Gold" is sitting over on a shelf in my room instead of in here, so I can tease her about it more frequently. "You better watch out, or I'll make you go dragon riding. And you know *exactly* what I mean by that." The ridiculous thing is too big to fit into a person. At least I think so. I've held it and teased her with it, but it's not going to work for the purpose I want now. But she does have this other interesting-shaped dildo...

I dig through the box until I find a strap to go with it that has a universal ring. My hands are shaking as I put the red and pink ridged dildo through it. I guess it's from the same company that made the dragon one and made of soft silicone with a narrow tip.

I shuck off my clothes, cloak, and horns from the D&D session earlier. I've never been able to successfully wear a strap-on. Not that I've had much experience in that department. Cristy and I tried once, and she got irritated at me. But I can do it for June.

I hear the buzz of her 'magic wand.' It's now or never.

I step through the black straps and adjust them to be tight around my legs and waist. I look ridiculous. June will be as likely to laugh at me as get turned on. But that's okay, too. I love making her laugh.

Dramatic entrance it is. I burst out of the closet, the absurd dildo leading the way. "Hey, what did I tell you about not without letting me watch?"

June's eyes go wide, and she gasps. She's naked, holding the vibrating wand to her front. "Shit." She squeezes her eyes shut. "I just came a little. Holy gods. You look..."

"Ridiculous?" I put a hand on my hip.

"Sexy as fuck. You found the demon dick." She pushes a button on the vibrator, and it turns off.

"Is that what this is?" I look down at it. I guess I can see that.

"Mmm." She nods.

"And this does it for you?" I put a leg up on the bed and gesture to myself, from my bare chest down to the new appendage.

She nods again, quicker.

I guess it does lend a certain air of...well, something. I'm not quite sure what to call it, but I like it.

"Lady Danamark, you better be careful what you wish for. You commanded me to use something on you, but I'm afraid this thing has a mind of its own."

"Mmm, Hunt," she moans again. She bites her lower lip.

I climb on the bed, straddling her body. She's gorgeous. I love everything we play in bed, and when we don't play at all, just sleepily rubbing against each other. Endless time with her would be my greatest fantasy.

I scoot up her body, tilting my hips so the dildo aims at her face. Holy shit. I think I unlocked some kind of brand-new desire in me. "Command, suck."

She puts the tip of it in her mouth. "Like this?" she asks, words muffled around it. God, the sight of her looking up at me...

I swallow, breathing fast. "Yes."

She dips a finger under the strap-on, rubbing my clit. The sensations zing through my body. "You're so stiff for me," she says, still muffled around the dildo.

"June...good God." I put a hand in her hair.

She moves her hand away, and I'm about to complain when I hear her wand again. She lifts an eyebrow, then presses the end of the wand up under where the thing is strapped to me, the tip of it still in her mouth.

I grind my hips, pressing hard against the wand, and come, my moan uncharacteristically loud. But there's never any judgment with June. Eyes closed, I have to breathe for a second before I can even hope to speak. I move the wand aside as the sensation is too much.

She pulls her lips off the dildo with a pop. That gets my attention. "I've heard legends of your perversion, oh paladin, even among tieflings. But you came so easily for me. Maybe my performance check is higher than yours."

Fresh excitement jolts through me. "You suggesting I won't measure up? I assure you, my lady, my constitution is unmatched." I pull the straps around my upper thighs tighter. "Flip over. I mean, command, flip." I climb off her.

She snickers, turning over so her ass is exposed to me. She wiggles it. "Like this?"

Fuck. "Yes." I take the still-on magic wand and bring it around to the front of her hips, pressing it against her clit. "Hold this, please."

She groans, doing as I say.

I straddle her again, spreading my legs over her thighs from behind. So beautiful from every angle. I trace my fingers over the round ass cheeks, tickling her lightly and making her wiggle. I dip two fingers between her legs, to her entrance. So warm and wet. I didn't know if I'd need to put lubrication on this thing or not. She moans again as I finger her entrance. I know how to touch her like this, but using this strap-on?

"June." I lean up and nibble up her neck to her earlobe. "I have to confess I've never successfully wielded one of these *weapons* before. You're going to have to tell me what feels good. I don't want to hurt you."

She looks over her shoulder at me, and I kiss the corner of her lips. "You won't. The design on that one is to be semi-soft on purpose. So you don't have to worry about injuring me."

I lean back to where I was, then start laughing as I position the thing to go into her. "I'm sorry. It's just so ridiculous looking."

"Don't insult your own demon dick! I mean, I can insult it if you want. If that gets you off."

"You already got me off." I grip her hip with one hand, loving how soft her skin is.

"Yeah, and I plan on doing it again."

With the other hand, I guide the tip of it into her. I'm not going to be able to see if she wants me to insert the whole thing. "Don't insult me. Tell me it feels nice."

"Your dick feels so good," she moans, drawing out the last word. "Hunt, please. Don't hold back."

I pull her hips, thrusting the whole thing in. Well, at least I think it's the whole thing. Kind of hard to tell. "Like this?"

"God, yes," she breathes. She grinds her clit against the vibrator as I move the dildo in and out of her, and in a few moments, she gasps and reaches around to hold my hips still against hers. "Yes, fuck!"

Definitely unlocked a new desire in me. I don't want to wear one of these, like, every time, but damn. "Was that adequate, my lady?" I murmur in her ear.

She releases my hips, and I slide the dildo out. I loosen the straps and climb out of the thing at the same time she flips over. I turn off the wand, put both items aside on the nightstand, and then lower my naked body on top of June's. Every inch of my skin seems to sing where we touch.

"So good. You're the hottest person on the planet, you know. Well, you and all your characters."

I kiss her lips, teasing them open with my tongue. "I'm dating the hottest person on the planet. That was...wow."

"Nova." She traces her hand around my face. "We're not going to lose this, right? By having to go places for our careers?"

I roll off her and lay my head on her same pillow, our noses inches apart. "Never. You can take that as my oath. You're my favorite person in the whole damn world, like, including all of history. I believe in you, and I know going to Seattle for this show is a great opportunity. But you have to know, no matter where life takes us, I'm yours. You could break up with me, and I'd still be yours."

Is that weird to say?

"I love you. Let's use a Time Stop spell, okay? Just stay here for as long as we want."

We have a week and two days left together. I...can't process that now. I want to pretend we have all the time in the universe.

"Please."

26
NOVA

June watches me as I wave the gold dragon dildo in the air. I'm packing boxes to go to storage, and she's on the phone with the show's social media marketing manager. It's been an irritating call—and I've only heard her half of it.

I hold the dildo up to the front of my pants, pointing at it.

Her eyes go wide—transfixed on me. "Hm?" she asks the guy on the phone. "Oh—I'm sorry! I just got distracted for a second."

Only a few more days, and we're both moving... I've been in total denial. It doesn't seem right. But I can maybe fly out to visit her if there's a break in the show's filming schedule, they allow it, and if the plane tickets are reasonably priced. We'll talk every day. At least text every day.

She'll move to Iowa with me when she's done. Right? I swallow. Unless there's another opportunity in Seattle. And of course, I wouldn't ask her to give that up. At the very longest, it'll only be two years until I'm done with my MFA.

After that, if I need to, I'll move to Seattle. I don't care where we go, as long as June is there.

"I need to put you on speaker so I can use both hands, okay?" She asks him, then a moment later sets the phone down as she sits cross-legged on the bed, typing something on her laptop.

"Consistency is the key," a baritone voice says over the phone. "Do you see what I mean about your older content versus your newer stuff?"

"I guess," June says, tucking a strand of hair behind an ear.

"Like, I'm not going to mince words because it seems like you're a pretty to-the-point person."

She makes a motion like she's holding a gun to her temple, rolling her eyes. "Good."

"I'd advise you to pick a lane as far as your branding. In some of your videos and pictures with the most likes, you're dressed like a fantasy pin-up girl. Take this one, from December of last year. You're in a holiday-themed outfit and kissing a poster of a buff male orc with a white beard. This other one from February is actually the one I presented to the showrunners when I suggested you out of our pool of applicants—the photo shoot where you're playing a lute as Awe while sitting on top of two men."

"Uh-huh." June is still looking at me, and I realize I'm still foolishly holding the dildo. She's busy—she doesn't need distractions. I smile at her, put it in a box, then pick the box up. I can fill it with the rest of the dragon figures from the shelves.

"But in your recent content, you're very into this Nova, who is on your game stream."

Hearing my name gives me a jolt. I pause. Do I really

want to listen to this conversation? At the same time, how can I not?

He mustn't realize I'm in the room and continues, "She? They? I don't know, but either way, this character isn't going to resonate with your traditional audience nor the majority of our show's target audience."

Character? Hunt or me? I put the box down.

"If I were you, I'd lean into your content that's likable across your entire audience. Female/female is too niche. You're losing over half of your audience."

"Nova is nonbinary." June's voice is cold. *"I'm so sorry,"* she mouths to me.

"That's even more niche."

I cringe. I hate that word. Niche. My whole life, I've felt like a weirdo just for being myself.

June holds my gaze as she picks up the phone. "Well, that can't be true. My channel has more viewers than ever after our latest campaign. A campaign I'm not getting to participate in because of this show. I don't see a reason or motivation for me to rebrand any of my content."

"I'm just saying, there's a reason why no popular television shows feature a pairing like this. Technically, I'm not supposed to mention anything about it, but your romance on this show will be with a male elf."

"Yeah, a fictional romance. That's different."

"Your contract says you must appear single during all your out-of-character appearances and channel content through the duration of the show's filming and until it airs so as to not spoil the plot. Is that going to be a problem?"

"No. I'm aware. However, my contract says nothing about having to change my existing channel and content."

"I'm only trying to help you. You're going to get more out of this opportunity if you trust professionals with more experience." He sighs over the phone. "Okay. It might take some rewrites of our plotlines, but what about presenting yourself as a gay influencer? You could play up a breakup with Nova and get back together or whatever when you're done with the show. For it to be effective, it'd be nice to see a social media presence from her."

They want...me to have a social media presence? I can't do that. I hate everything about it. Even leaving comments on other people's pages gives me anxiety.

June wrinkles her nose, shaking her head. "She's not going to be interested in that. And she's way too busy with her own career."

"I'd like you to come up with a plan then. Just make up your mind on how you want your image to go from here, tell me, and then streamline your content leaning in one way or the other."

"Well, I don't lean one way or the other. I make content based on what inspires me."

"That's fine. I just need to be able to do my job and make a marketing plan for you and your character." His voice sounds strained. "I'm happy to take ideas from you, so please decide what you want to do and send them to me as soon as possible."

"I will. Goodbye."

June hits the end button on her phone, then lets out a grunt, slamming herself backward on the bed and putting her palms over her eyes. "Can you believe that asshole? I've made a mistake. This is a step back."

I walk to the bed and lay next to her.

She closes her laptop. "This is so ridiculous! Why did I agree to this? You heard him. I'm supposed to have picked a lane. How is it so difficult to understand?"

I move my head up to lay on the pillow. "It shouldn't be."

"What if I belong nowhere? With the pin-up style stuff I've posted in the past that I designed to target straight men as viewers, I'm hardly a role model for the queer community, and obviously I'm not straight, so where *do* I fit?"

"You fit right here." I pull her to my chest. "Really well, I might add." She's perfect. Absolutely perfect. I hate that she doubts it. "That guy's an asshole. Pin-up style content does *not* make you a bad role model for queer people—I don't care who your target audience was. You can present any way you want, and you're always free to change your mind." I inhale the scent of her hair and kiss the top of her head. "And for the record, it doesn't bother me that you can feel attraction to other genders, too. There's nothing wrong with you."

"You're seriously not going to have a problem with whatever bullshit fake romance they're setting up for me? With seeing me interact with this guy?"

This feels like a trick question. Of course, it bothers me. How could it not? But I want this chance for her. She's been working toward it for years—whether she realized it or not. Her make it or break it chance.

There's an infinite list of things she could do with her life and career. I can't stand in her way.

"It'll bother me a little, yeah. But I still want the opportunity for you."

"Before, you said it wouldn't bother you. Or else I wouldn't have agreed." Her voice increases in intensity as she speaks.

"You know I'm autistic, right? I don't think I ever told you, like, in words. I mean, you probably figured it out. I'm never going to be a social media person." That sounded presumptive. "Shit, I mean, not that autistics are a mono-lith or anything. Plenty of people are great at that, but not me. Not online or in real life. I can't do those things he was talking about, and honestly, I don't want to. The most I could tolerate was having an author website and Twitter, and I sucked at using those." The words spill out, and I feel strangely disconnected from them. I'm ruining her career. Worse than she ever ruined mine. Oh God.

"It's fine. I love you how you are. Don't change anything. He's clearly a backward-thinking jerk."

"What I'm trying to say is I can't be the one holding you back from success. I won't be."

"What does that mean?"

It's a good question. What does it mean to let June explore herself? To give her true freedom? She can't be worrying about hurting me.

I brush pink strands from her forehead. "You don't need the stress of this. It was why I tried to keep our relationship from becoming so...deep."

She smiles with sad eyes. "Special friends?"

"Yeah. That. The problem is I fell so fast, June. Who couldn't love you?"

"Heh, the marketing guy?"

I shake my head. "He's wrong. I fell fast, and that's not fair to you. We're moving across the country from each other. You're going to have lots of stresses with this show."

"What are you trying to say?"

"Something I hate." God, I hate it so much. My heart feels as heavy as a boulder.

"What?" her voice drops to a cold whisper.

"We have to take a break."

June

I thought I could stomach this pecan waffle. That it would cheer me up, even a tiny amount, but it's sickeningly sweet with fake maple syrup and sugary batter. Even the smell turns my stomach. I pick at it with my fork.

Nova didn't even order anything. And she was the one who suggested going to the Awful Waffle. She stares off over my shoulder. I can only imagine what's in her head. I can't believe this. It's late, and we're one of only three tables with diners.

Our talk hasn't been going well.

I put my fork down. "In a way, you're giving me an ultimatum."

Her hazel eyes snap back to mine—panic in them again. "What? No, I'm not."

"You're saying that I have until December to figure out what I want more. A career or a relationship with you."

"No. That's not it at all! I'm saying take until December so you can do your show without having to worry about my feelings."

"I'm going to worry about them regardless! I love you."

"I love you too. That's why I want to give you this."

"You love me so much you're breaking up with me."

She closes her eyes. "Never. Not if I have a say in it."

"That's what taking a break is. A *break* up."

Someone in the restaurant starts a country music song from the jukebox. Fucking perfect.

Nova leans over the table. "I don't want to be with anyone else. But I don't want to hold you to officially dating me when you have industry people putting pressure on you. You're already moving all the way to Seattle. Like, at this point, you should go all in. Give it your all."

"I can give it my all and still date you."

"You'll be acting and role-playing. If we're a couple, in the back of your mind, you'll be thinking about if it'll hurt me to see the footage."

"You think it'll hurt less if we're broken up?"

She sits back in the booth and puts a hand over her face. "I'm trying to do right by you."

"By breaking up with me."

"By giving you this chance to figure out if it's what you really want! I'm afraid I pushed you into a relationship. I kissed you without permission."

"For the record, I give you permission from now until forever to kiss me whenever you want. Retroactively, too."

She shakes her head. "If I asked you three months ago, you would've said you were straight."

"I would've been wrong!"

"My point is we've been going fast. Really, really fast. I don't want to break up; I just think it might be a good idea to go back to what we'd agreed on before. Friends. Then in December, when you're done, we can revisit, and you can tell me how you feel. After I've given you time to live on your own. To think and breathe." She reaches across the sticky table and takes my hand. "I don't mean to sound at all like I'm judging, but have you ever lived on your own?"

"No," I whisper. Why do I feel embarrassed at admitting this? I lived with my parents, then Parker, then my parents again, and now Nova.

She nods. "It's okay. Don't be ashamed. I just think you should...try it. I don't want you resenting me later for all the things you could've had but didn't realize are out there. Before you commit again."

I pull my hand back and cross my arms. It's not the same. Nova isn't Parker, and she has way more respect for me than my family ever did.

"Remember back when I said that doing the right thing doesn't always give you a reward?"

I groan. "I don't see why we have to choose. We can still be a couple—it'll just be long distance."

"Imagine yourself ten years in the future. You're thirty-six."

I picture a more put-together me, boasting a collection of at least ten real gemstone dice sets, running a tabletop game like a master DM. "Yeah, and just as fabulous."

"What if you get to a decade from now, and you're stuck wondering if you gave yourself a chance to explore your options? You were in two long-term relationships in a row. And I'm not arguing that it's too soon to move on from Parker; obviously, you're ready. But should you really jump into a long-term relationship with me at such a big turning point in your life?"

"Yes."

Nova turns her face toward the window. "You're just being stubborn."

"I don't want you to be right!" It bursts from my mouth before I can stop it. Dammit. "I don't want to break up with you."

She takes my hand again. "I'm not going anywhere. You can take your time with this. I want you to be sure. I've never stopped loving you. Six months? It's nothing."

I've never stopped loving you. I didn't stop loving her either, even though I couldn't put into words or thoughts what it meant back when we were teens. A tiny flame of it burned in me during our separation. During my years with Parker.

Tears run down my cheeks. "I love you too. Don't think this will change any of that."

"That's right. And we're still going to talk and text all the time."

"Expect messages, like, every single day."

"Good. But also, don't let me hold you back from having fun. Meeting people." She squeezes my hand. "You said before you never got to live your carefree twenties because of your relationship with Parker. It's not too late, and this is your chance. Please, take it. I'm not going anywhere."

"You're going to Iowa."

"Well, yeah. But metaphorically." She gives me a little smile.

She loves me, but she's breaking up with me. How did we get to this place?

Why does gaining an opportunity I've wanted for years feel like I'm losing everything?

27
NOVA

I remind myself to unclench my jaw again as June and I walk through the final security checkpoint of the Atlanta airport, collecting our carry-ons from the x-ray scanner.

She gives me a small smile as she slings her backpack over one shoulder. I know she's worried about me.

This morning, I totally lost my shit over breaking a coffee cup, which was brilliant because it'll be the last thing June remembers of me. I was trying to wrap my favorite mug—one that brings me comfort every morning—in bubble wrap to put it in my carry-on, and I just dropped it, sending little pieces of shattered pottery everywhere. We didn't even have a broom and dustpan anymore, having already put them in storage. I couldn't stop insulting myself, saying how I didn't deserve nice things. I wanted to crawl out of my skin.

June listened, letting me finish ranting while picking up the shards with me by hand. Then she hugged me and said I deserved the world.

I don't. I barely feel like a functional adult. How am I

supposed to get a master's degree at one of the most prestigious programs in the country?

We walk together to the train that leads to the terminals. My plane leaves first, then June's in a few hours. She's going to go see me off.

A voice gives instructions as we step onto the train. I hold onto the same vertical rail as her, and when the train lurches forward, she falls into me. I wrap an arm around her shoulders to steady her, and she leans into me. The contact has me yearning for more. We haven't been intimate since I told her we needed a break three days ago. I'm such a fool. I don't know what my alignment is in real life, but I wish I could be different—do the more selfish thing and tell her to be exclusive with me when we're apart.

We had to finish packing everything for both of us, something neither of us is good at and put off until last minute. I managed to get the belongings coming to Iowa with me down to just a luggage bag that I checked plus one shipped box. June ended up needing several boxes to ship to Seattle—mostly cosplay stuff—but even teasing her about it didn't get the usual lighthearted reaction.

We get to my concourse number and exit the train. June takes my hand as we walk to the escalators. On the ride up, I bring it to my lips.

"It's going to be okay," she tells me.

It doesn't feel like it. So much can happen in these months we're apart. Of course, everyone at this show will love her. She'll be popular and get more jobs. Maybe a continuation of the show's campaign. And she'll be with other brilliant creators like her. Ones that can match her skill with people. A skill I'll never have.

If I were a D&D character, I know I'd be running with a charisma detriment. Minus one, at least, maybe two. It's probably why I wanted Hunt to be so charismatic. To impress June.

We walk hand in hand the rest of the way to my terminal. The airline is already boarding my plane. Shit. Don't they usually run behind? I'm not ready. I swallow down a lump in my throat. It can't be time yet. How can this be reality that I have to get on a plane and fly away from the person I love the most?

I turn to June. Seeing the tears well in her eyes shatters my resolve. I pull her to my chest in a tight hug. No, I can't cry here—I have to be brave for her. To show her how much I believe in her.

"Hey," I pull back and tip her chin up. "I'm so proud of you. You're amazing. A real bard. A star."

She chuckles, wiping her eyes with the back of a hand. "I don't think I count as—"

"Don't. You do. You're going to win this contest. Everyone is going to love Awe—to love you. I love you."

I can't keep her from the world, hidden away the way Parker tried. Damn this being on a break. I'm not leaving her without giving her a proper goodbye.

I close the distance between our faces, kissing her lips. Salty from tears, but soft, warm, perfect June. My person. The only one who ever understood the way I see the world. The only person to get me comfortable enough to go on stage, or be on videos, to role-play in front of strangers on the internet.

Please, I don't want this to end. I no longer care who's staring at us standing in the airport or about the steward who clears their throat at the Frontier desk.

She returns my kiss like we're back at the D&D session and she's trying to resurrect me again.

Someone makes an announcement—it's the last call for

my plane to board. I knew I was cutting it close, but I'm about to miss my flight. Maybe because I want to miss it. That plane is the last place I want to be.

I reluctantly break the kiss and touch our foreheads together one last time. These are going to be the longest months of my life.

"I love you, Nova," she says through sobs.

Seeing her openly cry, I can't stop myself. I'm crying in public—something I despise. I kiss her forehead, then pull my hood from my oversized hoodie over my head, covering my face with my hand.

Time flows in a wobbly way as I fish the boarding pass from my pocket and hurry onto the plane. My seat is the only empty one—of course, stuck right in the middle of two other people.

Tears pour down my cheeks. This is so embarrassing, but I can't stop. When I squeeze into the small space and sit, I pull my hoodie strings tighter and hide my entire face in both hands.

I'm vaguely aware of the airline staff making announcements and the eventual motion of the plane as it takes off.

The man next to me just said something.

I'm finally catching my breath. "I'm sorry?"

"I said, you need anything, son?"

"No." Humiliation floods through me again at being so upset in public. I just broke so many social norms.

"It a girlfriend? I bet it's a girlfriend."

He thinks I'm a boy, and I don't correct him. I just nod.

A flight attendant makes an announcement that they're turning back on the wifi.

I can't do this. I was wrong. This is the biggest mistake of my life. Who cares about an MFA? I pull out my phone, connect it, and start texting June.

Please, June, I'm so sorry. I made a big mistake. Taking a break is a terrible idea. I want to be with you forever—I want to marry you. As soon as I get off this damn plane, I'm buying a ticket to Seattle. It doesn't matter that we have to sneak around for a while. I love you so much. I feel like my heart is breaking in two.

Before I can send it, I get a picture from June. Her eyes are still red, but she's smiling, one arm around the shoulders of a teen with short green and black hair, the other hand giving the thumbs up. They're holding a copy of my book in between them.

Then the text comes after it:

"Nova, Hunt, my darling, my love, Rock Band pro, and loser of Smash Bros and D&D single combat. I feel like I can't breathe without you already. I'm sure your plane is taking off, and you can't get these texts yet."

Me too, love. It feels like I'm dying without you. My finger hovers over the send button.

"This picture is of Riley. They're only fifteen. I saw them reading this book you love and had to go say hi and strike up a conversation. Anything to distract myself, you know? They never identified with a character in a book, movie, or anything until they read about Hunt, who gave them the courage to tell their parents they're nonbinary. Isn't that cool?"

I wipe my face with the inside of my elbow. Yes, it's cool. It's why I fought through the uncomfortable steps of publishing the book—why I dealt with internet bullies and bigots.

"I wanted you to make sure you know how important your writing is. Like, I'm glad I can entertain people on my channel and encourage them to play D&D, but you're going to write books like "Curse of the Dragon's Gate" which can literally save lives. I know you, and I bet you're overthinking and worrying if

you made the right call getting this degree and taking a chance on your writing. You're where you're meant to be. I can't wait to read what you create next."

Should I send my text? I delete the line about my heart breaking in two.

"These months are going to be difficult, but we're both doing what we're supposed to. And we're going to keep our promise to each other and be best friends the whole time. I'm going to text you so often it'll run your phone battery down. You'll have to carry an extra charger. Then as soon as I can, I'm going to come to Iowa and kiss your ridiculous handsome, beautiful face. Then cast Command to make you to take me to bed. Got it?"

I select all of my text and delete it, then click on the photo she sent, zooming in on June. Tear-stained, messy hair, no makeup, gorgeous.

"That her?" The guy next to me—a middle-aged, gray-haired man who somewhat resembles my dad—leans in to look over my shoulder.

I nod, covering my mouth.

"Oh, damn. She's pretty. I'm sorry."

When the flight attendant comes by to take drink orders, the man buys me a whiskey, saying I need it.

I text June. *"You better, Lady Danamark."*

28
JUNE

I check my phone absently as Marie fixes my hair. Marie likes to give me intricate braids with long extensions that match my color—something I certainly never had the skill to do on my own.

No messages.

I haven't heard from Nova all morning, and it's almost eleven-thirty already.

"Yo. June." Soren slides into the chair next to mine. We're in the hair and makeup room before today's filming starts. At least they don't schedule us to start early in the morning. Apparently, most D&D fans are like me and night owls.

I don't dare move and mess up Marie's work. "Yeah?"

Soren's character, Sariel, is Awe's possible love interest. An elven barbarian, which is hilarious, and Soren plays him well. Without his alliance, I don't know that I would've lasted this long in the game.

"Rumor time."

Marie snickers as she secures a braid with a tiny elastic. "Oh, here we go again."

"Hush. My predictions are right fifty percent of the time."

"Great stats." I lift my phone and snap a picture of the work-in-progress that is my hair. "This is looking really cool, Marie." The room behind me was some sort of smaller dining room at one point, and the show repurposed it for the hair and makeup area. The main game happens in a formal ballroom, with the D&D table in the center and a stage area with lights that let the show shoot some dynamic shots of our characters.

"Thanks!" Marie weaves another braid.

I send the picture to Nova. She's in class, but I can't help it. I want her to message me. "What's the rumor?"

Marie sprays the braid she just made with hairspray. "That Sariel is next on my hair schedule, and if Soren doesn't hold still this time, I'm going to be a lot less careful with the hairspray?"

Soren chuckles. "Please, that's fact. No—it's about the next challenge."

"I'm not here for this." Marie sections another piece of my hair. Technically, we're not supposed to meta-game—to talk about any of the game's challenges outside of playing. But everyone is doing it.

This campaign has been a weird mix of scripted and live play. Reminds me if Squid Games met Critical Role with cosplay. The official lore is that a chaotic floating eye monster opened portals all over the realms, pulling adventurers from all backgrounds into his gameshow.

The show animators rendered a 3D version of this character, Xandriver, who floats around on big screens behind where we play. He has a single giant eye at the center of a large blue beachball-shaped body, with eight additional smaller eye stalks sticking out. In game, Xandriver is incredibly powerful. Even more so than Yhallister. He's made our characters his prisoners as we compete for the top spot in his gameshow. The winner becomes the eye monster's apprentice, and the losers die.

"Now that there are less of us, the producers are really digging into our characters' backstories," Soren says.

The in-game stakes are win or die. Out of game, the winner and their character will get to appear in the sequel to the D&D movie. Which would be really freaking awesome. Nova was right—I came all the way out here; I might as well win. And I think I have a good chance.

"Huh, how so?" I ask.

Soren leans in, dropping his voice even though the three of us are the only ones in the hair and makeup room. "They're bringing in the evil exes. Classic fuck-with-the-players move. I was DMing once, and I had our horny bard's entire gang of former spouses come in and yell at him. There were lots of persuasion checks involved."

Nova texts me back with the heart eyes emoji, making my real heart jolt. *"You're so cute oh my god"*

"The intricate braids in my hair are why I sent you the picture, you dork," I return.

"June. Are you hearing what I'm saying?" Soren asks.

"Yeah, evil exes hate bards. Got it." I wave him off, trying to decide what I should send her next.

"Are you texting *Nova*? How are they today?" he teases, putting emphasis on their name.

"Maybe. Shut up." I feel my cheeks flush a little. Soren and I have a very clear agreement—we're not interested in each other romantically or sexually, no matter what ridiculous plotlines the showrunners develop for us.

He shrugs, pushing his shoulder-length black hair back. "Anyway, the rumor is the producers are calling our former flames who play D&D and flying them out here for a specific challenge where our characters will have to fight theirs in single combat. Do you have someone who you had a public breakup with?"

"Um, I guess. I made a few videos about breaking up with Parker and the fallout. Then he played at our table to try to convince me to date him again."

He winces. "I saw some of those streams. Parker is probably a good bet for the one they call in to face you. I already know they're going to call Callie, my number one evil ex. We were together for a year until she cheated on me with our party's other warlock. That was eight months ago, then they left to form their own group. Hashtag sad eyes."

"That sucks, man." Soren's game stream is more popular with Discord viewers, and he runs darker story-lines than the groups I want to join. Still, the gods of D&D must like me because the showrunners could've paired me with a much worse player than Soren.

By the end of the show, even Soren and I will have to strategize against the other to win. We still have other contenders to beat first, though.

"I'll have to think about how to beat a 'lock. Casters can really fuck you up."

I laugh. "Nova's paladin found that out. Did you see our last session?"

"Maybe you'll get lucky and they'll bring them in." He nudges me with an elbow. "Lucky in more than one way."

"You're funny." Damn it, I wish I could see Nova in person. "But I doubt it. I already beat their character, and the writers will want to show viewers something new. Also, the whole thing with the marketing guy pushing my"—I make quotes with the first fingers on my hand not holding my phone—"*straight content.*"

"Ah, true," he agrees. "That guy said the same thing to me before the show. Tried to convince me to remove any bisexual memes I'd posted on my Insta. Marketing dude probably already knew the writers were going to play up the drama with our recent exes, and that's why he couldn't be more specific. That guy's being ridiculous, though. D&D has a huge queer following."

My phone buzzes, and I look immediately to see Nova's reply. *"I'm stuck in class so I'll have to text you more later, but here's the scene I was working on this morning. I'm so obsessed with finishing it, I even missed running prayers. And you know I never miss that."*

I smile. Even if the show asked Nova to come, she's too busy. She's been sending some of her scenes to me piece by piece ever since I assured her it was utterly impossible for her to send me too many texts and that I'd never, ever get sick of reading anything she writes.

I get another text from her of the scene she mentioned, so long I have to click on it to start scrolling through all the words. Getting this is making my day better—even after getting Soren's news about Parker likely coming to the show. I can only hope he'll be on better behavior than he used to be after life coaching and therapy, but I'm pretty sure I can wreck Jerald, even with the min-maxing he did.

Prove bardic superiority, win the evil eyeball's gameshow, and after, return victorious to my true love. Best quest ever.

29
NOVA

I'm not built for this kind of weather. It's only early November, and snow flurries stick to my face and hair as I walk through campus. It makes me want to curl into a blanket back in my apartment. My lonely, shitty apartment. I stayed up too late last night writing and then got up this morning to finish the scene. The time got away from me, and I was late to my class. At least I made it to class this time.

I hurry down the path toward my counselor's office. This semester hasn't gone well. There's the ideal college me, which I envisioned, and there's the me in reality. The one terrible at organization, meeting deadlines, and making my brain focus on lectures when my heart is somewhere else.

Seattle, to be precise.

And in a fantasy realm. Not only did the publisher want the sequel to *Curse,* but they offered a five-book contract—finishing this three-book series, plus another series after that. I've been unable to stop writing and editing the second book, shaping it into an even stronger story. It's embarrassing. I'm missing classes and assignments because I can't stop myself from writing something else.

By the time I arrive at Dr. Brown's office, I have to make a note on my phone of the ideas that sprung to mind. I don't trust myself to remember them.

"Ms. Dawson. Come in."

I walk into the small office in the historic building, with all four walls covered in bookshelves stuffed full of books, papers, and notebooks. It's five minutes past the time I was supposed to meet her.

"Thanks." I don't know what I'm thanking her for. She's the one who requested to meet.

Shit. Maybe I'm on academic probation. I missed classes and missed a recent assignment—though I did contact the professor and get an extension.

"Nova—I can call you Nova, right?"

I nod.

"Why did you want to come to school here?"

Fuck, I'm suspended or failing. Or both. "Um," I swallow. "To improve my writing."

She looks me over behind large glasses. "But you haven't been attending the lectures, and when you do, you're often late."

I stare at my knees. "I'm sorry." There's not an intent to skip class—I want to attend. It's just so difficult to get my brain and body to cooperate when I'm focused on my book. "You saw my email about the situation before. I'm under contract for my next novel, and the edit deadline is soon." And the sooner I turn it in, the sooner their editors can accept it, and then I can get paid again.

She nods. "I remember. I read your first book after I learned it was yours. Intricate, detailed world building."

"Oh." I can't tell if she means that as a positive thing or not.

"It doesn't matter if you're the bestselling author in the world; you can always expand your techniques and improve, and our school strives to meet individuals where they are."

I nod. *Get me out of here.* "Agreed. I'm so sorry. I'll do better."

"That's not what I'm saying. Let me rephrase. Sometimes, opportunities come up for our students, and the university set up our program to work with them, giving leniency so they can finish their degree at their own pace."

Wait. Maybe I'm not in trouble?

"If you think it would help, while you're at this pivotal moment in your writing career, we can put your education on pause after this semester, give you extra time to view the lecture recordings and complete the assignments you're still lacking. You're submitting your manuscript for your project, anyway."

It takes me a moment to process what she's saying. "I can put my degree on pause without failing?"

"Of course, if that's what you want. Even for years, and if it helps, we can look at transferring you to a remote program either here or at another school. We want you to succeed."

I nod. "Yeah. That'd be really helpful."

What a relief. I could finish my books without having to attend all the lectures in person.

"When I signed up for this program, I didn't have any prospects in publishing. Then, when the publisher came back and offered me more contracts, I thought I'd be better at balancing them and"—I gesture to the small office filled with books—"all of this. It's hard for me to juggle. My brain gets stuck on one thing."

She smiles. "I remember when I was a young writer—it felt like there weren't enough hours in the day for me to get done with what I needed. It's important to pace yourself, set realistic goals, and keep a work-life balance. I'll send you the paperwork and let your professors know. Is that okay with you?"

I squash down my irritation. She says these things like they're so easy. But she's helping me out. Apparently, I won't lose my place in the program like I feared. "Yes. Thank you so much."

I walk outside, heart feeling lighter with each step away from that office. Should I tell June about the situation at school? And more importantly—should I finally tell her about being the author of *Curse?* I've delayed so long I'm afraid it'll be a shock to her. And that she'd feel terrible all over again for a mistake she's already apologized for. I take a slow breath and let it out. She could be filming now. I look at the time. It's four in the afternoon here, but in Seattle, it's only two.

Back in my apartment, I unpack my backpack and open my laptop on the little coffee table. It can't hurt to look at flights to Seattle. If I get to finish these assignments and lectures somewhere else, I might as well finish them where June is. Never mind that it'll be a surefire way for me to not meet any deadlines—the school's or the publisher's. *June.* I want to see her so bad. I've tried to be good and give her space. But every day feels lonelier.

I could visit her—I bet I'll be done with my edits in less than a week.

There's about ten tabs open on my MacBook as I look between my bank account balance, airfare, and hotels near where June's show is filming when my phone rings. How annoying.

I stare at the screen, trying to decide if I want to answer it or not. I don't recognize the number, but it's not coming in as a scam likely. It could be an editor or maybe even someone at the school.

I slide the bar to answer. "Hello?"

"Am I speaking with Nova? This is Tara Manning. I'm one of the producers for *Dungeons and Dreams.*"

June's show. Why are they calling me? "Oh. Yes, this is Nova."

"Great! I was hoping you'd have a few minutes to discuss an opportunity to appear on the show."

"Wait, *me* on the show? Are you sure?" Must be a mistake. And so late in the season? The episodes air a few weeks behind, but half of the contestants have gone home.

She laughs. "Yes. I'm sure. We're setting up a new twist for our characters that'll happen in about a week."

She launches into a detailed explanation: they're bringing in ex-lovers of the characters for a face off— preferably if the player had a relationship with the player. They want either me or Parker, but she'd prefer me. She and the marketing guy must disagree.

"Don't you want to fulfill your paladin's quest for vengeance? Have a second shot to take down Awe? I watched your last stream. Fun stuff."

"Are you bringing me in to make things harder for June or to help her win?" I'm not on board if they expect me to ruin June's chances of winning.

"Is ex the appropriate label for you and June? Are you still dating June outside the game?"

Feels like a trick question. "No, I'm not seeing her now. I haven't since she came to Seattle. I was, and now we're not." I suppose it's true. We text every day as friends, like we promised we would. Where's the line between friends and lovers? I'm not sure anymore. We've never been good at staying in the lines.

"I see. Then you'd qualify for the opportunity I'm describing. We'd, of course, pay for your transportation and lodging, as well as food during the days you're filming. It's not a huge amount of money, but you'd be compensated for any episodes you appear on, probably one."

I glance again at the tabs with the airfare listings. "Really?" I could see June by next week. It's like winning the lottery. I'll finish my edits first, even if I have to stay up every night. "Yes, I'll do it."

"Great! Give me your email, and I'll send the contracts. Review them at your convenience, return them with signatures, and we'll iron the details out. There are a few things you have to agree to, like a confidentiality agreement to not give plot spoilers and to promise not to tell June you're coming to the show. We want the surprise to be genuine, so as soon as you land in Seattle, no calls or texts to her. Keep in mind, like the agreement with all our players, if your character dies in our game, you can't play them in games elsewhere unless there's an in-canon way to bring them back."

"Yeah, sure. My character shares a name with a character in my books, but they're technically separate. Is that okay?" Maybe June will finally figure out I'm the author, and the excitement of seeing me will outweigh her inevitable, crushing guilt over making that first video. I don't need an apology about the book situation from her, and I certainly don't want to cause her any additional stress.

"Works for me. I'm excited you're willing to appear. The

viewers from June's stream and NerdyPodCast's show are going to eat it up."

So many questions buzz through my mind as I give her my email address and other contact info. What if they let it slip to June that I'm *Curse's* author? Will she be mad I didn't tell her sooner? Will she feel so bad that it messes up her performance in the show?

How am I going to do this while not messing up June's chances of winning? If I don't go, they'll ask Parker, and I don't trust him.

After I end the call, I open up photos and look at the one June sent today, smirking at me, little flowers woven into her braids like a crown. She's so amazing...so good at this. Forget vengeance. I'll make a new vow if I have to, in-character and out—even if I lose my character's life.

30
JUNE

I rub the goosebumps on my arms as I wait backstage. They're setting up for tonight's show. It's been a week since Soren warned me about Parker, and sure enough, when I tuned in to Aiden's stream, he wasn't there. I didn't watch the whole thing. It would hurt too much to see Nova as Hunt carrying on without Awe—without me. We were able to transfer the podcast contract to Aiden continue. NerdyPodCasts would also be interested in doing another with me. Maybe one day after the show is done.

"The witch is in the castle," Soren mutters, walking up behind me.

"Callie?" I turn and throw him a sympathetic look.

"Yeah. Late last night, they tried to sneak in the new players, but I was hiding in the bushes." He gives me a thumbs-up and the crazed smile I've come to recognize as part of his humor.

I open my mouth and close it. Who am I to judge anyone doing something unhinged, considering what I've done in the past?

"Shut up. I had to know if she was here."

"I'm guessing you saw Parker too?" I roll my eyes, and an image of his rip-off character smirking jumps into my mind.

"Not sure. Before I had my stakeout, I went back and looked at his picture from your channel, but I didn't see anyone coming in who looked like him. However, there were several people who arrived in hoods or hats."

The show's makeup and costume departments are so good they're going to even be able to make his useless Jerald of Rivera look cool. Which will, no doubt, boost his ego. "I think we can go ahead and assume the worst. What's our plan if both of their characters come at us together?"

"You get that giant magic hand of yours to grapple the heck out of the fighter. I'll try to line both him and the warlock up for one of your line-shaped spell attacks."

Good idea. Soren's elf, Sariel, is a Bear Totem barbarian, so he takes half-damage from many attacks, and since he doesn't wear armor and relies on dexterity, he's likely able to dodge my spell attacks if he's in the way.

"And what's the plan if we're facing our respective exes alone?"

"Pray to a god of love to intervene and smite. Who's that in D&D?"

"Goddess, and Sune." My mind whirls with the scenarios that could happen. "Maybe we can try to swap our characters' places when they go in the portals. I can take on the 'lock for you. You'd have a good shot at Parker's fighter, provided he doesn't roll really hot at the start. He'll blow his action surge in the first round and renew his hit points as his reaction to your attack."

"Rather than swapping places, if I can get into your portal, we could team up. Our characters have enough of an in-game bond at this point, I can justify Sar running in with Awe."

"If you do that, I *might* be able to convince the eye monster running the game that your cheating shouldn't result in immediate death. Is that a risk you want to take?"

"If I have to face Callie's character, I'm dead. A warlock is a tank killer. I'd rather be vaporized by Xandriver or Polymorphed into his new goldfish buddy than have Sariel get taken down by *her* character."

Damn, I didn't even entertain until now what it might be like if Parker's character manages to kill Awe. He could— if he got that action surge off before I get a turn and he gets lucky enough to roll some criticals. That'd...be the worst ending to Awe's life I could think of. It'd make all the sacrifices to get here pointless.

I nod at Soren. "Yes. Agreed. If I could cast real-life Bardic Inspiration on both of us, I would right now."

"Would you or Nova care if I gave you an on-air kiss? You know, to make Callie jealous."

Nova wouldn't care—leaving me free to decide things like this was one of the reasons they wanted to take a break. "Nova and I aren't a couple. You can, but only on the cheek or hand, good sir." Old me would've agreed to it, even though it'd make me feel uncomfortable.

"Cool." He makes two fists. I bet he's regretting his character's choice of cosplay: no shirt and painted-on clan symbols. His wild hair sticks straight up in places, interspersed with small, vaguely Viking-inspired braids. "Team Bard-barian."

"Team Bard-barian," I echo, giving him a double fist-bump.

Soon, the stage managers have us take our places around the stage for the opening.

The session begins like the other ones have. The narrator gives a quick recap of the story so far, showing cartoon animations of our characters acting out the events on the screens behind the stage area. It's really damn cool to see Awe animated. It'd be even cooler for her—and me—to appear in the D&D movie sequel. They move the cameras around where we stand, filming us and our costumes from a few angles. Only six players are left out of the initial thirty.

"Okay, players, to your places," the director announces as the cameras cut and we walk to our designated places at the table. Sometimes, we play at the table with physical dice and other times, we're standing in front of the screens or even acting out actions with props, and they'll roll digital dice on the screens for us.

There's no live audience, so the show's team is allowed to cut and adjust things that aren't working. I probably should've expected it, but their DM is even allowed to stop and rephrase things when she wants to or replay certain sections that didn't work well for the story.

I can't go down tonight. Only six players left. Three unofficial teams. Soren and I must outlast them. When the show started, they were taking out several players at once. Now, it's likely only one of the six will go home each episode until the finale, and one going home will make the other in their team vulnerable.

The DM starts the scenario. Like before, the floating eye monster opens portals across the realm and drags our characters out of where they were previously. Awe and Sariel were sleeping in a pub after making an escape from last session's dungeon.

Xandriver fashions himself like a gameshow host, a show being put on for his only friend, his goldfish, the only member of the fictional audience. Xan's animation bops across the screens, explaining that today will test the hearts of everyone here, exposing what they'll do when their past loves confront them.

"Aren't you bored of this?" Soren, as Sariel, asks when it's his turn to address the eye monster.

Xandriver smirks from the screens behind us, revealing an enormous mouth of spiky teeth. The DM speaks for him, "Never! I was bored, but now, I'm not. My fish and I have learned so much about you humanoid specimens, but not about love! I desire to have desire!"

I touch the button in front of me to indicate I wish to speak. It turns green, meaning I can talk. "The language of poetry and music would teach you more about love and desire than battle. Instead, let me sing the language of love to you. Even the hardest of hearts can't help but feel when hearing the right words and songs. Let me be your apprentice and I'll not only teach you how to feel love, I'll teach you how to write words that'll make others love you. Send the rest of them home. They can't understand the desire for desire like you and I can." I gesture to the other five players sitting around the table. Some of their backstories have them motivated to win the apprenticeship Xandriver offers, and others just want to survive since the stakes are win or die.

"Persuasion check," the DM says.

I roll my custom d20, and my eyes bug as it reads back a twenty. A twenty on an ability check isn't an automatic success in these rules, but my score should be pretty damn high. I don't know what Xandriver's stats are, but he's not a god. It shouldn't be impossible for Awe to convince him, or else the DM wouldn't have called for a check.

"Cut," the director announces. "We're going to redo that section. June, roll that again."

Dammit, I was successful. They just don't want me to be.

"Persuasion check," the DM says again.

I reroll my die. A seven this time. My throat feels tight. It's not fair. If we're playing this game using D&D rules, we should be using them all.

"Awe, Awe, Awe. I understand you want me all to yourself. However, we have a lot of fun planned today. Without further ado...contestants, step on up to your portals!" On the last sentence, Xandriver's voice shifts into a caricature of a gameshow host. "Is anyone going to try to resist this time?"

None of the players say anything. Previously, a few fights broke out at this part of the sessions, and once a rogue even lost his life when trying to sneak attack the eye monster. I take a breath through my nose, trying to let go of the surge of anger from the reroll.

"We're going to play the next part as breakout sessions," the director says. "Going alphabetically, Awe is first, so the rest of you can take a break."

My stomach does a flip. I hate that I'm nervous. Will I ever be free of my ex-fiancé? Will they even let me win this game? It's starting to feel rigged.

Soren pushes his button, asking for a turn to speak. "Wait, I'd like to do one thing."

I glance at the director, and he signals for the cameras to continue rolling.

"Sariel doesn't resist, but at the last moment, he's going to charge into Awe's portal with her."

"Xandriver will try to stop him, as that's a big violation of the gameshow rules," the DM adds.

Soren shrugs. "The things we do for love. My portal is next to Awe's, and I have additional movement speed."

They roll it out, and Sariel succeeds—barely—making it into Awe's portal before the giant floating eye can cast Hold Person at him.

The DM laughs. "Animators are going to have to add a new angry Xan face for that."

"Already working on it!" someone announces from backstage.

"Then I suppose I need Awe and Sariel onstage for the next part. Everyone else can go backstage, take a break, and stand by." For the breakouts where our characters are in different places, we're not technically supposed to know what happens to each other.

Soren winks at me as he stands from his spot, and we both walk onto the main part of the stage.

"You step through the portal into what looks like an enormous dark cavern."

They cut the lights on stage and play music that sounds like it could proceed a battle in an epic fantasy movie. Here it is. They'll turn on the lights, and fucking Parker is going to be standing there in his fucking character's fucking costume.

Sariel managed to make it into the portal with me. We're going to kick Jerald's ass so hard. I guess, in a way, it'll feel good to get this revenge.

"Awe Danamark."

Nova's voice. My heart skips, and time practically stops, the seconds stretching out.

Someone turns on a spotlight, illuminating myself and the figure in front of me. It's Hunt—straight out of their book, our many game sessions, and my perverted imagination. They're wearing real armor, and it gleams in the stage lights. Their teal horns look spectacular, like the horns are really growing out of Hunt's forehead. Then I notice the longsword. Pointed at me.

"I've come to fulfill my vow."

Their vow to kill me. My world seems to zoom in until all I can see is Nova. My brain reels, refusing to believe that they'd do this to me. I put a hand over my mouth.

Nova—Hunt? Is there a difference?—kneels and turns the sword around, pointing the tip of the blade toward themself. They unlatch and pull their shiny chest plate to the side so the sword is aimed directly at their heart. "I forsake my vow of vengeance to Oghma and all that comes with it. Today, I make a new vow."

My feet are glued to the stage floor. What are they doing? How did the show get them here? "Hunt." Their name is all I can get out.

"I swear," Hunt begins, looking up at me under the stage lights, which illuminate their bright teal hair and Nova's absolutely gorgeous face.

They came here for me. Getting in front of my viewers is one thing, but this is a different level of 'doing things in front of people.' No one's ever shown up for me like this.

"...upon the demon-goddess herself and by the great power of the gargantuan gold, that I give you, Awe," *June*, they mouth, "my fealty and pledge to you my loyalty. If I ever raise a weapon to harm you, then may this holy mithril blade pierce my heart."

I can't stop myself. I run across the stage to them, knock their sword to the side, and throw my arms around their neck, kneeling with them. The longsword falls to the stage with a clatter.

"Hunt." I stare into their eyes and trail my hand along

their face, tracing it with my fingers. Nova. I can't believe they're really here.

If Xandriver wants an example of love and desire, he's going to get it.

I bring my lips to Nova's and kiss her with all the intensity of how I missed her over the past four months, passion kindling and burning inside like a wildfire. I don't want to stop. Her taste. Her warm lips. I thought this only happened in fantasy stories—my love showing up for me, swearing loyalty. The feel of Nova's hair under my fingers and the smell of her desire on her breath...it's pure bliss. Home.

Eventually, someone clears their throat. I can't stop smiling, my face burning as we break.

Nova's grinning and red-faced, too.

"Hello. Glad to meet you. I'm Sariel. You must be Hunt."

I turn to see Soren waving at us. Him and the rest of the whole damn world just disappeared for a few minutes. We're still being filmed—still playing this game. I stand and give Nova a hand up.

"I hate to be the bearer of bad news," Soren says, "but as of now, two of the three of us violated some very specific rules set by a very powerful monster. We might need to prepare ourselves."

"Having broken the pact with their patron deity, Hunt can't use any of their paladin abilities," the DM announces.

Nova fixes their chest plate and picks up their blade. Damn, they look hot holding a real sword. "Whatever it is, I'll face it with you."

31
NOVA

I came all this way to save Awe, not damn her. And yet, that seems like the most likely outcome. Our small party of three—Hunt, Awe, and her elven barbarian friend, Sariel have just defeated a string of traps. Xandriver sent a clone of himself to stalk us, which is summoning waves of increasingly difficult monsters as we try to escape through the tunnels from the old underground arena.

Xan pulled Hunt out of their group at the end of the last session I played with Aiden, as per instructions from the show writers, then dropped both Hunt and Awe into the middle of a cavern where duergar gladiators used to fight for crowds.

We, the players, sit at a huge gaming table at the front of the stage, complete with fancy chairs that look like thrones, inlaid maps, and spaces for each of us to roll our dice. I've never played D&D at something like this before, and I'm so used to the kitchen table in Aiden and Lyssa's dining room.

"Rule check." Soren nods my way. "Hunt violated an Oath of Vengeance but certainly never made a decision outside their true neutral alignment. Does it really stand that they'd have none of their abilities from Oghma? Wouldn't Oghma, as *the* patron of bards, feel like Hunt is justified in breaking this vow once they deemed that Awe was worth saving?"

My character is all but useless with no class abilities. June is having to blow through spell slots just for us to survive the waves of skeletons and undead.

June nudges me with her foot, and it brings back all the memories of flirting and playing D&D with her. God, I've missed her. I have to get her character out of here alive.

The DM laces her fingers together on the table. I've seen her streams before—she's good but really tough. "That might be the case if Awe wasn't a patron of his rival, Leira, Lady of Deception."

I look at June, raising an eyebrow. Lady of Deception. I'm going to tease her for that later.

She nods, grinning. "It's true."

I sigh. "Bards."

We keep going—what else can we do?—until my character is down most of their hit points, suffering a broken leg from failing a dex save on a trap.

"Okay. New plan," June says as our characters have a moment of breathing time between fights. "Sariel heads back to the portal, and we buy him the time he needs."

"What?" She can't mean that.

"Hunt. We're running low on resources. You can't walk, and I can't carry you. Even if you take all that heavy armor off."

I shake my head vigorously. "No. I can't accept this. You have to survive—you have to win! Leave me."

A smile ghosts across June's face. "What'd be the point? You and I facing Xandriver's clone can give Sariel the chance to escape. And if anyone is reckless enough to take down Xandriver, it's his wild ass."

How can I say this while staying in character? "I...came all this way because I wanted to save you. If you die, then you'd have been better off without me."

She reaches out and cups my face. "My darling. We're always better together. Promise." She turns to the DM. "Awe is staying."

It's over so quick. When the clone catches us, he casts Disintegrate on both our characters. He aims it at Awe, and I use my Shield Master feat—not connected to my paladin abilities—to absorb as much damage to her as possible, but it's not enough. After my character's hit points drop to zero, he's still able to one-shot her.

Sariel manages to get to the portal and the director says he'll return to do his breakout session later in the day.

I want to scream. I should've stayed away. If not for me, June could've won this game.

The lights and cameras cut. The DM gives a handshake to June and then offers her hand to me. I shake it, numb.

"Come on," June pulls me backstage, and it's all a blur. A few people speak to June—people she knows from the show. I follow her around like a lost puppy. How can she be so cheery after what happened?

"June, Nova, very nice!" Tara, the producer who invited me, gives us a thumbs up.

Nice? I let my healer die. I'm the worst tank in the world.

"Thanks! It's been a pleasure." June shakes her hand, too.

"You know, I was rooting for the two of you to get back together. That was an epic ending. Sorry to have to keep Nova's appearance a secret. Despite the opinion of our marketing person, I've been shipping Awe and Hunt since I saw your first session." She winks at June.

June laughs. "Same!" She takes my hand and squeezes it. "Is this all the filming you need of me and Nova today?"

Tara looks at her tablet, scrolling down a list. "Maybe. We'll let you know by text if we need to do any exit interviews or extra scenes for your characters. Otherwise, you have food and lodging for another night, then you'll need to find other accommodations and arrange your flights. Our accountants will reimburse you for the return travel."

"Excellent. Thank you."

June says goodbye to a few more people, then I follow her out of the large ballroom and into the castle hallway.

"June." I pause. How can I even begin to fix this? What can I even do now?

She hugs me, sighing deeply. "You're here."

"But you lost the game."

She puts a hand over her mouth. "Oh, no...so, anyway..."

Isn't that a meme? "You've been acing these sessions. Everyone says you're a top contender. And I show up and ruin it."

She grins. "Want to see my room? I had to share a smaller room at first. After one of the more famous players lost and went home, I convinced the B&B staff to let me have this nice big one. It has a huge attached bathroom with a double shower..."

What does the room matter? "It would've been better if I let Parker come. He would've attacked you like the instructions were, you would've killed his character, and then you'd still have a chance of winning."

She pulls my arm at the elbow, making us break into a light jog as she leads me down the hall toward the huge staircase. "It really doesn't matter. They weren't going to let me win. I should've won already. Or at least made the game go a different direction. Earlier in the session, before your character showed up, I rolled a twenty on a persuasion check against Xandriver. Now, a twenty doesn't necessarily equal success. But with only Awe rolling the check, the DM shouldn't have called for a roll if Awe had no chance. Xandriver isn't a god or anything, just a high-level monster. The director called cut, then they made me reroll."

"What?" Rage replaces my guilt. "But...how could they cheat?"

June runs up a few stairs, then turns around to face me. "The show is partially scripted. They were never going to let me win. Two of the remaining players are actors, trying to beef up their geek cred. My money's on one of them. Now, come on!"

Come where? Then I remember her talking about her big, private room. *Oh!*

My armor rattles as I follow her up the spiral stairs and down another ornate hall until we reach the last room. I got in late last night and didn't have a chance to explore the castle.

The producers insisted that I and the five other temporary players come in through the backdoor and stay in some of the smaller, bottom-floor guest rooms.

June pulls a large metal key from her pocket. It looks like a key from a hundred years ago. "Pretty cool, huh?" She puts the key in and opens the door. "Now that I've rolled high enough to convince the handsome demon-born knight to come to my room..." she runs around behind me, shoving me inside, "I'm going to play out *several* fantasies that've been going through my head." She locks the door on the other side.

"Convince me?" Her fancy, light-filled room is scattered

with the usual June messiness of clothes and empty cups, with a large, unmade four-post bed at the center, antique furniture, and a double window with white curtains. I look down at myself. "Don't we need to go return this to costumes or something? I still have the armor and horns on."

"Nova."

At the sound of my name, my eyes lock on her. She's wearing the intricate costume from the show, flowers embroidered into the edges of her pink cloak. She still has a laced leather corset, but this one's stamped with embossed roses. My vision catches on the lines of her neck where I want to kiss, her cleavage, her waist. This is real. I'm in June's room. And staring at her like a fool.

She cocks her head to the side, giving me a playful smile. "So, are we officially together again?"

"W-what kind of a question is that?" I sputter, staggering toward her. "I knelt and said a vow to you! In front of high-definition cameras. I thought I was going to throw up before I even finished saying everything."

She bites her lip as she regards me. "I'm trying to think of a way to tease you, but honestly, you're so damn hot it's making my brain stop. I'm glad you're here."

"You'd be the only person to think describing almost vomiting is sexy."

She goes on her tiptoes and pulls my head to her until our foreheads touch. "To put your mind at ease, you didn't ruin this for me. I've made a lot of connections, lined up opportunities, and even learned a good bit about how to make better videos. Awe might've died, but today's my favorite day. The love of my life got on a plane and flew hundreds of miles for me. I would've never asked you to get in front of people like that, and I know it was super uncomfortable, but you did it anyway."

The love of my life. Maybe I died with Hunt. Being here with June...it seems too perfect.

She takes a step back and stretches her arms out, gesturing to the room. "So, Hunt. You said a vow to your demon-goddess, and I guess since we both died, we're in the astral plane." She giggles. "Is it prayer time?"

Hell yes, it is. I close the gap between us and run my thumb over her soft lips. "You're such a dork. I love it." So am I. It's like she was made to fit perfectly with me, body, mind, and soul. "I love you."

"I love you, too."

I kiss her, and it's more magic than any fantasy.

32
JUNE

N ova stands as still as an unmanned suit of armor as I kneel, unlatching the leather straps that hold her leg plates. Damn, the costume designers weren't playing around with this.

I remove the plates strap by strap and pile them together.

"We should've stopped by costumes." She shakes her head, laughing.

"Shh, I've got this. I'm a pro at getting inside your armor." Under the silver pauldrons, I find thick linen pants and leather boots. "Ugh, they really have you in multiple layers."

"I know! It took me over two hours between costumes, makeup, and hair this morning."

I move up to work on her belt. "Two hours isn't *that* bad."

Nova reaches around, trying to get to one of the spaulders that cover their shoulders. "I might die again if I have to wait two hours."

"Again. So dramatic. Will you, now?" I pull off the

metal-linked belt, drop it with the rest, and then stand to start working on the pieces on their arms.

She sighs, giving up on reaching the shoulder pieces. "Next time, I'm rolling a monk. No heavy armor or weapons needed."

"Mm, but you look so hot in armor holding a sword." I go on my tiptoes to kiss her jawline, my hands finding the claps of the leather straps on her arms.

A groan rises from her throat, so I kiss that, too—across her neck and down. This metal chest piece is going to be a problem.

"June." Their voice already has a desperate tone. I love it when they moan my name. "You brought up prayers, but I haven't been doing them."

"Yeah? Which ones?" I drop the arm pauldron with the rest of the pile and get to work on the shoulder pieces.

Nova swallows. "Well, I've been slacking a bit on the running, pushing, and jumping prayers because I've been too focused on writing."

I stand on my toes to whisper in her ear. Her delicious closeness shoots pleasure through my body with every breath I take. "And the *other* prayers? The important ones?"

"I've been too sad. I haven't self-cared, as you put it once, at all."

"At *all?*"

They shake their head. I've finished removing the arm pieces. Just their chest plate left...and all the damn padding and clothing underneath.

I pat her head. "Aw, poor thing." I've been no saint during our time apart. Pleasuring myself while imagining Nova in my bed. Posing for and taking the sexy selfies to text to her. Venturing into the city during off days of filming to buy some specialty toys to surprise her. I thought

I'd have to fly to Iowa to see her after a few more lonely weeks.

"I felt too guilty, like I was a creep if I thought about you that way after I said we weren't together." Their fingers shake as they work on the straps on one side of their chest while I unlatch the other.

So literal. God, I love them. I laugh. "Aw, my gallant paladin. That was why I sent those dirty pictures of the titty nature."

"Oh. I...should've realized that. Those pics were really hot. Oh God, that one with you wearing a costume looking like a sexy Princess Zelda..."

Straps unlatched, I pull open the chest armor, then move it up and over their head. They have to turn their face to not catch their horns in it. I drop it on the pile with the rest with a satisfying clang.

Nova grabs me and twirls me around. "Finally. Come here." She scoops me up, lifting me in her arms like she did the night after she first kissed me, and carries me to the bed. She tosses me on, kneeling over me.

"I sent you pictures because I wanted to excite you." I run my hands down her chest, over the thick quilted wool gambeson. This thing needs to come off, like now. "Wanted you thinking of me all the time."

Their cheeks are delightfully pink. "Well, you could've sent me nothing, and I still wouldn't have been able to stop thinking of you. Okay, that's it. I'm getting out the rest of this damn costume right the hell now." They step back, yank off the boots, shuck off the pants and underwear, and then, on their way up, try to pull the gambeson over their head. "Oh, shit. It's stuck." Their voice sounds so muffled and frustrated.

Laughing, I yank on it until it pops over her head, taking one of her horns with it.

She wrinkles her nose as she laughs, falling naked next to me on my fluffy, unmade bed. "I see why they filmed that awkward sex scene with the armor still on in the movie *Excalibur*."

I unlatch my cloak. "At least mine's easy to take off. You already know that."

"June." She sighs my name, wrapping her arms around me and rolling me so I'm on top.

"I cast Command. Watch." I straddle them and take off my Awe costume piece by piece, setting it carefully off to the side. It might be the last time I wear it. Huh. I'm not sad. I leave the horns on my forehead and flowers in my hair, fluffing it over my shoulders.

Nova's eyes follow every movement I make.

Before we begin, I have to tell them. How do I even start to say it all, though? "I'm sure, by the way."

"About what?" Nova's hazel eyes are so wide, absolutely glued to my body. It makes me smile. I did order them to watch.

I roll off her to lay on the bed again so we're facing each other. "I'm sure I want to live with you. To be with you." I cup her face with one hand and her eyes flutter shut.

She's so generous with her love to trust me like this.

I'm going to do my best to be worthy of it. "I did what you said: I lived alone and thought for a long time about what I want. Not what my parents want, my friends want, or even what you want. But I found more than anything else, I want to be with you."

They put a hand over mine, looking into my eyes.

"You make me better, Nova. When I'm with you, I love myself more. I enjoy things more, all the little and big moments. Video games, work, eating dinner, cleaning. Even exercise. You're my best friend, and life is fun when you spend it with your best friend. I love you. I'm coming back to Iowa to live with you no matter what you say."

She opens her mouth, a cute, panicked expression on her face as she holds up a finger. "I...already sublet my apartment. I mailed most of my stuff to my dad and brought the rest with me in my luggage. The university is letting me complete my degree virtually. When I came here, I didn't really have a plan. I thought I'd try to find a cheap place to stay near you. If you rejected me...let's just say there wasn't a backup option."

"Oh!" I swat their shoulder. "I have money in my bank account for the first time in my life. Not my parents' money. Not Parker's. Mine." I hop off the bed and dig through my discarded costume's pockets until I find my phone. Then I open the banking app.

Is this showing off? I hope they're not offended. I've never felt confident in myself regarding money. The dollar amount doesn't matter—just, damn, it feels good to know my freedom isn't connected to or dependent on pleasing anyone else.

Nova blinks at the small screen. "That's...amazing. I'm proud of you." She lowers the phone and grins. "Hell yes, let's live together. I'm done trying to slow down our relationship or pretending to act chill." She leans over and puts the phone on the nightstand. "Let's buy a house!"

I snicker, and when she lays back down, I climb on her and straddle her again. "A tiny house, maybe."

She puts her hands on my hips, squeezing gently. "Tiny is fine. I don't care. I'd live in a shack in a haunted forest with you. In the Tiny Hut D&D spell. In Yhallister's creepy mega-dungeon."

I lean forward and kiss her lightly. Figuring out life with Nova is the best adventure scenario. "I think we can find a better place to live than *that*," I tease, letting my breath and words brush against her mouth.

Nova grabs the back of my head, kissing me with sudden passion. They pull my naked body tight over theirs. "You're so soft. So gorgeous. God, I've missed you." Their hands grope across my back and ass, and every touch thrills me. "I don't even know where to start."

I grind my hips into theirs, relishing the friction and jolts of pleasure. "Start anywhere."

Nova flips me over, tackling me as we sink into the white fluffy mattress topper.

It's such a comfort—her weight and warmth, like she's exactly where she's supposed to be. "Mm, yes, crush me with your large body. I've been missing this."

She tickles my sides. "Crush you, huh?"

"Eep, no!" I squirm, trying to grab her wrists. When that doesn't work, I decide to try to turn the tables, tickling her ribs.

They catch my hands and pin them above my head, grabbing and holding my wrists together. I like pushy Nova. And soft Nova. And silly Nova. They kiss me again, and when I part my lips, they dip their tongue inside, exploring, tasting, savoring.

Nova runs her free hand all the way down my body, starting by trailing it down my face and neck, around the curve of my breasts, squished into hers, and to my hips. God, the things she can do to me with those hands...

She releases my wrists and leans on her elbows, eyes catching mine. "You're beautiful. Smart. The bravest person I know."

"Ha. It's not like the show was real combat to the death."

"You're standing up for what you want out of life despite years of conditioning and society telling you at every turn to conform. It *is* bravery." Nova drops kisses down my neck where her hand trailed before, then pauses before biting lightly in the soft spot above my collarbone.

"That feels so good..." My voice sounds breathy now. If they make me wait longer, I'm going to be begging.

I run my hands through their hair, soft with a little pull of styling products. "Lower, Hunt."

"Yes, goddess."

I love it when they say that.

They kiss down my belly as they part my legs with their hands. "You colored your hair."

I cackle. The pink color conditioner doesn't show up as bright on my pubic hair without bleach, but I was bored a few nights ago and had been toying with the idea of sending naughty pictures to Nova. "What are you talking about? Pink's my natural color."

"Hm. Let's see if I can make all your skin flush pink, then." Nova inhales my scent and sighs, like even the smell of me turns her on. "You smell so good." She parts me with her fingers, then dips her tongue in, licking until she stops at my clit.

I close my eyes. I've missed this so bad. It's sensory bliss—their hair tickling the insides of my thighs, the firm softness of their tongue, how they drape my legs over their shoulders, the soft sheets under us. I'm lost in it all, at how singularly lucky I am to be here.

They find a rhythm with their mouth, getting me closer to the edge, then switch it up, prolonging the buildup. We've been apart for months, and already, our bodies are in sync, speaking the same language. It'd be so easy to finish here, but I want to feel her over me again, to kiss her and lose myself.

"Nova," I hold her head in place as she teases me, swirling her tongue around and adding a little suction.

"Mm?" she hums into me.

"Come up here and kiss me." I want it all at once. Multiple times. "Then I have a new toy I want to try." At that specialty toy shop I found something awesome, and, my God, I've missed being playful in bed with her.

Nova kisses my clit one more time and then does as I ask, putting her body over mine. I find her lips, kissing her deeply. Her lips trace kisses across my jaw and down my neck. She knows every place that makes me shiver, all my secrets.

Not wanting to get up, I reach for the drawer on the side table but fumble around. Ugh, I thought with such a unique shape that it'd be easier to find.

Nova's faster. "Let me get that for you." They yank the drawer open. "Um...what exactly am I looking for?" That face—their nose is all scrunched up and one eyebrow raised. I love it. Seems they might've spotted the toy.

I lose myself in a fit of giggles. I may have overdone it in the shop, but after seeing a freaking mimic grind toy, I couldn't help myself. Of course I was thinking of Nova. "Oh. You'll know it when you see it. Or maybe you won't. That's the danger of this foe. It may cause unexpected little deaths."

Nova pulls the toy from the drawer, squinting at it, and again, I admire my high skill score in shopping. The toy is mostly flat with a sticky back—for putting on a thigh— with a raised tongue coming out of a treasure chest. I can't wait to show Nova how it vibrates.

"June. What the fuck?" They burst out laughing too, which causes me to laugh again until we're both wiping tears from the corners of our eyes.

Nova waves the toy in front of me and then gives me a gentle bonk on the forehead. "Bad bard. Go to horny jail. A mimic should *not* be involved in any sexy times! It's arguable that a mimic shouldn't be involved in dungeon times either, and yet here we are."

I grin and stretch back, arms behind my head. "I figured if the dragon dick worked on wooing you, this could finish the job keeping you with me for eternity."

"Okay, fine." Nova turns it over, examining the soft silicone surface. "You want to equip this? Let's go." She slaps it on her upper thigh. "Ride me."

Fuck, that's hot to hear her say it like that. "Hell, yes." I draw the word out as long as I get up, we switch places, and I straddle her.

I reach down and turn on the vibration, and Nova's eyes go wide. Then I adjust the toy on the top of their thigh so that my leg grinds against their clit too.

"You shouldn't underestimate my magical powers." I add what I hope is a winning smile to the end of my statement.

"No. I don't." And suddenly, her hazel eyes are so earnest in the low light. "You're the most magical thing I've ever seen."

Damn, I love this. We can be silly together. Serious together. No masks and yet wear any persona we want. I grab the vibrating toy and push it between Nova's legs against her clit. No more waiting—I want to see her undone under me. I lean my thigh against the toy, giving her the pressure she likes while the vibration hits her in the right places.

"June." Their hands twine in my hair, pulling my mouth to theirs, kissing me deeply. "I love you." They murmur it against my lips and then cry out.

My heart is so full it feels like it could burst. So many times I've imagined Nova like this in the weeks we've been apart. Somehow, it's better than I could've dreamed.

"Grind on my thigh again," Nova barely gets out between breaths, pulling the toy away from between her legs. "Kiss me."

Damn, they could command me to do anything right now and don't even need the spell. "With pleasure." I place the toy on her upper thigh again and rub my body against hers. My mouth finds hers and, ah, the taste of me still on her lips is thrilling. I don't want to wait anymore, either.

An orgasm builds and spills over suddenly, waves of pleasure crashing over me.

I collapse against their side, and they remove the toy from their thigh, fumbling for the switch until the buzzing stops. This. I want this closeness every day. Awe might've died today, but I finally got what I wanted. Time with Nova, stretched out as long as we want. Our whole lives, if we're lucky.

I pull the covers tight over us, pressing my chest to hers and snuggling my chin against the crook of her neck.

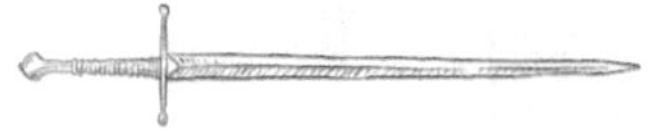

Nova

Something buzzes from the nightstand, and it takes me a second to get my bearings. June. That part I'll never forget. Her scent is everywhere, and her pink hair is in my face. I brush it aside and sit, reaching over to pick up June's ringing phone.

Huh, it's Drew. I glance at the digital clock sitting next to our phones. One in the morning. We fell asleep early after returning the armor and costumes, eating dinner, and then *reconnecting* several more times. It's gotta be, like, 4am in Georgia.

I slide the bar to answer. "Hello." June won't mind.

"Hunt, I was trying to reach Awe's communicator. Is she there?" Drew's using his character's voice. It's Saturday, right? Well, Sunday now. Are they really still playing D&D?

I hear Lyssa's cackle in the background. "Nova answered June's phone, didn't they?"

Looking at the gorgeous girl next to me, I'm struck again by how lucky I am. "Um, hold on. I'll get June. I mean Awe."

June blinks heavy eyes. "What's going on?"

"Namfoodle is calling you." I hand her the phone, then snuggle into her side, nuzzling my nose into her neck. We're both still naked, and it's glorious.

She puts it on speaker. "Okay. Are you injured or will I be injuring you? I assume you have a good reason for calling us in the middle of the night."

"Oh, I'm fine." Drew's nasally voice comes through. "Just wanted to tell you the news. We beat Yhallister. Well, I beat Yhallister. Everybody else is dead."

"Um, okay?" June seems unamused.

"Since far communication is wonky, I can't tell if you're on the astral plane or not."

Oh. He's asking if our characters are dead, but he knows we can't say it outright due to the agreement we signed.

"We...might be on the astral plane," June says.

"I thought there was a chance of that. Good thing I'm

using a special spell. After what happened, my deity inter-fered. I met Procan."

"The Storm Lord," I whisper in June's ear. She elbows me.

"God of the wind and seas," Drew continues. "Turns out the Yhallister was worth a lot of experience. Oh my Procan, I learned so much. You might even say that I can cast at the highest level now."

"He hit level seventeen," June translates.

I reach my hand up to fondle her breast. "I know what it means. He's saying he can rez us."

June bites her bottom lip, then takes a breath. "Wow. That's amazing, Nam. But you'd still need—"

"Really expensive diamonds. I've got three of them. And enough money to buy one more. I've got to bring Solla and Croga back first, but then I can rez you guys. I've made an executive decision to leave Jerald dead."

"Actually, I'm ready to roll a new character." Parker's voice comes from somewhere away from the phone.

"That's great. You died in the most useless way possi-ble," Drew says.

"It was a noble sacrifice."

"You jumped into lava." Cristy's there too. They really must've played all night.

"Yeah, but I took Yhallister's minions with me," Parker says.

"Which he summoned right back." Lyssa's voice. I hear Eleanor's coo answer her mom. "Baby's reverse sleep cycling. We were going to be up anyway."

"In retrospect, I should've grabbed Yhallister and then jumped into the lava," Parker says.

"That wouldn't have worked either. He can Misty Step at will." Drew's Namfoodle voice again. "It's okay. We understand. Jerald made bad decisions. RIP. Well, that's wrong. There is no peace or pieces. He's melted."

"I thought I'd have a chance to resist the fire damage!"

"You jumped into lava," Aiden's voice deadpans. "That's like, four million fire damage."

"So anyway," Drew continues, "thought you might be interested in knowing all of that."

June blinks. "Isn't it four in the morning there?"

"Yeah, we decided to finish the campaign. Go all in. Well, Jerald was all in the lava, at least."

"He went out doing what he loved," Parker says.

"Burning to death?" Lyssa asks.

"Being useless?" Cristy adds.

"There you have it," Drew says.

"I was going to say being heroic."

"Yeah, no one else would say that."

I hear everyone laughing. Moments like this are some of the best parts of playing D&D. Things we'll be able to joke about even twenty years from now.

I pull the phone slightly over to me. "Thanks for telling us. That's great you beat the campaign."

I hear a rustling sound. "We're gonna need deets on what's going on with you two," Lyssa says.

June looks at me. Her eyes are lovely, even in the dim light of the glowing phone screen. "We can't talk about the show. NDA."

I still haven't told her about my pen name. I'll find the right time. Eventually. Being here with June is so perfect it hardly feels real.

"Not what I meant, and you know it," Lyssa chides.

June giggles. "Okay, then. Which of you or Aiden guessed the closest to age twenty-six?"

"Damn. That'd be him."

June touches my cheek. "I guess you owe him a beer or something."

"A pack of cards from a game that doesn't exist anymore, actually." Aiden's voice comes through the phone. "So good luck, darling." He must be talking about some inside joke with Lyssa.

"Pfft. Ebay exists. I'll manage," Lyssa says.

We say goodbye to everyone, and June ends the call.

I kiss her lips. I'll never be tired of doing that. "What was that about?"

She traces a circle on my shoulder. "Ah. Back in high school, Lyssa and Aiden took bets on how long it'd take before you and I were official. I was the last to know."

"They could've let me know, too." But it doesn't matter. Truly. I'm in a castle with the woman of my dreams.

I kiss her again and revel in the sheer magic of it.

EPILOGUE
JUNE

Music plays through the speakers of the game bar. All of our friends in town sit throughout the place at tables. Lyssa is all ears, sitting across from me as I explain the last day at the castle and how I embarrassed the hell out of Nova.

"I got this text, which apparently came in while I was… otherwise occupied."

From my right, Nova glances at me, smirking over their draft beer. I love how we can say so much to each other without speaking a word.

I gesture with my hands as I speak. "Text was from the head of costumes and said, 'Have your special friend bring me back my suit of armor right the fuck now, or else I'm coming after you!'"

Lyssa cackles. "Everyone knew you were full of it with that 'special friend' shit."

Baby Eleanor is old enough to occasionally stay with Lyssa's parents, and it's nice to see Lyssa and Aiden letting loose outside their home. Aiden sips on a glass of beer-style mead to her right, an arm around Lyssa's shoulders.

Nova leans toward me, putting their arm around my waist. "Yeah, an entire real metal armor set apparently costs around four *thousand* dollars. No wonder she was pissed."

This wrap party back home is way better than anything they could've held in Seattle for the winners. In a few moments, the bar owner will play my last episode of *Dungeons and Dreams* over the big TVs as it airs online. We filmed it over four months ago, then they hit an editing snag over the holidays, and it's been really difficult to keep the details to myself.

"So, after Nova and I, uh, shower,"—and what a lovely shower it was, double shower heads, but we ended up under the same one—"I gave her one of my shirts—"

"A tiny shirt for tiny people, with a picture of a tiny frog and mushrooms on it," she adds. "Trust me, it added to my embarrassment."

I nudge her with my elbow. "It was a stylish crop top, you rocked it, and *anyway,* we decide we don't want to get flayed alive by the scary costume woman, so we gather up all the armor, my costume, plus Nova's wool gambeson, pants, and boots. It takes both of us to even carry it all."

"You know, I've never had to do a walk of shame before June."

I make a faux-offended sound, turning to glare at her. "Shame? That was a walk of pride!"

Nova's ears are slightly pink, even now. "Every single person in that castle knew what we were doing in your room, and then you dropped a piece of the armor, and it clanged all the way down the stairs!"

"Yeah, the costume director caught it as it bounced off the last step, and then she gave me an earful," I tell Lyssa, laughing. "She asked us if she needed to disinfect the armor. I think Nova died again. But she does that a lot."

"And somehow, it's always your fault."

"June?" My older brother's voice calls over the low roar of conversation and music.

I turn around in my chair, and Sage, Harmon, *and* Mom are walking into the building. I invited my family, but I never expected them to show.

I stand, grabbing Nova's hand to pull them with me. "Be right back." I wink at Aiden and Lyssa.

"Sure." Aiden tips his glass of mead my way.

Drew is here too, and we walk past him, sitting at the end of the longest table, playing a game of Last Imagination with Cristy and some of her friends. Looks like he's winning despite only learning the rules tonight. Typical.

"Hey, guys!" I wave at my family.

"Junie!" Harmon hugs me tight. "Congrats!"

I chuckle as I squeeze him back. "You know I didn't win, right?"

Mom hugs my shoulders from the side as Harmon shakes Nova's hand. "You're the winner in our eyes. Your dad would've come too, but he's babysitting Liam."

I brought Nova to their house when I visited for Christmas. It was awkward as hell—more so because Nova's a vegetarian from a secular family than because of our relationship—but my folks were kind.

Sage hugs me, too. "We're all caught up on the show. I can already tell you should've won."

"Thanks. I don't even know the winner yet since that episode hasn't aired. Soren won't tell me. Pretty sure he was part of the final three contestants, but my money's still on one of those actors trying to get geek cred."

It honestly doesn't matter. I'm glad I did the show, but

I'm more thankful to get to design my own content and videos again without any oversight. My channel exploded in popularity after the show, even without Awe—though I'll be able to use her again as soon as the show stops airing since Drew was able to pull off that in-game resurrection. Nova and I have been trying on some new characters and doing some role-playing videos where the viewer can practice along with us.

The theme song of *Dungeons and Dreams* starts playing. "Ooh, it's starting!" I grab Nova's hand. "You ready for this?"

They cringe. "Everyone's going to see my confession."

"Yep." I kiss their cheek. "What I'm looking forward to the most. It was very romantic."

"Everyone is going to see us—"

I cover her mouth with my other hand. "Spoilers." I turn to my family. "Y'all find a seat wherever you want! If you want to learn any games, everyone here is really nice."

I skip back to our seats, pulling Nova along.

We sit, and she takes a long drink of her beer. "I have something for you. I don't know if I should give it to you now or after the episode. Damn, I'm nervous."

I kiss them lightly on the lips. What could they have to be nervous about? "You're adorable." But I don't get a chance to ask further.

"Ahh, it's starting!" Cristy squeezes in a chair at my other side. "I can't believe I couldn't get you to tell me spoilers."

"No way. My chest is a much higher level since you last saw it."

Nova coughs on her beer. "What?"

Cristy and I both laugh, and I take Nova's hand under

the table. "You know, my ability to keep secrets. Like a locked video game chest."

She squeezes my hand. "That's locked? You just told Lyssa about our walk of shame."

"Parker wanted to come and support you," Cristy says, "but he also didn't want to annoy you by existing. And from what he's told me about your relationship, you definitely have a right to be irritated at the sight of him. He's sitting in the back corner."

I wave her off, watching the show give the usual intro to the episode's remaining characters. "Nah, it's fine. I don't hate him or even pity him anymore." And I mean it. He has no bearing on my life. "Though you can tell him the show almost cast his character for this episode. And I would've murdered him."

Cristy's eyes light up. "Ooh, I will."

As the episode plays, I glance around the packed bar and restaurant. Nova and I still haven't decided where we want to live and are renting an apartment together a few miles from here toward the mountains. My only stipulation was good internet and a soft bed. She likes being able to find close trails and places to write in nature.

But I have to say, it's nice to know people, and I've been surprised by how many kindred spirits I've found near this small town that seemed so backward when I was younger.

"June," Nova whispers.

"Yes, my dashing paladin?" We're almost to the point in the episode where Hunt shows up. I can't wait to see it, especially on this big of a screen.

"I can't do it."

"Hm?"

They lean in close to where they're whispering directly in my ear, their soft breath sending shivers down my body.

"I had this big plan to get on a knee here in this bar and give this to you at the same time Hunt gives that vow. I can't make myself draw that much attention. So, here. I got the author copies early." Nova presses something into my hands under the table. A book.

"Hm?" I lift it. *Vow of the Demon Born*. Wait. This cover art is of Hunt and...another tiefling that looks a lot like Awe. This is the sequel to *Curse* and...Nova said 'author copies.' Nova is the author?

What? I turn to her so fast, I almost knock my drink over.

She puts her hands up. "Don't be mad. I tried to drop hints. Like, a lot of hints. You know I have a hard time talking about some stuff, and I didn't want to make you feel guilty you'd made that video and—"

"Nova, oh my God!" I squeal, tackling her in a hug and squeezing her tight. Maybe a part of me knew after a while. Maybe I was in denial because I didn't want to think I hurt her the way I did the author. But things click into place. Of course *Curse* was my favorite book, even before I knew Nova wrote it—my favorite person in the world had created this character and story.

She barely manages to stay in her seat, holding me around the waist. "There's more. Read the dedication."

My hands shake as I open the beautiful cover and flip to the dedication page.

To June,

Every day spent with you is my greatest fantasy.

Under it, they hand-wrote, *Will you marry me?*

Wait, *I* had plans about this, and was going to propose to them at the next Renaissance Fair joust. Even messaged my contact about it.

Nova's face is bright red, eyes closed. "But will you? I mean, you can think about it. I know it's a big deal and—"

"Yes." I kiss her lips. "Yesyesyes," I say against them, kissing her three more times.

She opens her eyes, and the trust and love reflected in them nearly take my breath away.

"I don't want anyone else." I grin. "Just you...and all the characters you ever make."

Nova puts a hand in my hair and kisses me again.

ABOUT THE AUTHOR

Erin Branch (she/they) is passionate about writing queer stories full of romance, comedy, and heart. Outside of writing, they love spending time with their partner, kids, and pets. She practices and competes in martial arts, enjoys hiking and running outdoors, and is always up for a new adventure.

www.erinbranch.com

Coming April 2025:

Kicks and Kisses, a sapphic contemporary romance of karate rivals

Available now:

The Pull of the Tide: A Sapphic Fantasy Romance Anthology

ACKNOWLEDGMENTS

To my partner, Ev, thank you for seeing this book through all its (and my) evolutions, for pushing me to be a better author and person, and for making this writing dream come true. I love you and I want to write 100 books together.

To Adam, thank you for your endless support, all the times we bounced funny scenes back and forth, nsfw discussions on dragon parts, and countless D&D (and beyond) adventures through the years. P.S.—you're not actually Parker.

To Julie, Theresa, Heidi, Laurel, Nicole, Elaine, Mindy, Liz, and all other critique partners and beta readers, thank you for lending your wisdom and time to help hone this story into its best.